ONLY THE GOOD

Susan Brooks loves her great-aunt Ella, whose kindly nature is constantly put to the test by the rest of the family. But now matriarchal Aunt Ella lies sick in bed, and has called the family together to make an announcement. A recent stroke has postponed her revelation, how--- le the family gathers a--- domineering \dsome husband Tony, ·l, and their two kids; 's mother Amelia, who ha ui Aunt Ella at birth and wh ııad never met.

They all have their secrets. Then Aunt Ella's trusted maid, Parsons, disappears. After Susan discovers her murdered body the next day, Sheriff Atwood is called in. One thing becomes clear to him right away… this is a family that protects its secrets well. Unfortunately, it also becomes obvious that his likeliest suspect is Susan herself!

Mary Collins Bibliography
(1908-1979)

Novels:
The Fog Comes (1941)
Dead Center (1942)
Only the Good (1942)
The Sister of Cain (1943)
Death Warmed Over (1947)
Dog Eat Dog (1949)

Crime Stories:
Sirens in the Night (*Street & Smith's Detective Story Magazine*, April 1943)

ONLY THE GOOD

Mary Collins

Introduction by Curtis Evans

Stark House Press • Eureka California

ONLY THE GOOD

Published by Stark House Press
1315 H Street
Eureka, CA 95501, USA
griffinskye3@sbcglobal.net
www.starkhousepress.com

ONLY THE GOOD
Originally published by Charles Scribner's Sons, New York, and copyright ©
1942 by Mary Collins. Reprinted 1948 in paperback by Bantam Books, New
York. Copyright renewed August 21, 1970 by Mary Collins.

Reprinted by permission of the Mary Collins estate. All rights reserved
under International and Pan-American Copyright Conventions.

"Mary Collins and Her Golden State Mysteries" © 2022 by Curtis Evans

ISBN: 979-8-88601-000-8

Book design by Mark Shepard, shepgraphics.com
Cover design by Jeff Vorzimmer, ¡caliente!design, Austin, Texas
Cover art by Tom Lovell
Proofreading by Bill Kelly

PUBLISHER'S NOTE:
This is a work of fiction. Names, characters, places and incidents are either
the products of the author's imagination or used fictionally, and any
resemblance to actual persons, living or dead, events or locales, is entirely
coincidental.
Without limiting the rights under copyright reserved above, no part of this
publication may be reproduced, stored, or introduced into a retrieval system
or transmitted in any form or by any means (electronic, mechanical,
photocopying, recording or otherwise) without the prior written permission
of both the copyright owner and the above publisher of the book.

First Stark House Press Edition: August 2022

MARY COLLINS AND HER GOLDEN STATE MYSTERIES

by Curtis Evans

Between 1941 and 1949 Mary Collins (1908-1979) published six mysteries, her entire oeuvre, all of which she set in the state of California, where she resided for four decades from 1911 to 1951. Like classic soap opera, Mary Collins' California mysteries concern crimes which scandalously implicate wealthy families when their dark, restless secrets are dragged shockingly into light. With their buried pasts haunting the present like malignant specters, Mary Collins' books recall those by another "Mary": influential, bestselling mystery maven Mary Roberts Rinehart, to whom she often was compared. The younger woman's tales move with greater celerity, however, in part due to the snappy narration of her wry and spirited female protagonists. These women are frequently independent "career gals"—in the parlance of the day— but in any case always refreshingly irreverent and independent-minded. "Janey Jeffries can eavesdrop and get conked as well as any Had-I-But-Known heroine," sardonically observed *San Francisco Chronicle* crime fiction reviewer Anthony Boucher about the narrator-protagonist of Mary Collins' fifth novel, *Death Warmed Over* (1947), adding, however, that there was a major difference in that "Janey has a fine salty spirit of her own and...her creator conceives murder as a real and unglamorous fact." These qualities made the advent of the author's new novel "a joyous event" in the eyes of Boucher, who himself was by no means a slavish admirer of Rinehart's literary acolytes.

Mary Collins, whose career as a crime writer began and ended during the alternately war-torn and precariously peaceful 1940s, was born in St. Louis, Missouri on January 14, 1908 to Edward Gordon Garden, a noted American architect of Canadian Scottish descent, and Edith Agnes (Banta) Garden, a woman of New York Dutch extraction. At the time of her marriage to Edward Garden in 1905, Edith Banta was a divorcee with a six-year-old daughter, Elizabeth, nicknamed "Betty," having previously wed another man—unhappily as things turned out—nine years earlier. Three years after her marriage to Edward,

Edith gave birth to the couple's only child, Mary.

In St. Louis, Edward, Edith, Elizabeth and Mary resided, along with a cook, Mary's nursemaid, and a mixed-race butler, at a fine, brick Georgian-style house located at Windermere Place, a private street—a sort of "gated community"—of about two dozen attractive dwellings. Edward, the junior partner in the firm of Mauran, Russell & Garden, worked on a series of impressive commissions for buildings in the beaux arts style, including the First Church of Christ, Scientist, the St. Louis Racquet Club, the Cabanne Public Library and the Second Baptist Church, this last described as a "tour de force of brickwork." In 1911, however, the Gardens picked up stakes and moved to Berkeley, California, later relocating to San Francisco, where they lived at the foot of fashionable Russian Hill. Thirteen years later, when Mary was just sixteen years old, Edward Garden died tragically in the prime of his life at the age of fifty-three.

The previous year, Edward's popular and outgoing twenty-four-year-old stepdaughter Betty—a graduate of Miss Head's School for Girls in Berkeley and a prominent Bay Area debutante and society page habitué who during 1917-18 had taken up film acting in Los Angeles, appearing in ingénue roles in several pictures, and dressing up in elaborate costumes for charity cabarets—had wed wealthy California fruit grower William Flanders Setchel. Setchel was a native of Fresno, not far from Edward's own age. His first marriage, to the similarly youthful Minnie Helene Wilson, had ended after only four years in acrimonious divorce in 1921 and was followed by five years of bitter litigation from his ex-wife, as she pursued back alimony eventually totaling $5700 (approximately $83,000 today). Setchel finally made partial payment to Minnie in 1926 only after being hauled into court and threatened by a judge with incarceration. Mary later became permanently estranged from Betty, rather extraordinarily never mentioning to her son, Jeff, who was born in 1944, that she even had a half-sister. Perhaps Betty served as a model for the unpleasantly selfish female relations whom heroines encounter as menaces and obstacles in Mary's mysteries, with nasty Bea Forrester in *Only the Good* (1942) being a particularly repellent example.

After her half-sister's marriage and her father's death, Mary lived, in somewhat reduced circumstances, with her mother in Oakland. She was successively educated at Miss Burke's School in San Francisco, Laurel School for Girls in Shaker Heights, Ohio (this when she and her parents lived for a couple of years in Cleveland), University High School in Oakland and, for a single year (what Mary herself dismissed as "a brief whirl"), the University of California at Berkeley. At this point money for her education became depleted and Mary found employment in San Francisco as a stenographer, commuting daily from Oakland to the Financial District. She took pride in her work and had ambition to accomplish bigger things in her career, but felt stymied by the prevalent sexism of the day. Once when she proposed to her boss a plan for improving the efficiency of the office, he crushingly told her: "That's a great plan, Mary, I know *just the man* to implement it." This aspect of her life comes through as a form of wish fulfillment with Jane Jeffries, the insatiably curious protagonist of *Death Warmed Over* who works as a sort of efficiency expert and has a secretary of her own.

In 1929 Mary, an attractive, twenty-one-year-old brunette, became engaged to Hampton Mauvais, a young man in the insurance trade; however, this engagement was broken off and two years later she wed Richard Hesketh Bovard, a Stanford University senior majoring in business and engineering. After graduation Richard and Mary resided at an apartment in the San Francisco neighborhood of Nob Hill, where Richard operated a service station for the Associated Oil Company (later Tidewater Associated Oil Company). Their union, however, ended in divorce after a few years, and by 1936 Mary was again living with her mother, this time at the Hotel Claremont in Berkeley, which then was operating as a residential establishment for respectable ladies of genteel social standing. During these years Mary tellingly changed her political party declaration from Republican—Richard's own political persuasion—to "declines to state." Her son Jeff, who recalls attending "Ban the Bomb" rallies with his parents as a teenager, has confirmed that Mary, like contemporary California crime writer Bernice Carey, became something of a "fellow traveler" with the Communist Party, sympathizing greatly with the workers' plight while recognizing wrongdoing as well on the part of the Left.

In 1937 Mary wed again, altogether more happily, to John Edward Collins, a native of Wisconsin of Irish descent and son of a prominent lumber and chair manufacturer in the northern Wisconsin town of Antigo. 5'9", 178 pounds, blonde-haired and blue-eyed, the handsome, athletic and outgoing John, two years younger than Mary, graduated in 1928 from Antigo High School, where he played football, baseball and basketball, was a member of the Drama Club and served as class treasurer and editor of the *Antigonian*. ("The world is blessed most by men who do things," was his appropriate motto.) He then matriculated at Dartmouth College, from which he graduated in 1932, and received an M. B. A. from Harvard two years later. In Wisconsin he owned and operated a cheese factory, appropriately enough, and after moving to California he ran various business ventures and worked as a security analyst and money manager in the San Francisco Financial District, where he met Mary, with whom he decidedly clicked.

Three years later the young couple was residing some twenty miles across the bay from San Francisco in Contra Costa County in the small town of Lafayette, a situation to which Mary later plaintively referred as being "marooned…where she knew nobody." In desperation she and John, both of whom were detective story fans (they eventually compiled, their son Jeff recalls, a large library of both detective and true crime fiction) decided to while away their idle time by collaboratively composing a mystery novel—an endeavor which, Mary later jokingly avowed, nearly brought about the demise of their marriage. "Somehow the psychologists and the marriage counsellors have never mentioned book collaboration among the more lurid causes for broken marriages. I don't know why not," Mary mirthfully mused in 1948, adding:

> We fought more over the first thirty-five pages of that book project than we fought about anything else before or since. My gripe was that he insisted on reveling in technicalities of football as played in Hanover, N. H. I forgot what his gripe was.
>
> Anyway, I literally "threw the book at him" in a towering rage, in the course of which I managed to come out with the comparatively sane ultimatum that if our marriage was to last, I'd go ahead and write my own books. Of course I didn't know then how many times I'd have to write the same one over. By that time I imagine John thought he was well out of it. He could still give advice—with lots less time and bother, not to mention wear and tear on the disposition.

Mary wrote this novel, *The Fog Comes*, three times over before she finally felt satisfied with submitting it to Charles Scribner's Sons, publishers of mysteries by, among others, Leslie Ford and August Derleth. (She dedicated the manuscript *In Affectionate Memory of My Father Edward Gordon Garden*, lost from her life for sixteen years now.) Upon receiving from Scribner a detailed reply pointing out the flaws which remained in her novel, she painstakingly rewrote it one more time, after which it was accepted (a process which should prove inspirational to future mystery writers reading this introduction).

Scribner published *The Fog Comes* in March 1941, by which time Mary and John had moved to Sacramento, where John had accepted a position at Sacramento Junior College from their mutual friend, the new president, Richard Rutledge, a native Missourian who would die tragically the next year from pneumonia at the age of forty-eight.

(From Dr. Rutledge Mary likely derived the surname of the wealthy Rutledge family in her third novel, *Only the Good*, published six months after his own untimely death.) Scribner would publish all six of Mary's novels over the decade, all of which also were reprinted in paperback by Bantam, who likewise reprinted the beloved classic detective fiction of Elizabeth Daly, something of an East Coast counterpart to Mary Collins.

At the height of her success as a mystery writer, however, Mary, like Elizabeth Daly, simply stopped writing. In 1951 she and John and their young son Jeffrey or "Jeffie" as they then called him, moved to Portland, Oregon, where John manufactured electrical circuit breakers. During the Fifties, Mary found another outlet for her creative energies when she became the costumer to the theater department at Reed College, something which should not surprise anyone who has noticed the descriptive interest she takes in cloths in her crime fiction. Why did she cease writing, however?

Partly, one supposes, because, as she later told her son, she deemed mystery writing *really hard work*. Likely it also was because, as many another woman at the time found, raising a child and keeping a house was, as well, really hard work, which she took very seriously. Between the three-year period from 1941 and 1943 Mary published four crime novels. After she gave birth to Jeff in 1944, only two more novels would appear from her typewriter over the next five years. Upon the publication of her final mystery, *Dog Eat Dog*, in 1949, Mary gave an interview with the *Oakland Tribune* in which she made it clear that in her case crime had to give some ground to housewifery:

> Now she has worked out a [domestic] schedule somewhat like this: Up at 7:30; breakfast for husband John and son Jeffrey; get Jeffrey ready for kindergarten; dishes whipped through the electric dishwasher; beds and "tidying."
> At her desk by nine, she works through till lunchtime. Afternoons are for "chores": washing, ironing, cleaning, while keeping an eye on Jeffrey. Evenings for reading and diversion.
> She loves cooking and cleaning and is now learning to sew....She also finds all these activities conducive to the planning of her novels. Ironing is especially favorable to creative thinking. "I get many of my best ideas over the ironing board," she says.

After the recent war, American cultural institutions urged women—who during the conflict, led on by Rosie the Riveter and her sisters ("We Can Do It!"), had entered the labor force in greatly heightened numbers—to return to their "traditional" roles as wives and mothers. Mary Collins was not the only woman mystery writer in the late Forties who, in newspaper puff pieces, found herself more extolled for domestic competence than writing capability. A 1951 publicity photo of crime writer Helen McCloy, for example, showed her seated on a couch with her husband, mystery writer Brent Halliday, standing at her side and her toddler daughter Chloe, "their only collaborative effort to date," clamped rather grimly to her lap. The accompanying *Boston Globe* article by Elizabeth Watts which accompanied the photo evinced far more interest in Chloe's care than McCloy's mysteries. Women crime writers at the time obligingly tried to give the impression that they could "do it all," but, contrary to how newspapers would have it, juggling jobs was not easy.

After ironically dedicating *Death Warmed Over* (1947) to *Jeffie, in spite of whom this book was written*, Mary found that her son, whom she wryly nicknamed "the perpetual crisis," inadvertently posed an even greater obstacle the next year to completing her last crime novel, *Dog Eat Dog*, when he came down with a case of measles. Fortunately, "John stepped nobly into the breach," as her *Oakland Tribune* interviewer explained: "He shut his office, announced that he was going away on vacation, installed Mary on the premises with paper, carbon and typewriter to finish her book—and stayed home to see Jeffrey through the cantankerousness and incarceration of measles." A relieved Mary was tempted to put John's name right up there with hers on the title page of *Dog Eat Dog*, for without him she could never have completed the book by deadline.

Whatever the reasons, no additional Mary Collins crime novels appeared over the last three decades of the author's life, and her name became largely forgotten in the mystery field, although noted San Francisco author Gertrude Atherton, to whom Mary dedicated *The Sister of Cain* (1943), lauded Mary in her 1946 biography as a "brilliant" writer who deservingly "won a wide reputation as a writer of unusual mystery stories" with her "imagination...remarkable flair for character psychology, style and magnetism." The feminist Atherton, who herself felt stifled in her marriage, pointedly added: "In 1944 Mary had a baby, and that form of creation drives the loftier faculty into a remote brain cell and padlocks the door—and that padlock has to be wrenched open and the poor dormant 'creative faculty' dragged out, coaxed, petted, implored, scolded, abjectly apologized to, before it finally condescends to pour its light through the upper story and get back on the job." Clearly Gertrude Atherton did not believe that women received creative inspiration over the ironing board!

In retrospect, Mary's 1950 appearance in San Francisco at the third anniversary celebration of the Northern California branch of the Mystery Writers of America—in the distinguished company of, among others, Anthony Boucher, Lenore Glen Offord, Virginia Rath, Dana Lyon and promising new girl on the block Bernice Carey—was something of a last hurrah for the author. At the head of the *Oakland Tribune* article about the gala event, Mary appeared in a photograph clad in a stylish back slit dress and laughing as one-hit wonder Cary Lucas, author of *Unfinished Business* (1947), provocatively held her in his arms and with a long dagger demonstrated "an expert way to deliver a stab in the back." (I believe the pair of authors were intentionally mimicking the lurid cover of the 1950 Dell paperback edition of Lucas' novel.)

"Mary is lovely to look at," observed the admiring Gertrude Atherton. "She is tall and slender, has charming manners, and knows how to dress." But Mary Collins was no slouch either at the fine art of stylish murder, as vintage mystery fans happily will now have a chance to see for themselves.

Only the Good

Mary Collins' third mystery novel, *Only the Good* (1942), is set in the village of Rutledge, which she based on Lafayette, where she and her husband John had recently resided (see above). Susan Brooks, the novel's heroine-narrator (and Mary's stand-in), is the owner of *Susan Brooks, Interiors*, a decorating firm she started with the financial assistance of her kindly Great-Aunt Ella Rutledge, renowned wealthy widowed mistress of Oak Hill, an opulent Greek Revival mansion built not long after the Civil War by Ella's late father-in-law Jonathan Rutledge. "[S]ince the tunnel through the Berkeley Hills was completed in 1938, a lot of people have built in the country," Susan observes. "Fortunately for me they've found it handier and cheaper to have me do their houses than to go to San Francisco to shop."

Enterprising Susan has worked hard to get what she has got out of life, but then she has had to, even with Ella's help. As Susan explains it, she is the product of a short-lived, ill-advised French Riviera marriage between Ella's niece Amelia Rivington and an Englishman named Lawrence Brooks, who not long after their inevitable breakup was killed at the Battle of Gallipoli. After divorcing her wayward husband, Amelia casually handed Susan off to Aunt Ella, who generously raised the child at Oak Hill, and departed for "South America and marriage with an Argentinian named Ortiz." Ella's own daughter Eleanor having died tragically from tuberculosis at the age of nineteen, Ella lavished her remaining maternal devotion upon Susan.

Ella had Susan practically educated for a career, in contrast with Susan's pampered in-law Beatrice "Bea" Forrester, the granddaughter of Ella's late husband Henry Rutledge and his first wife Rachel Taylor ("from all accounts a bit of a shrew"). Not only is Bea, as a Rutledge, the proud heiress to Oak Hill, she also nabbed Susan's hunky former boyfriend, Tony Forrester, whom she now spurns, chasing instead after another man.

Of the situation with Bea, Susan rather witheringly observes:

> I knew I was [Aunt Ella's] own true love, but Bea was a Rutledge and was brought up accordingly. There was, naturally, no question of Bea's having to earn a living when she was grown—her parents had left her plenty of money—so she went to different schools from mine and made her debut when she was eighteen and was always very social in a labored sort of way which was quite all right with me. My life, I considered, was a whole lot more interesting than hers."

Anyone knowing something of Mary's own life and that of her socially prominent, debutante half-sister Betty can be forgiven for wondering if the author is drawing on personal experience in her depiction of Susan and Bea.

Just as unappealing as the privileged and selfish Bea is the sanctimonious Will Starr—first cousin, once removed, of Bea—and his wife Mabel, a pious "pillar of the Long Beach Methodist Church." Yes, Susan's Rutledge relations are an unsavory lot indeed, and the reader will not be surprised to find that when the ailing Ella summons them all to Oak Hill to discuss The Will and other matters, the foul play is indeed in the fire—and sizzling! Is it coincidental that Susan's mother, now known as Amelia Ortiz, shows up at the doorstep as well, with a fancy-pants Latin son, Carlos, in tow?

All in all, readers of *Only the Good* are presented with what might almost be a classic British mystery, at least in terms of its idly wealthy setting and ravening relations. At one point the first of the novel's slayings is blamed on "some tramp." Not only is there a butler, Glore, but six maids (including Ella's longtime English personal maid, Parsons, who is promptly bumped off), a nanny (Bea, like Betty, has a son and daughter), a laundress, a gardener, a chauffeur, and "an Italian to come in with a tractor to plow and spray the orchards." We might almost be sojourning at Gosford Park or Downton Abbey, in terms of the number of house servants flitting though the story. Of course, Mary Collins was one of the few mystery writers of whom I am aware whose family actually employed a butler.

All this notwithstanding, the novel benefits greatly from Susan's (and the author's) skeptical take both on her relatives and Ella's vulgar, nouveaux riche neighbor, odious businessman "Clare" Opal. The good may die young, but Death eventually catches up with their elders as well, and in Mary Collins' acerbic American mystery most of these characters well merit murder. In the *New York Times Book Review* Isaac Anderson deemed *Only the Good* "a well-integrated novel of greed and suspicion and murder"—an apt description of this mystery.

—May 2022
Germantown, TN

....

Curtis Evans received a PhD in American history in 1998. He is the author of *Masters of the "Humdrum" Mystery: Cecil John Charles Street, Freeman Wills Crofts, Alfred Walter Stewart and British Detective Fiction, 1920-1961* (2012) and most recently the editor of the Edgar nominated *Murder in the Closet: Essays on Queer Clues in Crime Fiction Before Stonewall* (2017) and, with Douglas G. Greene, the Richard Webb and Hugh Wheeler short crime fiction collection, *The Cases of Lieutenant Timothy Trant* (2019). He blogs on vintage crime fiction at The Passing Tramp.

ONLY THE GOOD
Mary Collins

For
My Mother

*All characters and incidents in this book are fictitious.
The Village of Rutledge is also an invention of the author.*

CHAPTER 1

"Oak Hill is the most beautiful *old* house in California...."
That is what the man had written in the magazine. He had described the house carefully, and then had gone on to prove his points with four pages of big shiny photographs. He wrote quite a bit about the beauty of its setting, too. The lovely little valley about a mile wide, nestling in the hills east of Berkeley, embraced the gracious old house like "a tender lover," he'd said. He wrote about the five huge oak trees on the knoll where the house stood, and the gardens and the outbuildings and the orchards.

He told about how Jonathan Rutledge came to California in 1866 with a carefully drawn plan of his father's South Carolina plantation house and the contents thereof in a ship that fought her way through the gales off Cape Horn. The writer told, in a very polite way, about how Jonathan was smart enough to marry a California Spanish heiress whose land grant had been approved by the Land Commission.

And that old house had been my home for twenty-four years until I moved into a little white cottage a quarter of a mile down the valley where I could still see Oak Hill and love it, and be thankful for Jonathan Rutledge's sentimentality which prevented him from building the usual gingerbread horror that was popular in the early seventies.

I stood on my neat little brick terrace looking up at the house with the September moonlight pouring over it in good imitation of the most successful Hollywood searchlights, and then I let out a deep sigh and called the dog—who didn't come—and sat down in a canvas chair.

"That you, Susan?" A throaty male voice called to me from the shadows under the trees near the creek, and I heard footsteps crunching on the brick path that led from the bridge.

"Yes," I called back. "Come on up, Joe."

It was young Doctor Hilliard walking over from his sister's house at the other side of the valley.

He flopped into the other long chair and lit a cigarette and said something like whew.

"It's too much," he said, gesturing toward Oak Hill with his cigarette. "It looks like a sentimental illustration for a calendar. Moonlight! That house doesn't need it."

He was right. The great six-pillared portico across the main wing of the house was sheer drama of moonlight and black shadows and darkened windows.

"I came over to talk to you about your aunt, Susan." His voice was very serious, and I wished that I could see his face. "I'm worried about the old girl."

I stood up and felt my heart pounding uncomfortably. "Let's go in the house," I said.

He followed me through the French door, and I turned on some lamps and sat down on one of the blue love seats by the fireplace and motioned for Joe to sit down, too, but he shook his head and leaned against the mantel.

"What's the matter with her?" I said.

"Blood pressure. It's way up again. I'm afraid of another stroke. It'd be bad."

Mrs. Rutledge, the owner of Oak Hill, was my great-aunt. She and my grandmother were sisters, and when my parents got a divorce and wanted to get rid of me, as well as each other, Aunt Ella brought me home to Oak Hill and took care of me, and I didn't want to think of life without her.

"You mean it would kill her or just make her completely helpless?" I looked up at Doctor Hilliard and tried to think with half my mind whom he looked like. He shrugged his shoulders and turned his hands up eloquently.

"One's as bad as the other. For her. She hates the wheelchair as it is, even if she doesn't say so."

He sat down and kicked gently at the coffee table and leaned earnestly toward me. "Listen, Susan, they don't take care of the old lady. She's tired all the time, and I suspect that old hag of a maid of slipping her raw beefsteaks. The place's full of your cousin's guests—has been all summer—and Mrs. Rutledge can't stand that." He shook a finger at me in an irritated manner. "Why aren't you up there? You'd look after her."

I could feel my jaw setting. "That's not my home anymore, Joe. I don't belong up there. I'll do what I can." I reached for a cigarette, and Joe picked up the lighter and held the flame toward me when he got it going.

The worry about Aunt Ella was making my mind do funny things. I could feel myself smiling. "I know," I said. "You look like Fred Astaire. Exactly. Only you're bigger."

Joe grinned and showed his handsome teeth. "Dope," he said gently. "You look like hell, young lady. Don't you ever sleep?"

"Some," I said. "I have a lot of work. There's a building boom on now, or didn't you know? Lots of people want their houses decorated, and Susan Brooks is glad to oblige."

"Yes, I daresay." He stood up. "Well, drink some hot milk and go to bed." He looked around. "This is a pretty room, Susan. A good ad for you. Not as handsome as Oak Hill, of course, but a whole lot cosier. In fact, if I decide to marry you, it'll be because your house is prettier than my sister's." He grinned appealingly, and I grinned back.

As he walked past me, he patted the top of my head. "You go see Mrs. Rutledge tomorrow and give her hell for ignoring her diet, will you? And give your cousin Beatrice a good swift kick in the pants for me, too. Of all the self-centered, selfish women ..." His voice trailed off in disgust.

"Shame on you, Joe. Bea's all right," I said, family loyalty winning against truth.

"Nuts is the word for that. Anne says for you to come to dinner tomorrow night." He waved his long, sensitive hand and sauntered through the door. I called after him to say thanks to his sister for her invitation. Then I whistled to the dog. She came slowly into the house in her most deliberate Scotch terrier manner and indicated that she would consider going to bed.

"Oh, Bonnie," I remarked to the dog, "life is loopy."

The next afternoon I closed up Susan Brooks, Interiors, promptly at five and told the girls in the workroom to go home. My shop is in the village of Rutledge, and since the tunnel through the Berkeley Hills was completed in 1938, a lot of people have built in the country. Fortunately for me, they've found it handier and cheaper to have me do their houses than to go to San Francisco to shop. For a while I was so busy I had to refuse a few jobs, but lately I'd been taking them all. After all, it didn't require genius for me to see that the building would soon be over because of the government's needing all the materials for defense. I had to make money while I could.

I drove the mile and a quarter out of the village to Oak Hill wishing that I'd worn something decent and hoping that Bea's guests would be skulking around the halls.

Glore, Aunt Ella's ancient butler, opened the big panelled front door for me and smiled a heart-warming welcome. The poor old man looked very tired, and I knew that Bea had been needing a lot of service. Glore would be glad when she and her husband and two little children and their nurse went back to San Francisco in October.

"Good afternoon, Miss Susan. We haven't seen you for several days." Glore closed the door behind me, and I said yes, I'd been busy and asked where Mrs. Rutledge was. He said upstairs, and when I was half way across the great white-panelled hall that bisected the main wing of the house, Bea burst out of the blue drawing room on the right with a highly irritated expression on her carefully made-up face. A few sparks blew out of her brown eyes as she turned to Glore.

"Glore," she said in a quiet voice full of asperity, "I've rung three times.

We need ice."

I could hear voices in the room behind Bea, but I couldn't see anyone.

"Hello, Bea," I said. "Glore was letting me in."

Bea turned quickly on her heel and looked at me. "Oh," she said. "Well, all right.... How are you?"

Bea is twenty-four and very smart-looking and competent and impatient. She bore her two children with a minimum of fuss, because she said she might as well do it and get it over with. She takes her social life and her clothes and her house—and Aunt Ella's—very seriously, and I really don't think she has much fun.

"That old Glore," she said after he had disappeared into the service part of the house. "All these ancient servants. They're awful. They should be pensioned."

"They like it here," I said calmly. "Aunt Ella says it's their home. That's a good-looking dress."

It was, too. About eighty-five dollars' worth of simple yellow linen that did a lot for her deep tan and long, loosely waved chestnut hair.

"Thanks," she said. "Do you want a drink? I have some people here."

I went on toward the magnificent spiral staircase. "No, thanks. I came to see Aunt Ella."

Bea went back into the drawing room, and I was very conscious of my not-too-fresh twenty dollars' worth of blue linen that did very little for my deep tan and blonde hair.

In the upper hall I met Parsons, Aunt Ella's English maid, whom she brought back from Europe when she brought me. I remembered Joe's remark about her being a hag and I decided she was, in appearance at least. She looked very skinny and dried up and sere in her black skirt and white blouse, and inky-black dyed hair didn't help her poor old face much either. But I'd known her so long that I don't suppose I'd really ever thought about how she looked. I called to her.

"Hi, Parsons," I said. "Come and talk to me. I'm supposed to give you hell."

She turned back from the door to the linen closet.

"My, Miss Susan, you did give me a turn! What have I done?" Parsons' false teeth made a little clicking noise when she spoke.

"Doctor Hilliard suspects you of slipping rare roast beef to Mrs. Rutledge. She's not supposed to have it." I sat down on the window seat.

Parsons' face got very red and full of righteous indignation.

"Miss Susan, I never. Mrs. Rutledge never has a thing that isn't on the list. Why, I never heard of such a thing."

I laughed. "Okay, Parsons. I'll tell him. Where's Mrs. Rutledge?" I stood up.

"In Miss Eleanor's room, Miss Susan." She hesitated as though she wanted to say something, and I asked her what. "Mrs. Rutledge's worried about something, miss. That's what's making her ill. *Not* meat!"

I stood there thoughtfully studying the panelling on the doors and the crystal chandelier that hung in the stairwell. "Any idea what, Parsons?"

"No, miss." She clamped her mouth over the fancy porcelain teeth, and I knew she did have an idea but wouldn't tell.

"All right," I said, and walked down the hall and knocked at the door of the long-dead Eleanor Rutledge's room. Eleanor Rutledge was Aunt Ella's only child. She died of tuberculosis at nineteen and broke her mother's heart at the same time. Afterwards Aunt Ella built a magnificent tuberculosis sanitarium for girls and spent millions to make it one of the best in the country, and when people spoke of her generosity she always said it was so little to do for young girls who had the frightful disease.

Aunt Ella called to me to come in, and I opened the door to see her sitting in her wheelchair near one of the west windows. Her first stroke had paralyzed one leg, and she had sat patiently and without complaint in the wheelchair for four years. She raised her arms to me, and I ran across the room.

"Why, Susan darling, I'm so glad to see you, child. I thought that was your car." She kissed me, and I stood off to look at her.

Her hair was very white and lovely, cut off short for convenience and allowed to curl in short ringlets all over her head, but her great dark blue eyes looked weary and almost glassy. Her skin looked dreadful. Hot and a sort of brownish-red. The skin on her hands felt hot and papery, too. I smiled hard.

"You look very elegant. That's quite an outfit." I patted the arm of her robe—heavy white crepe beautifully cut and evidently costly. She had a fluffy white afghan over her knees, and she wore her pearls.

She smiled and looked pleased. "Why, thank you, darling. I've decided that white is more cheerful for an old lady in a wheelchair. I got tired of that eternal lavender that Bea got for me." She laughed and looked at me conspiratorially. "She doesn't approve of this. Says it's inappropriate."

"Oh, stuff," I said. "It's lovely." I plopped down on a tufted hassock thing and pulled it near Aunt Ella. Then I had to get up and get an ash tray.

We had a very nice visit. I told her all about what was happening in the shop, and she told me all about Bea's entertaining for the week and what the two babies had been up to and what people had come to see her and who had given how much money for the new wing on the Eleanor Rutledge Memorial Sanitarium.

She sent for some tea for me, because she said I looked as though I needed it and asked how much sleeping I'd been doing and why didn't I have more help in the shop. I told her I didn't think it was fair to take in another girl and then have to let her go when the building boom let up. Aunt Ella said I was probably right but not to kill myself in the meantime as it wasn't good for girls of twenty-six to get run down. A shadow of old sorrow flashed across her face as she spoke.

"When's Bea going back to town?" I asked, to change the subject.

Aunt Ella opened her mouth, shut it, and opened it again. "The first of October," she said, and shifted a little in the wheelchair. "Susan, I want you to do something for me, and I don't want you to say anything about it."

I raised my eyebrows. "All right, my aunt," I said smiling, "I'll do your dirty work for you. What is it?"

She sighed deeply and took my hand, but she didn't say anything for a long time. We sat there in a pool of silence and sunshine that poured in the west windows. The lovely old mahogany of the room's furniture glowed in the afternoon light, and the sun brought up the fresh color of the rose and white and blue wallpaper. The silver toilet articles on the dressing table winked and sparkled, and I thought about all the Rutledge women who had used the things in the room and died young, and the things stayed on, still good and useful and lovely to look at.

Aunt Ella finally spoke, her voice quite strong, as though she had decisive thoughts in her mind.

"I want you to wire Will Starr and tell him to come up here this weekend and bring his family. I want all of them here. And you and Bea and Tony, too. There's some business we must all discuss."

She wanted to see the whole family!

My mouth hung open in surprise, but my requests for enlightenment met with polite but flat refusal.

CHAPTER 2

Will Starr, a cousin of the Rutledges, wired that he and his wife Mabel and daughter Peggy would arrive Friday evening from Long Beach, also son Bill if he could get leave from Fort Ord where he was a buck private.

And Bea raised particular hell when she heard of the week-end arrangements.

She stormed into my shop and with iron self-control restrained herself from evicting my client, Mrs. Applegarth.

Bea threw herself into a chair and with a lot of sharp, irritated movements she got out a cigarette, lit it, took three puffs, put it out. Then she did over her face which didn't really need it. Finally she just sat and glared, and Mrs. A. took her departure, with an abashed nod for Bea who ignored her.

"Of all the asinine things you've ever done, Susan Brooks, this is tops. *Why* did you let Aunt Ella ask those awful people up here? You know she can't stand much. Why?" Bea dumped her bag and sable scarf on the floor and pulled off her little black hat. I knew from her clothes that she had been in San Francisco.

"Calm yourself, toots," I said in a manner designed to be irritating. "Aunt Ella's got something up her sleeve that's worrying her. When she gets the business settled, she'll feel better." I started folding up samples and putting them back on the shelf.

"What business?" Bea asked.

"I don't know. She didn't tell me. Parsons says she's worried, and Hilliard says her blood pressure's up. So we have the Starrs for the week-end."

Bea gave me a long, wary look, opened her mouth to speak, and then shut it. She sighed. "It didn't have anything to do with me?" Her eyes were narrowed.

"How should I know?" I said impatiently. "You've had the house full of people all summer. Maybe Aunt Ella's tired of it. Your conscience bothering you?"

Bea gathered her belongings together and stood up. "Is that any of your business, Susan? I think not." She walked to the door. Then she turned back. "You'll have to take the Starrs off my hands Sunday. I've got a lot of people coming for lunch, and I'm not going to put them off."

"Okay," I said, grinning. "I get it."

Bea tried to slam the door as she left, but she was foiled by the automatic closing device.

I worked hard through Thursday and cursed the weather which kept getting hotter and drier. On Thursday at five-thirty when I went up to see Aunt Ella, I met Joe Hilliard in the hall. His face was drawn and serious.

"What's up?" I said.

"Mrs. Rutledge isn't at all well," he said. "I've given her a mild sedative. She needs sleep. Go say goodnight to her, and I'll wait for you."

It was cool in the big old house, and the hot north wind that had blown for two days had obligingly stayed outside so that the brittle dryness that filled the rest of the valley was absent. I was glad for Aunt Ella.

She lay in her four-poster bed, and the sheets and pillows looked especially white and cool in contrast to her flushed face. I walked over and took her dried, hot hand.

"I came to say goodnight to you," I said. "Joe says you have to get lots of sleep and take care of yourself."

She smiled up at me. "I'm all right, child. Only the good die young, you know." Her voice trailed off in weariness. "You come up here this winter and stay with me, will you?" I could hardly hear her.

"Of course." I nodded hard. "I'd love to."

She moved her head from side to side on the pillow, and with deepening alarm, I saw that her tired eyes were filled with tears. "Poor Susan," she murmured. "What have I done? What have I done?"

I was horribly frightened. Frightened and puzzled and almost overwhelmingly sad. As far as I knew Aunt Ella had never in all her life done anything that wasn't good and kind and fair. Now, when she was old and ill and should have been at peace, some strange thing had come to trouble her.

"Go to sleep, darling," I said, with a lot of unwelcome tears in my own voice. I kissed her and walked quietly out of the room.

I was heavy with depression.

The long white hall was cool and empty. I went down to the south wing where Bea kept her children and went into the big day nursery. Two-year-old Sandra was running around the room like mad defying Nanny to catch her. She let out a loud yell when she saw me and flung herself at my legs.

"Sandra's being a naughty girl. She doesn't want to go to bed." Fat old Nanny in her stiff white uniform tried to look very severe. Actually, I think she thought Sandra was displaying proper spirit.

The child arched her back away from me when I picked her up, her funny soft brown hair bobbing around her little face. "No bed! No bed!" she shrieked. Her childish body felt wonderfully firm and strong under the pink batiste nightie.

"You're a fool, Sandra. You don't know how lucky you are to be able to go to bed." I headed for the night nursery where six-months-old Rutledge Forrester was already sound asleep in his crib, and after a little more persuasion, I convinced Sandra that bed was an attractive place.

Nanny and I went back to the day nursery, and I sat down and lit a cigarette. Nanny brought me up, so we are pretty close.

"What's the matter with Aunt Ella, Nanny? She's terribly upset about something."

Nanny nodded vigorously, all three chins waving in unison. Her sharp black eyes were filled with worry. "I know it. Parsons told me she's sent for the Starrs." She looked at the door and then looked back at me. "Your dress needs pressing, Susan. Parsons says Mrs. Rutledge got a letter."

When I had recovered from Nanny's irrelevancy, I gulped. "A letter? What kind of a letter? Who from?" I find that grammar frequently disappears under stress of emotion.

"We don't know. She got it last Saturday, and she's been upset ever since. Parsons said it came from New York."

I stood up. "Well, she'll probably settle things this week-end. Then she'll feel better." I winked at Nanny. "She asked me to stay up here this winter."

"Oh, Susan!" Nanny enfolded me in a frantic embrace. "That's wonderful. I wish I could stay, too. The girls cleaned your house today."

I said that was fine and left. As I stood at the top of the stairs, I heard voices in the lower hall.

My heart pounded and banged and beat with horrible intensity, and I cursed myself for a dreary fool and wondered if the day would ever come when I could hear that particular male voice without going to pieces. Gazing into the chandelier, I tried to analyze what it was that made my emotions crash to bits. Love? Not at this late date. Pride? Possibly. Humiliation? Doubtless.

Gritting my teeth, I walked downstairs to smile and smirk at Joe and Tony Forrester, my cousin Bea's husband.

Tony turned on his automatic charm valve and let me have it. His brown eyes crinkled with delight as though only Susan Brooks had been needed to make this a perfect day.

"Hello, love," he said. "Haven't seen you for ages. You and Joe must stay and have dinner with me. Bea's gone to bed with a good book—resting up for the Starrs—and I dread eating alone."

He hovered his six feet four of height over me until I felt like giving him a good push. He had a habit of standing so close to women when he talked to them that they felt they were going to be kissed any minute, and his male smell of tweeds, tobacco, and lavender shaving soap, flavored with Scotch, was overpowering. I got my hand loose from his without much dignity or tact and backed up a few inches.

"No," I said. "I'm going to imitate Bea. I'm going to have dinner in bed, too."

Joe said he expected to have to catch a baby some time during the night and would dine at home with his sister and get some sleep while he could.

Tony, still reeking of charm, walked out to our cars with us and helped me into mine as though I were some precious bit of Imperial jade and not Susan Brooks, Interiors, very self-sufficient.

"Lousy weather, isn't it?" I said.

Tony agreed and prattled for a few minutes while I looked at the too blue sky and the brown hills and the orchards that were dingy and gray with dust. Only the great lawns around Oak Hill looked fresh, and I knew that that was because Magruder, the gardener, had the sprinklers going twenty-four hours a day.

I leaned over and turned on the ignition as a polite hint for Tony to get off the side of my car. The sun flashed on his white teeth, and his blond hair looked almost silver against his sun-browned face.

"Aunt Ella's pretty bad, Joe says." An expression of concern flashed over Tony's face. "Too bad we can't put off the Starrs, isn't it? But she insists on having them."

I said yes and stepped on the starter and drove down to my house. That Tony. My stomach felt knotted. The dry heat and Aunt Ella and Tony made me *sick*.

I watched Joe's car disappear across the creek road into the big oaks around his sister's house and remembered that I must call Anne and tell her how much I'd enjoyed myself Tuesday night. In fact, I really thought that Joe was very lucky to have a nice widowed sister to keep house for him and be hospitable and make social life easy for him.

Bonnie, the dog, came around to the back door to bid me a polite good evening and hint that she'd be glad to get something to eat. I fixed her dinner and gave it to her and then walked around to inspect my house.

It was sparkling clean—brass, silver, and woodwork gleaming, slip covers straight, fresh curtains in both bedrooms. The icebox was full of vegetables and chicken and milk and cream and butter. There was white and whole wheat bread in the box, and six quart jars of pickled peaches had been added to the preserve supply. Every room in the house had bouquets of white flowers which are my favorites because they look best with a chintzy background. My clothes closet was in perfect order, and all my dresses had been mended and pressed, and my shoes had been cleaned.

I had a bad catch in my throat as I contemplated this perfection for which Aunt Ella was solely responsible. Once each week the maids from Oak Hill did this for me, and Mrs. Griggs, the cook, saw to it that I always had an icebox full of good food.

My own parents had got themselves a divorce *before* I was born. In fact, Aunt Ella once told me that she doubted very much if my English father, Lawrence Brooks, even knew that he had had a child a few short months before he was killed at Gallipoli and my mother, Amelia Rivington Brooks, had handed me at the age of two months to Aunt Ella and taken her departure for South America and marriage with an Argentinian named Ortiz. My mother had apparently forgotten my existence, because as far as I knew she had never communicated with Aunt Ella in the twenty-six years since my birth. I was brought home from Mentone where I was born and installed in the Oak Hill nursery and loved and cared for more deeply than many children who have a full complement of parents. I had, in small measure, taken the place of the Rutledge daughter who'd died.

I was given a good education, and when I chose decorating for a career, I was sent for two years to an excellent school in New York. When I came back, Aunt Ella set me up in business and built my little house for me. We both knew, of course, that on Aunt Ella's death, Oak Hill would go to the Rutledge side of the family, and Aunt Ella said that I should have a nice home of my own.

Well, I had it, but it looked as though I wouldn't have the love and kindliness of Aunt Ella much longer.

Bea's arrival at Oak Hill when I was nine years old had not, of course, been an unmixed blessing. Her parents, Albert and Amy Rutledge, had been drowned in 1924 in a storm off the California coast, and because Bea was the granddaughter of Henry Rutledge, Aunt Ella's husband, she had to be taken in. However, I always took a malicious and rather childish comfort from the fact that Bea was no relation to my great-aunt. Her father was born of Henry Rutledge's first marriage to one Rachel Taylor, from all accounts a bit of a shrew.

But Aunt Ella had been fair to the point of bending over backwards. I knew that I was her own true love, but Bea was a Rutledge and was brought up accordingly. There was, naturally, no question of Bea's having to earn a living when she was grown—her parents had left her plenty of money—so she went to schools of a different type from mine and made her debut when she was eighteen and was always very social in a sort of labored way which was quite all right with me. My life, I considered, was a whole lot more interesting than hers.

Actually, Bea and I had had a pretty good time together until her marriage. Then a lot of things had happened and we'd taken to snarling at each other, and I was very bored with her thoughtlessness as far as Aunt Ella was concerned.

CHAPTER 3

On Friday morning I woke up feeling fresher and much nearer my age than I had in weeks. The north wind had died down so that my skin no longer felt flakily dry, but in place of the wind was quavering, heavy heat. At nine o'clock when I left my house to go to the shop, a slow stillness lay over the valley. The trees drooped in the dust, and the big oak that shaded my house didn't rustle a leaf.

In the little village that lined both sides of the highway, the townspeople and their pets moved languidly. The postmistress and I exchanged views on the weather when I stopped for my mail. We agreed that it was going to be a scorcher. "It's eighty-nine right now," she said. "Imagine what it'll be at three this afternoon."

The girls in the workroom of my shop were taking off their dresses. Sophie, the young genius of the needle, was standing in her slip when I walked in.

"We're just going to put our smocks over our slips, Miss Brooks," she said, shoving her heavy red hair off her forehead. "And a very good idea, too, Sophie."

Wilda, who lacked Sophie's flair but made up for it in reliability, said she thought she'd start the sprinklers in the little patch of garden in back of the shop. "It'll help to cool the air." I said that would be fine and went into the office to telephone Oak Hill and inquire for Aunt Ella.

Parsons, with distress in her voice, said that Aunt Ella hadn't slept too well and that she, Parsons, had telephoned to Doctor Hilliard to stop in. "The house is nice and cool, though, Miss Susan." I said I'd be in late in the afternoon to see Mrs. Rutledge and hung up.

I worked hard at estimates all morning, and when I finished my figures, I typed them out and took them to the post office to mail to the clients. I bought a pint of milk at the market and brought it back to the shop. The thought of food in that heat was impossible.

Joe Hilliard was waiting for me when I got back. He looked hot and very tired, and I imagined that the new baby had kept him up all night. He stood up quickly when I came in.

"Listen, Susan, your aunt can't transact business this weekend. Can you get hold of those people and put them off?"

My heart gave a nasty, sickening lurch. "Oh, Joe, is she really that bad?" I sat down with a plop.

He nodded.

"They're driving up, Joe. From Long Beach. I don't see how I can stop them."

Joe nodded wearily and left. He looked dispirited, and I laughed inwardly at my own maternal concern for him.

At four o'clock, when I had finished an interview with a client, I shut up the shop and told the girls to go home. "You can't work in this heat. It's inhuman," I said.

They both protested that they were behind in the work as it was. "We promised Mrs. Applegarth's hangings for next Thursday, Miss Brooks," Wilda said.

"Well, if this heat keeps up, we'll fix it so that you can work at night. You'll pass out if you stay in here with all the pressing irons going," I protested. The workroom felt like a steam bath.

The great central hall at Oak Hill with its dignified white panelling and black and white marble floor was so cool in contrast to the heat outside that it felt like a tomb. When Glore let me in, he told me that Mrs. Rutledge was sleeping and that Mrs. Forrester would like to see me in her room.

Bea was in bed in her lush, frenchified, pink room which never failed to annoy me. Its decoration was entirely Bea's idea and was completely out of keeping with the rest of the fine, dignified house. She lay in her pink satin tufted bed between pale blue flower-sprigged sheets looking so cool and self-possessed that I wanted to shake her. She had a large pink wooden tray on her lap and was busily writing letters when I came in.

"Oh, it's you," she said, shoving the tray aside and reaching for the bell. "You look revolting, dear. You should try bathing after a hard day at the foundry."

"Yes, love, I intend to—after I find out how your step-grandmother and my aunt is, or are? Taken to your bed for the duration?" I inquired nastily.

Her nice young maid, Katherine, came in answer to the bell, and Bea ordered long, tall, cold ones for both of us.

When Katherine went out, Bea turned back to me. "As a matter of fact, I have a raging headache, my cousin, and I shall stay right here until it's gone. Anyway, Hilliard says Ella can't do anything about the Starrs. We'll send them home tomorrow."

I said that was all right with me, but how about tonight? Bea said that I could cope with them, and did I think Hilliard knew anything. "Ella looks about the same to me. I think he's an alarmist."

Katherine brought us beautiful big drinks full of lime and ice. Never in all my life had I tasted anything as good. "You do have occasional strokes of genius, Bea. How about your party Sunday? I suppose you've put it off."

"Of course not. Why should I?" She looked at me over the edge of her glass, her large brown eyes phonily innocent.

"Because you've no business having fifty people milling around this house when Aunt Ella's ill. That's why." I set my glass down hard on a little fruitwood table, and it slopped over. Bea glared at me.

"Wipe up the mess, Susan. My guests aren't noisy, you know." Then we really went to work. I told her she was thoughtless, selfish, and inconsiderate, and she told me to mind my own business, and that I was a dull clod. She also got in a few licks about me and Joe Hilliard.

"You shouldn't chase him, Susan. It's too obvious. Men don't like that sort of thing."

I shut my eyes and counted ten. I was mad all over and couldn't finish my nice cool drink. Then the telephone on Bea's bedside table rang, and she picked it up. A nice pale pink telephone enamelled to go with the rest of the room. It had an unlisted private number and no connection with the rest of the Oak Hill telephones.

She said hello, and I watched an alien, softened expression creep into her eyes. "Oh, it's you," she said almost breathlessly. "Wait a minute." She turned to me and asked me to leave, which I did with great pleasure.

Well, well, well. It sounded very much like monkey business, and I would have given a whole lot to know just what kind.

I told Glore that I'd be back for dinner. "I suppose Mrs. Forrester's told you where to put the Starrs."

He said yes, and I left.

I drove down to my house and parked my car in the shade and climbed slowly out. I noticed that my hand shook as I fumbled with my keys, a combination of heat and anger, I supposed.

The dog ran through the orchard from the direction of Oak Hill, and I stooped down to pat her. "Hot enough, pal?" I said, marvelling at her ability to run in such weather. Her red tongue was dripping, and I felt her coat. "Come out in back, and I'll take some of this hair off of you." I had a stripping table out near the garage, so I walked around the back of the house with the dog dancing along beside me.

I turned to look back at my terrace as I passed it, and I got a jolt. There was a woman standing there, and because I had walked on the lawn, she hadn't heard me coming. She stood looking intently up at Oak Hill.

She was a big woman—tall and well-padded with solid looking, carefully corseted flesh. Her clothes looked unbearably hot—all dull black drapery—and on her iron-gray hair, she wore a black shiny straw hat swathed in a long mourning veil. Her shoes and stockings and gloves were black, too, and I caught the gleam of a jet pin at her throat.

I walked over to her, and she started almost imperceptibly when I spoke to her.

"I'm Susan Brooks," I said. "Did you want to see me?"

She said nothing for a full minute. She just stared at me until I thought I would crumple under her intensity. Her eyes were black in tune with the jet pin. Her large mouth was firmly compressed above her heavy jaw. Even her eyebrows were black and heavy.

With astonishing self-control, I made myself stare back, and for some wild reason I was afraid. An unreasoning terror made the skin tingle on my spine.

The woman finally spoke, and my ear caught a tiny trace of an accent which I couldn't identify.

"So you're Susan Brooks," she said. She smiled with an effort and showed large, white, determined-looking teeth. "You've grown very pretty."

I could see no reason to speak, so I kept still.

She spoke slowly. "I am your mother, Amelia Ortiz," she said.

CHAPTER 4

My mother! I, Susan Brooks, had a mother. This big black stranger was my mother.

My face must have been the well-known open book, because Amelia Ortiz smiled wryly, apparently hugely amused at my discomfort. At least she made no effort to touch me.

"Do not distress yourself, Susan. I am not a sentimentalist. I didn't come here for a touching reunion."

She sat down on a straight chair, very erect and unsentimental-looking.

I heard myself laughing nervously. "I'm relieved," I said. I sat down, too, and picked up a cigarette box which seemed to leap in my trembling hand with a life of its own. I offered Amelia Ortiz a cigarette, which she took. She pulled a black-enamelled lighter out of her big bag and lit it with a competent twist of her strong black-gloved hand. If she'd pulled out cigarettes with black mouthpieces, I wouldn't have been surprised. She held the lighter for me, too.

"Isn't the heat awful?" I said, feeling that I should make some sort of conversation until we got our bearings.

"It's not bad," she said. "It's dry. In Buenos Aires we have much humidity."

"You're in mourning?" I asked.

She nodded. "Yes. For my husband. He died two months ago." I muttered perfunctory sympathy.

We smoked in silence for a couple of minutes, Amelia Ortiz staring up at Oak Hill. I began to wonder how she had found my house, so I asked her.

"I came to Rutledge on a bus from Berkeley, and I saw your shop, but it was closed. Then I asked where you lived. I came here in a taxi. You don't live at Oak Hill. Why is that?"

"Aunt Ella wanted me to have a home of my own so that when she died I'd be comfortable."

I simply could not think of this strange woman as my mother. I even had the feeling that she was thinking in a strange language and translating as she spoke.

"And Ella? How is she?" She knocked ashes off her cigarette.

"Not too well," I said, distress filling my mind. "I was up there a while ago, but she was asleep. The doctor's afraid she'll have another stroke."

"So? That is most unfortunate. I would like to see her."

"Well," I said, standing up and summoning good manners with an effort, "we'll go up there for dinner. We dress for dinner on week-ends. Did you bring luggage?"

My mother nodded. "Yes, a small bag. I shall go back to the hotel in Berkeley tomorrow."

I took her into the house and got her bag from the front porch where she had left it. I showed her into the guest room and looked around to see if she had everything that she needed.

"Would you like a drink or something?" I asked.

"Just some coffee perhaps?" She stood at the dressing table taking off her hat. "Your house is charming, Susan. You have fine taste, but it is strange for a young girl to live alone, is it not?"

I shook my head. "I'm a career girl," I said. "That makes it all right."

I went out to the kitchen to make coffee, of all ghastly things to make on a hot afternoon, and I fumed and shook and felt mad all over. Did this woman who had abandoned me so casually at birth think she could turn up and criticize my way of life?

When the coffee was ready, I put it on a small tray with cream and sugar and a plate of Mrs. Griggs' cookies and took it to my guest. She was sitting in a chair when I came in, and she said nothing. She just *looked* with her deadly, penetrating stare.

"I hope this is all right," I said and turned to leave the room. Then I turned back. Mother or not, this woman would have to account for her actions. Certainly twenty-six years of cavalier behavior demanded some explanation. I imagine that my expression was not too friendly.

"Would you mind telling me how you happen to turn up here at this late date? I think I have some right to know." My voice sounded disagreeable in my own ears.

My mother quietly set down the little silver pot when she had finished pouring her coffee.

"So?" She spoke very softly. "Later perhaps after I have seen Ella Rutledge. You will ask her, please, when she wishes to see me. Who else is in her house?"

I gasped for breath. This astonishing woman had put me, the injured party, on the defensive. And then surprisingly I found myself explaining about Bea and Tony Forrester and the Starrs.

A smile that had a hint of cynicism in it played over Amelia Ortiz' heavy features. "I see. My aunt has in her house and in yours all her remaining relatives. This is most interesting. And the good Parsons? She is still alive?"

"Yes, very much so." A paralyzing frustration had crept into my mind. Couldn't I get anything out of this woman who bore me? I had the feeling that years of living in a tropical country had slowed down her reactions until they were sluggish and her mind without fire. All in good time, she seemed to say, and maybe never.

My mind churned and roared and beat in sympathy with the heavy stream of tepid water from my shower. Aunt Ella *did* have all her surviving relatives around her, and she wanted to discuss business with them, and what the business could be I hadn't an idea in the world.

Will Starr was the son of Conchita Rutledge Starr, and Conchita had been the sister of Henry Rutledge, Aunt Ella's husband. And the woman in the other room was my mother, the daughter of Aunt Ella's sister. Bea, of course, was Henry Rutledge's granddaughter.

When I had dressed in the coolest thing I owned, a white chiffon dinner dress, I pinned a white flower in my hair and picked up my silver kid bag. Then I laughed aloud. My black-clad mother and I would make a very dramatic entrance at Oak Hill.

We did, too. My mother had put on a black crepe dinner dress with long sleeves and a high neck, and over one arm she carried a black lace scarf, very beautiful and silky. I grudgingly admitted to myself that she really had great distinction.

When Glore opened the door to us, I told him there would be one more to dinner. I gestured toward Amelia as she walked ahead of me. "My mother, Mrs. Ortiz, Glore."

The dear old man gasped very faintly. He quickly recovered his impeccable butlerishness and said, "Yes, Miss Susan," and bowed and smiled and told me that the others were on the terrace at the back.

Privately I thought it a horrid shame that Bea couldn't see my mother and me in the black and white hall, but we went on to the terrace.

We stood in the east door for a minute soaking up the cool green loveliness before us. Beyond the brick-paved terrace stretched acres of perfect lawn under the great somber oaks. The sprinklers were turned on full, and shafts of light poured through the leaves of the trees making a million tiny rainbows. The swimming pool at the southeast corner of the house was temptingly lined with turquoise tile. The heat lay heavy around us, but what we looked at was cool. It helped a lot.

Tony Forrester, beautiful in white flannels and navy blue jacket, all but ran toward us in his eagerness to display his perfect hospitality. When I introduced him to my mother, his smile of delight in having another guest almost covered his amazement.

"Of course. Mrs. Ortiz. But this is marvellous. How exciting for you and Susan." I could see him trying to decide whether to kiss my mother's hand or not. Her bow and "how-do-you-do" were so impersonal and dignified that Tony was almost abashed. But not quite.

Bea, to my amusement, had recovered from her headache. Her mouth dropped open in bewilderment as Tony made effusive introductions of "our own dear Susan's mother." Then I noticed with a rising tide of joy that my mother stopped Tony with quiet irritation.

"Mr. Forrester, I have known Will and Mabel Starr since before you were born." She shook hands with the pudgy Mabel who was got up in a hopeless printed georgette, bowed with great cordiality to the pompous Will, and spoke pleasantly to young Bill and Peggy. Then good old Amelia, as she had become in my mind, sat down with great aplomb and said she'd have Dubonnet.

Bill Starr, a nice young colt of twenty-two, looked hot, awkward and speechless in his soldier's uniform, so I went over to talk to him. I asked him how soldiering was, and he said it was fine and lapsed into gloomy contemplation of a glass of ginger ale which he was drinking for his mother's benefit. Mabel was a pillar of the Long Beach Methodist Church and went about making a fool of herself by telling everyone that her children had never tasted beer, wine, or spirits. I made a mental note to see that poor Bill got a drink somehow, as I knew that he took one whenever he got a chance.

Daughter Peggy was gazing with rapt adoration at Bea, and no wonder. Bea's pale gray and white printed dress was a masterpiece of the dressmaker's art, and Peggy's pink satin "formal" was not. Even as I looked at Peggy, she was surreptitiously removing her pink pearl necklace and her earrings. Peggy didn't have Bea's chic, but she had something Bea had never had. She had a kindly, generous-hearted expression around her mouth, and a real look of youth glowed in her big gray eyes.

In answer to my questions, she told me that she was still going to Long Beach Junior College but expected to go to Southern Cal after Christmas.

With one ear flapping in the breeze while the other listened to Peggy, I heard my weird female parent evade with pleasant impersonality all inquiries as to where she had come from, why, and for how long. When I got a chance, I asked Bea about Aunt Ella. She shook her head and said seriously that Ella wasn't so hot and that I could go upstairs before dinner and see her.

In my aunt's pleasant sitting room, I found Parsons looking weary and ancient. She motioned to me to go on into the bedroom. I was glad to see that the big room was fresh and cool. The full white curtains hung motionless at the windows, though.

Surprisingly, Aunt Ella looked pretty good. Her color seemed less red and flushed, but her voice was quavery and thin and old. She said hello and that I looked nice and that she was glad to see me. Then she closed her eyes, and I stood there smiling and prattling like an idiot about nothing.

I knew, of course, that she couldn't see Amelia Ortiz that night, and I decided to say nothing of Amelia's arrival. It might upset Aunt Ella, and there seemed no point to spoiling the night for her.

We talked about the Starrs for a minute—she hadn't seen them yet—and I told her that Peggy seemed a dear child and very pretty.

"Will's still pompous and mousey, though." I laughed a little. "The real estate business must still be bad."

Then Aunt Ella smiled faintly, and I leaned over and kissed her hot, dry forehead.

"The doctor says I can see them tomorrow if I sleep well. You tell them that, Susan." I said I would and walked quietly out of the room.

Parsons was still in the sitting room, fiddling with the chintz slipcover on a chair. She looked very tired.

"Listen, Parsons," I said, "why don't we have Doctor Hilliard send a nurse? You're worn out."

"No, Miss Susan," she said, clicking her teeth with an emphatic rattle. "I can take care of Mrs. Rutledge. We don't need a nurse. All we need is quiet."

"But, Parsons, you're so tired you'll get sick, too. Then where'll we be?" I said.

"No, Miss Susan. I don't want any nurses around here. I'll do my own work."

I sighed. "All right. Have it your own way." I looked around to make sure that the bedroom door was closed. "Listen, Parsons. Guess what? My mother, Mrs. Ortiz, is here."

Parsons drew a sharp breath. A look of agonizing terror swept across her haggard, wrinkled face. Every bit of color drained from it, leaving her lips blue. I was terrified. I thought the woman would faint. I shoved her into a chair.

"Good Lord, Parsons. What's the matter? Tell me quickly. What is it?" My heart was hammering so that it hurt.

She leaned back in the chair and shut her eyes. Then she groped for her handkerchief and wiped her lips with hands that shook until I expected the bones to rattle.

"I don't know, Miss Susan. It just gave me a turn. It's so long since we've seen Mrs. Ortiz and not ever hearing from her and all."

I could feel my eyes drawing into slits. I *knew* Parsons was lying.

"Listen here," I said sharply, "you tell me what's up. If my mother's here to make trouble for Aunt Ella, I'll see that she leaves. She has no claim on us. What is it?"

Parsons seemed to draw her skinny body farther into the wing chair. She shook her head. "Really, Miss Susan, it's nothing. I was just thinking of when Miss Eleanor died and all. Mrs. Ortiz was there then—after you were born and all. It was so sad for Mrs. Rutledge. That's all. Really."

Like hell it was. But there was no information to be got out of Aunt Ella's faithful servitor.

I went downstairs determined to work on my mother, and if necessary to send her away, but I had little hope of success with my plans.

Dinner was a strange meal. We sat in the big, cool dining room eating off Lowestoft plates set in dark, old mahogany that gleamed in the light of the candles with eighteenth-century Rutledges staring down at us from the walls—we, the remaining Rutledge connections, except for the tired old woman who was undoubtedly dying upstairs.

The room seethed with unasked and unanswered questions, and uncomfortable silences fell frequently. Glore and Jane padded quietly around the room serving us, and not even young Bill, whose appetite was normally huge, paid much attention to the delicious food that was set before us.

Only Amelia Ortiz, all black and white distinction, seemed to retain her unshakable poise. She chatted amiably with Tony, and when the conversation lapsed, she seemed quite content with the silence, but her food left the table almost untouched, too, I noticed.

The dreadful meal was finally ended, and when we went onto the terrace to drink our coffee, Bea told Glore to take away the candles shielded by hurricane lamps. "They attract the bugs, Glore. It's cooler in the dark," she said.

We sat in the black heat without even stars to light the night because of the thick leaves on the oaks that shielded the sky. There was the glow of cigarettes and Will Starr's cigar and the faint rattle of spoons on silver saucers and silence and occasional sighs. When Glore had gone, I said that Aunt Ella would be able to talk business on Saturday if she had a good night.

My wire-taut nerves told me that I really did hear a sharply indrawn breath as I finished speaking. But I didn't know where it came from.

As my mother and I were leaving the house, Bea waylaid me in the hall and pulled me into the powder room. The well-known Beatrice Forrester poise had vanished into the night. Even her impeccable grooming was disintegrating in nervousness that was almost desperate.

"Susan, for God's sake, where did that woman come from? What's she here for? Does Aunt Ella know she's here?" She lit a cigarette and burned herself on her lighter and said "Damn!"

For the first time in a long time, I was very sorry for Bea. She had trouble—what kind I didn't know—and no experience in coping with it.

I shrugged my shoulders. "You know as much as I do. I found her on the terrace, and she isn't talking. 'Later perhaps.' I didn't tell Aunt Ella she was here—she needs her sleep. But, Bea, I told Parsons, and she damned near fainted."

Bea sat down on the little stool in front of the mirrored dressing table. Her eyes were wide, and her mouth unattractively open. She rubbed a long beautifully kept hand across her forehead. "Something around here stinks if you ask me," she said eloquently.

I agreed and said that I'd work on Amelia, but that she was a button-mouth if I ever saw one. "Come on," I said, "we can't keep the good woman standing around the hall forever."

Mrs. A. Ortiz emerged from the blue drawing room as Bea and I came into the hall. The Starrs had disappeared.

"Yes," my mother was saying to Tony, "it is a most magnificent house. The things in the Huntington Museum in Pasadena are no better than these things." She gestured toward a Chippendale settee as she spoke, and then Glore came into the hall.

He told me I was wanted on the telephone, and I went into the library to talk. I came back quickly.

"It's Mr. Opal, Bea. He called to invite you and Tony and me to tennis at his house tomorrow. I declined with thanks."

Bea raised her pretty eyebrows. "That was decent of him," she said.

Tony roared with laughter. "Good old Opal," he said. "You know, Susan, I love that man. He studies *Esquire* faithfully every month. Then he rushes over to his tailor and orders his clothes. Does Opal love a good loud check!"

Bea let out a snort of disgust. "You're a nasty pair of cats, you two. Opal's really very decent. I shall go over there and play tennis if I can." She turned on her heel, waved, and walked upstairs, so I shouted after her.

"As a matter of fact, I thought we'd be busy." I said. "Maybe we can all go."

Tony walked out to the car with me and my foundling mother. "Opal's going to be a country gentleman or die trying," he said, as he helped us in with a lot of unnecessary gallantry and gestures.

My efforts to pump Amelia were totally fruitless. She said with great aplomb that she was tired and would go at once to bed. Trailing down the hall after her without dignity or even good taste, I managed to get in my two cents' worth.

"Parsons," I said in an unnecessarily loud tone of voice, "almost fainted when she heard you were here. Can you imagine why?"

Mrs. Ortiz turned around, raised her heavy black eyebrows, and said, "Really ?" Then she said goodnight politely and shut the door.

I was so mad that I knew that there was no point in trying to go to bed. Besides, the house was still a stuffy oven, so I marched out onto the terrace and stood there smoking and looking up at Oak Hill. There was a light in Aunt Ella's sitting room in the north wing, but the rest of the house was dark. Then I decided to walk over to the Hilliards, as I knew I would slowly perish of frustration if I didn't talk to someone.

When I was down at the bridge, Bonnie joined me, and we walked along under the trees until we had covered the quarter of a mile of path that separates my house from Joe and Anne's. Their house was dark, which was most unusual as they are in the habit of staying up until two or three.

I walked all the way around the seven-room white Cape Cod cottage hoping that the noise I made might even awaken them. Then I saw that both cars were gone from the garage, so I gave up and went home and to bed. The light in my guest room was out, too, and I wondered if Amelia slept well after all the excitement she'd caused.

I rolled and turned in the heat and got up and drank water and finally shamelessly took off my nightgown and lay on top of the sheets. With fine self-discipline I forced all baffling questions from my mind and at last went to sleep.

In the morning the clamoring jangle of the telephone wakened me. I made a dash for my living room before I realized that I had no clothes on, then stumbled back to the bedroom to put on a negligee, with a half-witted notion that it was immodest to talk on the telephone unclothed. I picked up the telephone, giggling at my own nonsense, but Bea's nerve-ridden voice quickly sobered me.

"Susan, for God's sake, come up here right away. Aunt Ella's had a stroke, and that fool Parsons has disappeared."

My heart stopped in space. "Oh, Bea. When?"

"Some time in the night. Hilliard's here now. Nanny just happened to go in there, or Lord knows when we would have found her. That Parsons!"

CHAPTER 5

"The morning Aunt Ella had her bad stroke."

That phrase is enough to call to my mind a picture of complete chaos. The well-oiled machinery that ran Oak Hill had a monkey wrench in it that day.

Glore opened the front door for me, and in spite of worry and downright fear, I realized that he had a stubble of white whiskers fringing his old face that was so worried that he looked like an elderly and careworn bloodhound. It had taken a crisis to force Glore to appear in public unshaved.

"Oh, Glore," I said, making a dash across the hall, "isn't this awful?"

He muttered something behind me, and I ran upstairs to find most of the household staff and all the house guests milling around the hall. Will Starr's mousey fringe of hair was standing on end, and he was futilely trying to fasten a suspender to a non-existent button. Mabel, wearing non-glamour-girl negligee and hairnet tied under her chin, kept squealing over and over, "I can't understand this. I can't understand this."

I thrust open the door of Aunt Ella's sitting room to find Bea pacing the floor, smoking furiously, her pretty face laced with lines put there by trouble and worry.

She turned swiftly at my entrance. "Thank God you're here, Susan." She pointed to the closed door of the bedroom. "Hilliard's in there. Nanny's helping him. Go see what's happened to my brats, will you?"

The hell with Bea's brats, I thought, sitting down hard on a small Sheraton chair: "They can wait. What happened? Is she going to die?" It was difficult to say that last word.

Bea shoved her hair off her forehead. "I don't know. She looks ghastly. She's paralyzed and can't talk."

"Where's Tony?" I said, thinking that he might look after his children just this once.

Bea kicked the train of her lace-encrusted, satin negligee. "I don't know," she said, a petulant expression crossing her face. "He's *never* around when he's needed."

I went to the hall door and told Jane to go in and stay with the children until Nanny got back.

"Hilliard had me call the hospital for nurses—three of them," Bea said. "I'd like to murder that damned Parsons."

I jumped up as soon as I'd sat down. "Listen, Bea. This doesn't make sense. Have you looked for her? Why, she wouldn't leave Aunt Ella for anything on earth. She's too faithful to be human. She was dead tired last night, but she wouldn't let me get nurses to help her."

Bea sat down and crossed her legs nonchalantly. "Well, her bed's empty, and she isn't in the house. Glore looked all over for her."

Parsons had her room in the service wing of the house and kept her clothes there, but ever since Aunt Ella's first stroke, Parsons had insisted on sleeping in the day bed in Aunt Ella's dressing room. She loathed nurses and was so jealous of her prerogatives as Aunt Ella's personal maid that we'd let her have her own way.

I went into the dressing room to look around. It was a good-sized room with three walls lined with mirrors which concealed the closets and cupboards for Aunt Ella's clothes. A long dressing table was in front of one window and the day bed, neatly turned down, was in front of the other. The white percale sheet which Parsons used for a blanket cover was marked as though her bony little body had laid down on it for a few minutes' rest.

The room was as blank and impersonal as a hospital operating room. The beautiful bathroom beyond was equally empty and immaculate. The walls were made of glass with murals painted on the back by a talented young Russian who'd been Aunt Ella's protégé. The underwater scene of tropical fish and long spears of seaweed seemed to move and float in the shaded green light that filtered through the blinds.

I stood near the bedroom trying to hear sounds of activity in the bedroom, but the door was too thick.

Then I went back to the service wing to look at Parsons' room. It was a nice room, and like everything about the little Englishwoman, it was orderly and fresh and clean, its woodwork spotless, the white curtains perky with starch. The narrow blue metal bed was untouched.

I opened her closet to see her clothes hanging in a careful row, her hats—Queen Mary style—on little stands covered with transparent bags. Her sturdy black pocketbook was in a cellophane bag in the top righthand drawer of the dresser. There was a five-dollar bill in the coin purse, nothing else.

I opened the drawer of the blue writing table, and then I closed it. There seemed no point in reading Parsons' personal papers until we had a better idea of where she'd gone.

The rest of Parsons' domain was the sewing room next door. It, too, was empty and impersonal except for Bea's gray-and-white dinner dress which Katherine had doubtless brought in to press.

The other rooms in the servants' wing were as nicely furnished as Parsons', but they all contained unmade beds and more signs of having been lived in, Mrs. Griggs' especially with dozens of snapshots and photographs of Bea, the children, and myself. But there was no Parsons anywhere.

I went down the back stairs and into the vast white-tiled kitchen. Mrs. Griggs was seated at the center table consoling herself with coffee. She stood up as I came in.

"Sit down, Mrs. Griggs, please," I said.

She shook her head sadly. "This is a bad day for Oak Hill, Miss Susan. Mrs. Rutledge is helpless, they tell me."

"Yes," I said equally sadly, "it's horrible, but, Mrs. Griggs, what do you suppose has happened to Parsons? Mrs. Forrester says she can't be found, and I'm sure she didn't go out. All her hats and things are still in her room. When did you see her last?"

Mrs. Griggs' fat cheeks, mute testimony to her own fine cooking, wobbled in bewilderment. "Miss Susan, I couldn't tell you, I'm sure. Parsons was that faithful—jealous, too—she'd never leave Mrs. Rutledge without she was chloroformed. She came down at nine-thirty last night and had a cup of coffee with me in the servants' dining room. She said Mrs. Rutledge was resting nicely, and that was the last any of us saw of her. Jane said she thought she heard her in the bathroom about ten-thirty, but she didn't see her."

I sighed and shook my head and went into Glore's pantry. He was busy unlocking cupboards and getting out silver. He looked up as I came in, and I smiled to see that he'd managed to shave.

"Glore, Mrs. Forrester told me you'd looked all over for Parsons. Did you look in the attic?"

Glore's face looked blood-houndier than ever.

"Miss Susan, Jane and I looked in every room in this house from attic to basement. We even looked under furniture and in closets and cupboards. I don't see what could have happened." He set down a handsome Georgian coffee urn as he spoke.

The buzzer sounded then, and Glore and I looked up at the indicator. It said front door, so we both went to see what it could be. As we walked through the dining room, I told Glore to have Magruder search the grounds and outbuildings. "And be sure to ask Robert if he's seen her." Robert is the chauffeur. "And Glore, when did Mr. Forrester go out?"

"I don't know, Miss Susan. Katherine says his bed hasn't been slept in."

We had reached the front hall by that time, and Glore opened the door to admit my mother, still unruffled and dignified and black-clad. She said good morning to both of us and inquired what the excitement was.

As I told her, I watched a queer expression cross her face. It was there for only a second, but I had a distinct feeling that it was fear, pure fear. Then it was gone as quickly as it came to be replaced by an appropriate expression of grief and compassion.

Glore waited until we had stopped talking to tell us that there would be breakfast in the dining room in half an hour.

Mrs. Ortiz and I went into the blue drawing room, so called in honor of the fine old faded blue damask set in the panelling and to distinguish it from another drawing room on the other side of the hall.

"You dashed off in such a hurry," Amelia said calmly, "that I was sure something was wrong."

"Yes, something is very wrong," I said, "and on top of everything else Parsons has vanished—completely and without trace."

"So?" She drew the word out. Then she made a strange sound that was half-laugh and half-snort. "That is most unfortunate."

Joe Hilliard came to the door of the drawing room. The lines from his nostrils to his mouth were deep, and he looked as though he needed about fourteen hours' uninterrupted sleep.

"I thought I heard you in here, Susan," he said, patting my shoulder. "Well, I've done what I can. Nature'll have to do the rest."

He spoke pleasantly to my mother when I introduced them, and they both lit cigarettes.

I sat there afraid to speak, afraid almost to listen. My heart pounded dully, and my mouth was dry.

"Joe," I said at last, "will she get well?"

A little grin twisted Joe's mouth. "It's too soon to say, Susan. Her general condition is pretty fair, but ..." He lifted his shoulders in a shrug. "I've called in Bromley. I don't want this responsibility by myself." A frown knotted his eyebrows. "Say, Susan, what happened to that hag of a maid? She just plain deserted her post, that's what. Why—"his voice rattled on under the impact of his anger—" Mrs. Rutledge was lying there with one leg out of the bed and her pillow on the floor. Damn it!"

He stood up, and I could feel horror crawling up my spine. "You mean she tried to get help, and no one was there?"

"I don't know. It's queer. I don't see how she got her leg out of the bed, but she did."

He stood up. "I think I hear those nurses. I'll get them started, and, Susan, I want all three of them to stay right here in the house."

I said I'd make the arrangements and asked when I could see Aunt Ella.

"Any time," he said, and I followed him out into the hall where Glore was admitting the three nurses. They were all from the Rutledge Memorial and all greatly distressed at Aunt Ella's condition. Glore and

I discussed their lodging, and he said he would make the arrangements, and the three women went upstairs with Joe. Mrs. Hill, the plump, middle-aged one; Miss Conover, the young, spunky redheaded one; and Miss Quincey, the thin, middle-aged one.

The door at the back of the hall opened to let in a flood of sunlight, also Tony Forrester wearing a yellow terry-cloth robe and straw slippers. I couldn't see his face, but he could see mine, and I must have looked like a shrew.

"Tony, where have you been? Aunt Ella's had a stroke—a bad one—and Parsons has disappeared."

He let out a long, low whistle. "Gad, Susan. That's awful. I had a swim down at the pool last night, and it was so hot I slept on one of those couch things. I just woke up."

"All right," I said. "Go get dressed. Are you going to the city today?"

With one hand on the stair rail, he stopped. "Hell! I've got to—for a while—but I'll get back as soon as I can. Tell Glore to send me up some breakfast. I'll eat it while I dress. Then I can get started sooner."

The Starrs, Amelia, and I had breakfast together. Peggy, very young and pretty in powder-blue slacks, and Bill, young and attractive in his khaki shirt and trousers, were quiet and subdued. I wondered what they really felt about this serious illness of their rich relation.

Will, who always bought his real estate dear and sold it cheap with plenty of alibis thrown in, was feeling his oats. He seemed to wish to convey the impression that as a man of affairs, he could be counted on in an emergency.

"We're going to stay over, Susan. I've explained to Bea that she needs an older man in the house," he said, attacking his scrambled eggs with zest. "We'll just stay and see Ella through this crisis. Of course, Tony's a lawyer and all that, but he's very young, too."

I had a pretty picture of Will pawing around in Aunt Ella's papers, and determined to see that he didn't get the chance. Mabel, not bothering to wait until Glore and Jane went back to the pantry, bristled with housewifely importance under her pink shirtmaker dress. "You know, Susan, servants get awfully slack when the head of the house is laid up. I think I ought to be here to keep an eye on things."

I blushed and was glad that Glore and Jane had the good manners to leave the room.

Good old Amelia put in her two cents' worth. "I rather imagine, Mabel, that this house runs itself. The staff is marvellously well trained, and of course, Bea is very competent."

I couldn't eat, and I couldn't stand the silly squabbling so I drained my coffee cup and excused myself. "I've got to call the shop, and I want to see Aunt Ella," I said, getting out fast.

Aunt Ella's quiet, cool bedroom seemed to bristle with starched nurses moving swiftly and efficiently about the business of taking care of her.

As I stood by the bed looking down at her, I felt sure that my heart must explode under the pressure of my sorrow and distress. Her kindly face sagged grotesquely, her mouth misshapen and unreal. Her eyes might have been chunks of glass for all the expression they contained.

I hoped that she could hear the things I said to her, the things that contained all my love and gratitude for all the years of her love and care, and I took what comfort I could from the fact that I knew that everything was being done to make her comfortable. I worried, though, about what she must think of Parsons' absence. I wondered if she were aware of it, or if she lived in some remote, unreal world of her own, untouched by the lives around her.

The day dragged on somehow. Glore reported that Magruder had found no trace of Parsons. Joe came with Doctor Bromley and told us that there had been no change, either for better or worse. Doctor Bromley even went so far as to say that there was a possibility—very faint—that Aunt Ella might recover to the extent of being able to speak.

We ate luncheon in the dining room because it was too hot for the terrace where we usually lunched in summer, and no one made the slightest effort to talk.

Afterwards Bea suggested that I take Peggy and Bill over to Mr. Opal's to play tennis, but they both said they'd been outside, and it was too hot to play. "I'd rather swim," Peggy said diffidently, so the two youngsters went down to the pool, and I called Mr. Opal and told him that none of us would be able to come to his tennis party, after all.

He said he'd heard in the village that Mrs. Rutledge was ill and asked if he could do anything, and I said no, but that he was very kind.

Tony took his time about coming back from the city and showed good sense as well as selfishness. San Francisco was bound to be much cooler than the country as it had been hot over there for the usual three days, and now the fog would come in and cool it off.

Amelia Ortiz went back down to my house after lunch, explaining that the siesta habit acquired in South America was impossible to break, and I was glad to see her go. She was unnerving, and the atmosphere was bad enough without her calm impersonality which caused me to bristle with questions. A long-lost parent was no pleasure in my life.

I helped Bea send wires to the guests she'd invited for Sunday lunch, and when we had finished, Bea made me very happy by grinning broadly.

"You won, Susan," she said. "No party, and now I'm going to take a nap."

I grinned back at her. "I wish you'd been able to have it, pal. That'd be better than having Aunt Ella laid up. And, Bea, what are we going to do about Parsons?"

She turned back from the door. "What can we do? We can't find her, and we've looked, Lord knows."

"Do you suppose we should tell the police?" I asked.

"Police!" Bea shrieked. "What have the police got to do with it?" She advanced upon me with anger blazing out of her eyes. "Are you crazy? Making fools of ourselves in the papers just because that half-witted maid takes French leave!"

I sighed with irritation. "Bea, you know very well Parsons'd never leave here under her own power without telling us she was going. All her hats and her pocketbook are in her room. Something's happened to her."

Bea trembled with anger. "You mind your own business. Parsons is crazy as a loon—has been ever since the war started—and we're not calling in any police. She'll turn up. She probably went to work at the Red Cross or Bundles for Britain. And she could have another hat and another pocketbook, you know." Bea tried to force a wavering smile about something that wasn't at all funny.

I stood up. "All right, my cousin, but if Parsons isn't back here tomorrow morning, I'm going to report her disappearance to the police."

I walked out of the library without looking back. What had got into Bea? I didn't know, but I certainly had no intention of keeping Parsons' disappearance out of the public prints just to please Mrs. Anthony Forrester.

Glore bore down upon me in the hall. He was carrying a little silver salver with a note on it.

"This note is for you, Miss Susan. Jane found it in the powder room," he said.

I took the note and said that was a funny place for it to be, and Glore walked off.

The heavy white envelope with the Oak Hill address engraved on the back flap was sealed, so I ripped it open. It was typewritten, and as I read it, I could feel myself breathing fast and trembling and hating myself.

The note said, "Will you meet me down at the Farm House at five this afternoon? We can't talk with all those Starrs in our hair. Love—"

It was signed "af," just like that in lower case, and I knew what "af" meant. It meant Anthony Forrester.

"Damn," I muttered and went out and got in my car and drove down to my house.

CHAPTER 6

"Now what?" I thought venomously, and banged my car door shut and slammed into my house before I remembered that a South American siesta was taking place in the guest room.

I went in to my room and took off my messy, damp dress and put on a negligee and sat down at my dressing table. I brushed my hair two hundred strokes, and as I counted I thought about Tony Forrester, and some of the thoughts were not exactly printable. Would Tony never learn? Did he think that he could play upon my sympathy, use me, year after year, when all the old business was long since finished? Didn't he know that he'd done quite enough?

I called the shop and talked to Wilda who seemed to have the situation well in hand. "Don't you worry about a thing, Miss Brooks," she said in a voice of kindly sympathy which I greatly appreciated. "We'll get the work out of the workroom, and we'll just tell the other clients they'll have to wait. Everybody loves Mrs. Rutledge. They'll understand."

I thanked her, and we hung up.

I went back to my room and got Tony's note and read it again. He must have written it in the morning before he left. Then I took it out to the kitchen and dropped it in the incinerator and waited until it had burned up.

In the shower I had a long and consciously phony debate with myself about going to the Farm House, and when five o'clock came, I went as I had known I would all along.

When Uncle Henry Rutledge was alive, he farmed the whole valley—fruit, dairy cattle, and some wheat at the far end of the valley about five miles from the house—and he had a competent farmer who lived in a fair-sized house across the creek. After his death, Aunt Ella found that the management of the farm was too much for her, so she sold off the wheat land and the cattle, except for two or three cows which supplied the house with dairy products, and sold the fruit on the trees. The Farm House was an attractive, white clapboard building, and I had wanted to remodel it for myself until we found that it was riddled with termites. We knew that it ought to be torn down and the lumber burned, but we hadn't got around to it. It had been empty for about twenty years.

I followed the path that led over to the Hilliard place until I got across the creek. Then I stood there debating about being sensible and going up to see Anne or going on to the Farm House. Of course, I went on to the Farm House, following the old, unused road inches deep in dust.

The heat lay over the valley, even that late in the afternoon, with the heaviness of water on the ocean floor. My big white straw hat seemed to weigh forty pounds, but it was better than the sun. My white sandals were coated with dust after I had taken ten steps and I tried walking in the orchard, but that was even worse as the plowed chunks of sun-baked adobe cut into my feet and made the going unutterably difficult. The pear crop had been harvested, but the orchard was teeming with thousands of nasty little fruit flies feasting on rotted pears that had dropped to the ground before the picking. I brushed them away from my face with irritation and plodded on through the dust and heat. The valley seemed to hang suspended in silence. Even the birds were too hot and uncomfortable to sing, and the creek was a joke. There was nothing in it in the way of water except a foot-wide, slimy green ribbon.

"You fool," I kept muttering to myself. "You fool."

I nearly jumped out of my skin when the heavy silence was suddenly broken by a loud bawl coming from somewhere on my right.

Then I laughed. It was Virginia, the cow, down in the creek bed. With the ingenuity of her kind, she frequently managed to break out of her pasture, and she always made for the creek. After she had eaten her fill of whatever delectable green thing she craved so violently, she could never get up out of the little ravine. She'd just bawl until Magruder or one of his assistants came and showed her an easy place to get out.

I laughed at her and called her name, and she let out a couple more bawls, and as it was time for milking, I knew she'd soon be rescued. Then I went on the remaining hundred yards to the Farm House looking for Tony as I walked. I didn't call out. I didn't want the cow-searchers to see me, but the silly, clandestine antic was distasteful to me.

There was no Tony to be seen. I walked clear around the house and up on to the porch in front before I thought of the termites and got off. Then I headed for the barn, all the time brushing fruit flies out from under my hat and cursing myself for an idiot. I looked down at my feet and legs and gagged with revulsion at what I saw. I was barelegged, and the skin on my feet was streaked with sweat and dust.

Half-way to the barn, I turned back. If Tony was sneaking a conversation with me, he certainly wouldn't be hanging around the barn at five o'clock when the milking was taking place. Even at that moment, I could hear Magruder's voice at the back of the barn urging one of the cows along, so in spite of heat and overwhelming discomfort, I turned and ran back to the Farm House before I could be seen. I stood panting behind a crooked old apple tree near the back porch and watched Magruder lead Genevieve into the barn. Bea and I always named the cows, and we liked nice elaborate names. The third one was called

Josephine.

Then I called softly, "Tony. Tony. Come out, come out, wherever you are."

There was no answer. No sound at all except the faint murmur of Magruder's conversation with Genevieve coming from the barn.

I walked around to the north side of the house and gingerly sat down on a stone step that led to the side door of the house. The stone was hot, and I was careful to ease myself down gradually. I pushed my hat to the back of my head and wiped my face with a piece of Kleenex and lit a cigarette. My watch said five-thirty, and I had got to the rendezvous late, but with good reason. Tony had been late for everything all his life, including his wedding. If he didn't come by the time I finished my cigarette, I would wallow back through the dust, take another shower, dress for dinner, and that would be that.

I took my time about smoking the cigarette. My surroundings weren't especially attractive, but I seemed to be at peace for the first time in days. Of course, Aunt Ella was still ill, I had my strange parent hanging around, I'd been a fool to walk half a mile in the blazing heat for nothing, and doubtless my business was deteriorating from neglect, but it was quiet there on the step. Even the fruit flies seemed to find the tangle of ancient blackberry vines across the path more attractive than my face.

I put out my cigarette in the dust and wiped off my face and mouth. Then I put on more lipstick and pulled my hat back where it belonged. I sat still for just a second longer, just one more moment of peace before I had to plunge back into the sea of trouble that seemed to surround us.

Then I saw it.

Something white behind the blackberry vines growing over a wire fence. Something white that looked out of place, inappropriate.

Jerking little nerves twitched across the back of my neck. I shivered hard, convulsively. Then I walked forward, faster and faster, until I knelt before the vines, tearing at them with hands that didn't even feel the ripping, slashing thorns.

The horrible crumpled thing, bloody and misshapen and staring, was Parsons. Dead!

I staggered to my feet and started to run, jerking at my dress that was caught in the vines. I wanted urgently, painfully to scream, but no sound came from between my dry lips.

Stumbling and panting and dirty, I ran until I fell on the concrete in front of the barn, the heel of my sandal broken.

CHAPTER 7

It took me a long time to get up on my feet and limp inside, and I still couldn't make a sound. My throat's paralyzed, I thought insanely, just like Aunt Ella's.

The barn was clean and quiet and smelled only faintly of the animals that lived there. It was a lot cooler than the outside, too. I kept on walking until I came to the stall where Magruder was milking Genevieve. He heard me, but he didn't look up.

"You find Virginia, John?" he said, steadily splashing streams of rich milk into the shiny pail.

Then he looked up, his eyes widening in horror. He jumped to his feet.

"Great Scott, Miss Susan! What's happened to you?"

He reached out his bony hands to steady me, and that did it. A torrent of words broke from my throat and poured out of me.

"Parsons! I found her. In the blackberry vines. You must get her out right away, Magruder. She's dead. And the flies! It's horrible!"

Then I sobbed and sank down onto the concrete floor of the barn, all control gone.

I'm ashamed of that performance, and even at the time, I was sorry for Magruder, who stood helplessly above me, his good face lined and wrinkled and confused.

John, Magruder's helper, came in, leading the other cow, and he, too, stood there confused and helpless until some spark of sense lit up my brain, and I pulled myself together.

The men helped me up from the floor and followed me out of the barn and across to the Farm House and around to the north side. I pointed at the blackberry vines which I had pulled aside to reveal their grisly secret.

"Get her out of there, Magruder. Quick. It's ghastly," I said. He and John stood there peering into the vines. Then Magruder turned back to me. His face was blue-gray with horror.

"My God, Miss Susan! This is terrible." He looked at me steadily. "I can't move her, Miss Susan. We'll have to call the police. Looks to me like she's been stabbed. Murdered."

Then Magruder, a true executive, took charge. He sent John to telephone the police and told him to have Robert come down with the station wagon and get me. He told John to say nothing about Parsons up at the house. "No need to get everybody excited."

"You better go home and lay down, Miss Susan," he said seriously, after

John had gone on his errand.

He had brought a chair out in front of the barn for me, and I sat on it clutching my head between my hands and trying to squeeze the sight of Parsons out of my mind.

"I *knew* Parsons wouldn't just go off," I said with tears rolling out of my eyes. "I knew it."

"Sure a terrible thing," Magruder said, "and Mrs. Rutledge so bad and all. I wonder...."

His voice trailed off, and I wondered too.

You certainly don't crawl under blackberry vines to commit suicide, but who on earth would want to kill the harmless Parsons?

"Have you seen any strangers around, Magruder? The last couple of days?" I said.

He shook his head gravely. "Hasn't been anybody around except the family since the pears were picked early last month. There's almost never any strangers up this valley on account of the road doesn't go through."

John came back in the station wagon with Robert, both of the young men looking excited, half in horror and half pleasurably. To my infinite disgust, Robert asked if he might view the remains before driving me to my house.

"All right," I snapped, "if you're that kind of a fool." I turned to John. "You got the police?"

He nodded his round, blond head. "Yes, Miss Susan. I got the sheriff's office. They'll be right over. I didn't tell anybody else."

I stood up, happy to see that Robert came back from his nasty errand looking very green around the gills.

"I guess I'd better go up to Oak Hill," I said. "I'll have to tell Mrs. Forrester."

I dragged myself up the stairs, leaving Robert to break the dreadful news to Glore, who had looked shocked silly at my condition and no wonder. My hands were bloody and full of thorns, my dress torn and dirty. I was carrying my sandals.

Bea jumped up from her chaise longue as I walked into her room.

"Did you fall?" she cried.

I shook my head and sat down on a white satin chair, and Bea looked apprehensive about the upholstery.

"Parsons," I muttered. "I found her in the blackberry vines back of the Farm House. She's been stabbed in the throat...." I could hear my voice disappearing into the black tide that came up to flood over me.

From the bed where I lay I could see a patch of sky full of enormous stars. Then I sat up quickly, my mouth dry and my heart pounding turgidly. There was something awful that had happened. I lay back. Ah, yes. Parsons violently murdered. Aunt Ella very ill.

Apparently I had passed out and somebody had put me to bed in Eleanor Rutledge's room, which was my room when I lived at Oak Hill.

With my knees feeling like overcooked macaroni, I managed to struggle out of bed and into a blue crepe negligee and down the hall to Aunt Ella's sitting room.

Mrs. Hill, the nurse, jumped up from a sofa, shoving her knitting aside. "Oh, Miss Brooks. You poor girl. You shouldn't be out of bed," she said, coming over to me.

"I'm all right," I said. "How's Mrs. Rutledge?"

A nice smile creased her plump face. "Pretty well, Miss Brooks. Not much change. She seems to be resting comfortably. Here, sit down."

She shoved a chair at me, and I was glad to use it. I put my hand up to push my hair off my forehead, and the hand hurt like fury. "Look," I said. "All these thorns. Can we get them out?"

She examined my hands and said she'd have to use tweezers.

"Where is everybody?" I asked.

"I think the family's at dinner, Miss Brooks. Aren't you hungry? Miss Conover and Miss Quincey are having their dinner with the family. Shall I order something for you?"

"No, thanks," I said. "I don't want anything to eat."

Mrs. Hill got the tweezers and went to work on my hands. It hurt a lot.

"How about it, Mrs. Hill? What do the police think about Parsons?" I said, wincing as the thorns came out.

She shook her head. "I don't know, Miss Brooks. Mr. Forrester talked to them. Of course it was some tramp." She tsk-tsk-ed and went on pulling thorns.

"Mrs. Hill, does Aunt Ella know anything?" I said. "Does she realize Parsons is gone or is she, well, out? Unconscious?"

Mrs. Hill looked very thoughtful, and she stopped pulling thorns for a minute. "I think she probably doesn't know anything, Miss Brooks."

I sighed. "Well, that's a blessing. She'd be insane with worry about Parsons. Poor Aunt Ella. Strokes are horrible things, aren't they?"

Mrs. Hill finally finished my hands and put some pink stuff on them. I thanked her for fixing them and said I thought I'd go downstairs. "I'll have some milk or something and talk to Tony."

Tony! The name crashed in my brain like a bomb. I'd forgotten about him completely. Tony, who'd told me to meet him at the Farm House. Tony, who hadn't shown up.

Mrs. Hill grabbed at me. "My Lord, Miss Brooks, what's the matter? You're not going to faint again, are you?"

"No," I said, pushing her out of the way. "I'm not. I'm going downstairs. Right now."

I ran out of the room and down the stairs. Glore was standing in the hall talking to a strange man.

"Miss Brooks," he said, "this gentleman asked for you." Glore looked very apologetic and half sick and no wonder. He and Parsons had been friends for twenty-six years.

"All right," I said, very conscious of uncombed hair and of being downstairs in a negligee of which Aunt Ella would have disapproved greatly. I walked toward the man.

He looked at me out of the most impersonal blue eyes I have ever seen in my life. "I'm the sheriff," he said. "Atwood's my name. I understand you found the Parsons woman's body."

He was a short, stocky man without any neck, and he looked as though he lived on starches and raw meat. The skin on his face was dark red and streaked with little purple veins. His black hair, sprinkled with gray at the temples, receded from his forehead in a great peak that made him look devilish. His ears were pointed, too.

"Yes," I said. "I did."

He held his Stetson hat in pudgy hands that had a lot of curly black hair on them.

"I'd like to ask you some questions," he said.

"All right," I said. "Glore, please take Mr. Atwood's hat. We'll go in the library."

Atwood followed me across the hall and into the library. I poured a glass of water for myself and offered him one. After we had both lit cigarettes, I sat down behind the leather-topped Chippendale writing table.

The man said nothing for a long time. He just looked at me and made me uncomfortable. I frowned.

"Listen," I said. "I don't feel very well. Shall we get this over with? I'd like to go back to bed."

"Okay," he said, sitting up straight in the red leather chair. He got a grubby-looking notebook out of his pocket and flipped over the pages. "Now, I understand that this woman was Mrs. Rutledge's personal maid, been with her twenty-seven years, very devoted, and so forth. Some time last night, she disappeared, and during the night Mrs. Rutledge had a stroke. This morning you people searched the house and grounds, but found no trace of the maid. That right?"

"Yes," I said, "that's right."

He put his cigarette out in a big Belgian crystal ash tray that lay on the desk. "It seems that this Elizabeth Parsons was very faithful. Wouldn't think of going off without telling someone?"

I nodded. "Yes, that's right. And we could tell from her clothes that she hadn't gone far. Her hats and her pocketbook were in her room."

He leaned forward and looked at me intently out of his glassy blue eyes. "But you didn't report her disappearance to the police. Why is that?"

I lit a cigarette off the stub of the one I'd just finished, and I felt like a fool for doing it. It's a sure indication of nervousness.

"Well, we thought we'd wait until tomorrow. If she hadn't turned up tomorrow morning, I was going to call you." The man nodded. "What do you think about this business?" I continued. "Who do you think killed her?"

He shook his head. "I don't know—yet. But I'll find out." He looked at the notebook again. "Apparently the cook, Mrs. Griggs, was the last person in the house to see her alive. Was this Parsons in the habit of walking around the grounds at night? Of going outside?"

I smiled a little. "No, Mr. Atwood, she wasn't. Bea—that's Mrs. Forrester—and I used to wonder how she lived. She never went outside if she could avoid it. She was always awfully pale—like a prisoner."

He stood up and walked around the room for a few minutes. "What a mess," he said sadly, and I agreed with him. Then he sat down again and leaned toward me. "Did the woman have any enemies that you know of? Any quarrels with the other servants. Anything like that?"

"No," I said emphatically. "The servants in this house get on together very well. The older ones have been friends for years, and they have a pretty rigid caste system of their own. They never interfere with each other's work. Of course, Parsons was, well, privileged, because she was so close to Mrs. Rutledge. But I'm sure the other servants wouldn't think of trespassing on her ground."

"How about family? Parsons have any relatives?" he asked.

I was beginning to get a dull, sickish feeling around the solar plexus. What was the man driving at? Why didn't he just go outside and pick up the tramp that had killed poor old Parsons instead of prying into her private life? I was distinctly edgy when I spoke.

"Parsons had a sister, brother-in-law, and two nieces—in England. She's been worried about them since the war started. She sent them clothes and sugar and coffee and money and things. But they're in England, not here."

The cold blue eyes glinted. So he could get some expression into them after all.

"How much money did the woman have?" he snapped.

I looked at him blandly. "I'm sure I don't know. She'd hardly discuss her financial affairs with me, but I imagine she had quite a nice tidy sum. She was well paid, and her expenses were almost nothing."

A prickly silence hung between us for several seconds. Then I stood up and pulled the boner of my life. I, in one sentence, earned Atwood's undying antagonism.

"Sheriff Atwood, I think you'd find Parsons' murderer a lot sooner if you'd get out of this house and spend more time looking for tramps and less in discussing Parsons' financial situation." I walked past the desk on my way to the door. "Now, if you'll excuse me...."

"Wait!" The man's voice whipped out at me. I turned around and lifted my eyebrows questioningly.

"I have good reason to believe that Elizabeth Parsons was murdered in this house!"

I grabbed a chair for support. The blood pounded and roared in a giant pulse in my throat.

"What do you mean?" I said. "You must be mad." My voice was a frantic whisper.

"No," he said evenly. "I'm not crazy, if that's what you mean. That woman's body was moved in a wheelbarrow—a blood-stained wheelbarrow—and taken down to the berry vines."

CHAPTER 8

I hobbled back to the desk and poured some water into a glass, slopping it all over the tray as I did so. When I drank it, I looked up at the sheriff. The desk lamp, shining up into his face, made him look like some devilish creature out of Albrecht Dürer's medieval imagination. Fear crawled over me like a thin coating of ice. Fear for Oak Hill and the people in it. And as I looked up at Atwood's eerily lighted face, I heard myself gasp from the pressure of my fear. Quick pictures of Parsons in the upstairs hall telling me about Aunt Ella's worry, Nanny's story about the letter, Parsons turning blue when I told her about my mother's presence in the house, my mother's expression when I told her of Parsons' disappearance, Aunt Ella's insistence on having the Starrs. All the strange tension of the last few days flashed across my mind, and I *knew*, right then, that the key to Parsons' death lay in Oak Hill. And it would have taken the tortures of the Inquisition to make me admit it.

I licked my rough, dry lips. "Tell me about this wheelbarrow," I said. "What makes you think somebody in the house used it?"

Atwood sat down again. He glanced at me, and then down at his square hands. "The wheelbarrow was taken out of the locked tool house. Somebody had to have access to the keys to get it. Now, this Magruder tells me that there are two sets of keys to the outbuildings. He carries one set with him, and the others are hung on the board with labels on them in the back service hall."

I interrupted the man. "But, heavens," I said. "Magruder's not infallible. Maybe he left the tool house open last night."

Atwood shook his head. "No, he didn't, because this John Peavey went to the tool house at seven-thirty to get a trowel, and it was locked. Magruder had gone to town on the 7:15 bus, and he didn't get back until midnight. He had to walk out from the village, and he got the bus that leaves College and Ashby in Berkeley at 11:15."

A tight net was drawing around Oak Hill. I could almost feel it trapping us, and God alone knew what hell we'd have to endure before the net was loosened.

"Where was this wheelbarrow?" I said in as matter-of-fact a tone as I could muster.

"Dumped in the creek bed. Peavey found it when he went to get a cow that was down there. He used the wheelbarrow yesterday, and he couldn't find it this morning when he needed it. Naturally, he was surprised when he found it in the creek bed—with a pair of canvas gardening gloves right alongside it. New ones that had never been worn until the murderer wore them last night and got blood on them."

I gasped for breath.

"And you're sure it was Parsons' blood on the wheelbarrow?" My voice was faint and quavery with emotion.

Atwood sighed. "Listen, Miss Brooks, it's no pleasure for me to come over here and cause an uproar in a house like this. I don't like tangling with important voters in the county, but when we were told that there was blood on the wheelbarrow of the same type as the dead woman's—a rare type, too—I had to come back." He stood up and walked around a few steps. "Hell, I'd a whole lot rather some tramp had killed Mrs. Rutledge's maid, but what am I going to do? I've got to do my job."

I was almost sorry for the man, but I was a whole lot sorrier for the residents of Oak Hill.

"All right," I said. "I understand. You have to do your job. Now, if you've finished with me, I'll get out." I gestured toward the door. "You can talk to the servants all you want, but"—I could feel the blood mounting in my face—"I'm damned if I can imagine one of them a murderer. It's all nonsense. When was Parsons killed?"

"Probably between ten and midnight. We can't be sure yet." He lit another cigarette from the box. As he talked, clouds of smoke issued from his nose in my direction. He leaned his arms on the edge of the desk. "Miss Brooks," he said, "I'd like to know how you happened to find the body?"

"Why," I said casually, "I was sitting on that stone step down there, and I just saw it. That's all."

He flicked a curious glance at me out of the side of his eyes. "How long did you sit on the step before you saw it?"

"As long as it took to smoke a cigarette and do over my face. I was just going to leave when I noticed something white—her blouse, of course. Then I tore the vines away and went to find Magruder. He was in the barn." I held out my pink-spattered hands to show him the thorn marks, and he nodded his head. "How'd you happen to go down to that old building?" he asked quietly.

My heart did a quaint little double-beat. I kept still three seconds too long. Atwood spoke.

"I looked around that place, Miss Brooks. It isn't a very nice place to sit on a scorching summer afternoon, and I saw your tracks in the dust of the old creek road. Why did you take that long walk and then just sit there long enough to smoke a cigarette? Will you tell me that?"

I waited a long time before I answered. I could lie and protect Tony, who might or might not need protection, or I could tell the truth and perhaps make an awful mess for all of us. But plain horse sense told me that I really needed a reason for having walked in the blinding heat to a hot, unattractive place. Atwood's voice interrupted my debate.

"It seems very queer to me that you'd go there instead of staying up here in this big cool house or having a swim in the pool. How about it?"

"All right," I said, throwing Tony to the wolves and taking a kind of vicious pleasure in my act, "Mr. Forrester sent me a note asking me to meet him there. He didn't show up."

As soon as the words were out of my mouth, I regretted them. I'd not only thrown Tony to the wolves but Bea and her children and Aunt Ella. I had, perhaps, hurt them all, and Tony had only hurt me—long years ago.

Atwood jumped up from his chair. "Where's Mr. Forrester?" he snapped.

I motioned to the bell pull by the fireplace. "Give that a yank," I said wearily. "Glore will find him."

Atwood and I waited in a seething silence until Tony bustled in full of his usual charm and affability.

"Hello, Atwood," he said cheerfully. "Back again, huh?" He came over to me. "Susan, darling, you poor thing. You look like death. You've had such an awful time."

He hovered over me, and I motioned for him to get away.

"Stop it, Tony. The sheriff and I both want to know why you sent me that note and then didn't show up?" I looked up at him with all the force of my large blue eyes that felt as though they had two tons of sand in each one.

Tony's face sagged in bewilderment. "Note, love? What note?"

"Tony, for God's sake," I said angrily, "the note you put in the powder room."

Tony shut his eyes and clutched his head dramatically. Then he smiled at Atwood as though only men could understand such things. "Susan, darling, it must be the heat. I didn't put any note in the powder room. I didn't put any note anywhere."

Making a scene in front of a stranger was no fun, but I saw I'd have to do it. I stood up and walked over to Tony and grabbed one of his lapels.

"Listen," I said through clenched teeth, "this is no time to play coy secrets. I'm in a jam. You've got to tell Atwood about the note you wrote asking me to meet you at the Farm House at five. Please, Tony."

I had to admit that Tony was as dazed as any human being I'd ever seen in my life. He put his long hands on my shoulders and looked, with complete candor, down into my face.

"Darling, I give you my word, I did not write you any such note."

Atwood seemed to be taking quiet pleasure in this touching scene.

CHAPTER 9

There was no doubting Tony's sincerity. He hadn't written the note. But somebody had, and, I believed, for the sole purpose of getting me down there to find Parsons' body. But *why?* She was carefully hidden in the vines, and how could anyone have had the faintest idea that I'd go around and sit on the step? I drew a sharp breath as realization came. The step was the only place to sit, and naturally I would sit down in the broiling heat to wait. To wait for Tony!

I clenched my teeth. The plan had been devilishly ingenious. Somebody in Oak Hill knew that I'd go to meet Tony, and as far as I knew only Aunt Ella really knew what had happened between me and Tony four years before.

I looked up at Tony and Atwood from the chair where I had flopped, weak with horror.

"I don't get it," I said slowly. "The note was signed 'af', Tony, the way you used to. You know."

Tony shook his head, a worried frown creasing his forehead.

"And it looked like Mr. Forrester's handwriting?" Atwood asked.

"It was typewritten," I said. "On the Oak Hill typewriter." I pointed to a closet door. "It's in there. I recognized the type. It's old-fashioned."

"But, Susan," Tony said urgently, "you know I can't type. For the love of God."

I groaned. "Yes, yes," I said. "I know it. It was the signature that got me."

Atwood spoke quickly. "Where's the note now, Miss Brooks?"

I groaned again. "I burned it," I snapped. "I burned it in my stove."

Atwood asked me to show him the typewriter. I opened the closet door and pointed to the machine which I had neatly covered up that afternoon when I had finished helping Bea send her wires.

"There it is," I said.

Atwood pulled it out into the room, being careful to handle only the stand to which it was screwed.

"Don't touch it," he said. "There may be prints."

I could feel my face twisting in a hopeless grin. "Yes," I said, "and they'll all be mine. I used the typewriter for an hour after lunch. The note was written before then."

Atwood jerked around to look at me.

"How do you know?" he snapped.

I sighed. "Because Glore gave it to me right after I left the library."

The Sheriff whistled softly, and I walked over to sit down on the couch. I looked up to see Tony glaring at me with unpleasant malevolence, the muscles along his jaw standing out like knots. There was a strange, baleful expression on Atwood's face, too.

"Susan," Tony said coldly, "what reason did you have to believe that I'd be asking you for a clandestine rendezvous? I really don't understand."

A slow, painful blush mounted toward my ears. I shook my head. "I don't know," I said feebly. "The note sounded like you, and I thought you might want to tell me something about Aunt Ella or something."

With an effort, Tony turned on the good old charm valve and laughed unconvincingly. He turned to Atwood. "We've all been pretty upset about Mrs. Rutledge, Atwood, and of course, it's been terribly hot. I guess that'll explain Miss Brooks' rather impulsive behavior."

He patted my shoulder. "Poor kid," he said kindly, "you go on back to bed. You must feel pretty rotten."

Atwood shoved his hands away down into his pockets and hunched his shoulders up until they were level with his pointed ears—almost.

"If Miss Brooks can stand it, I'd like to ask her a few more questions about the maid—friends and habits and so forth. It all helps."

Tony looked doubtfully from Atwood to me. Then he shrugged his shoulders as though the whole thing were a trivial matter. "Okay," he said. "It's up to Miss Brooks."

I nodded my head. "Tell somebody I'd like a chicken sandwich and a glass of milk, Tony, will you? I'm all right."

Of course I wanted to go to bed, but I was afraid to. I had to stay with Atwood and try to find out something about the hellish plan someone had devised to involve me in Parsons' death. There simply wasn't any other explanation for the note.

Tony sauntered off, and I was left alone once more with Atwood.

We were silent for several minutes. Then Atwood walked around behind the desk and sat down. He put his notebook on the desk and got out a pencil.

He licked the pencil and wrote something with it. "All right, Miss Brooks," he said at last. "I'd like a list of the servants in this house and the length of their service."

I gave it to him.

Glore, butler, 30 years.

Jane, parlor maid-waitress, 26 years.

Nanny, nurse to Bea and me, later returned for Bea's children, 26 years off and on.

Katherine, Bea's maid, 4 years.

Selma, upstairs maid, 2 years.
Viola, upstairs maid, 5 years.
Mary, kitchen maid, 1 year.
Hulda, laundress (Magruder's wife), 10 years.

When I had finished, I told Atwood that I wasn't sure about the length of time. "It's all approximate, of course," I said. "You can ask the servants for exact dates."

He nodded his head and flipped over a page. "How much help outside?" he asked.

"Magruder," I said, "is the head gardener. John Peavey helps him, and so does Robert, the chauffeur, because my aunt doesn't need a driver anymore except for errands. There's an Italian who comes in with a tractor to plow and spray the orchards—Martinelli's his name. That's everybody."

He sighed and smiled just a little bit.

"That's a lot of people to look after one old lady, isn't it?" he asked.

I nodded soberly. "Yes," I said, "it is. But of course this is a big house with a lot of valuable things in it, and Aunt Ella's always felt that it was a kind of trust that she had to look after."

Jane came in then bringing my sandwich. She, too, looked very badly. I thanked her and told her she'd better get to bed. "You look awfully tired, Jane. Tell us if you need extra help. There's a lot of work with the nurses and all the rest of us."

She said it was all right. Then I asked her to tell Atwood about the note she had found in the powder room.

"I just found it, Miss Susan. It was on the dressing table when I went in to tidy up after lunch. I didn't know where you were, and Glore said he'd take it to you."

She was visibly nervous, and she jerked her hand spasmodically when Atwood spoke to her.

"What time did you find it?" he asked.

"It must have been about three-thirty, sir. I went in to straighten the powder room in case anyone had used it since lunch, but no one had." She made a smoothing gesture at her apron.

"How do you know?" Atwood's voice was unnecessarily unpleasant, rude.

Jane's eyes widened and her lips were pursed.

"The towels which I put on the rack this morning had not been disturbed, sir. Will that be all?"

With a wild desire to laugh, I watched Jane's ramrod back as she left the room. It takes a well-trained, slightly snobbish servant to show outsiders their place, I thought.

Then I started on the sandwich and let Atwood do the talking for a while.

"As I understand it," he said, "this Magruder and his wife live in a cottage and Peavey lives with them. Robert, the chauffeur, lives over the garage. How long's he been here?"

"Oh, yes," I said, "I forgot. Five or six years, I think. He was married when he came, and he and his wife lived in the garage apartment, but she got a divorce a couple of years ago and left. She was a shrew—made trouble with the other servants."

"Know where she is now?" Atwood asked, writing busily.

"Nope," I said between bites. "You'll have to ask Robert." For some reason I felt impelled to do a little explaining. "We have those three young maids—Viola and Selma and Mary—because the other servants are pretty old and need help. Aunt Ella offered all the old ones very generous pensions some time ago, but they said they'd rather stay. I think they felt she wouldn't last long, and they ought to stay until her death."

Atwood looked at me with his mouth open. "Mrs. Rutledge is a very fine woman, isn't she?" he said seriously, and I smiled back at him, liking him a lot, at the moment.

"You're darned right she is. She's wonderful." I had a paralyzing catch in my throat. "That's why it's so awful to have all this terrible mess. She's really very ill."

I shoved the tray away from me and fished in my pocket for a hanky. When I had pulled myself together, I found that the food had made me feel a lot better.

"And all these servants got along fine with this Parsons and each other—as far as you know?" Atwood asked.

"Yes, they did, really. Until the tunnel was finished, there weren't very many people out here, and they were pretty dependent on each other. Of course Parsons was fanatically devoted to my aunt, but they all knew it, and nobody poached on her preserves." I sighed. "Of course, since Mrs. Rutledge's first stroke, Parsons was pretty much of a nurse, and she took over quite a bit of the housekeeping, too. Linen and stuff."

"Who were her friends, Miss Brooks?"

I tried to think, but I drew a blank. "I don't really know," I said. "She was English and reticent, but since the war started, she always went to the city on Wednesday to work for Bundles for Britain. You might look in her desk. She may have letters or an address book, and of course, the other servants may know."

He drummed on the desk with his pencil for a few minutes. Then he looked up. "You never heard of Parsons being interested in any man or *vice versa*, did you?"

In the worst possible taste, I grinned broadly. "No," I said, "I did not. She was very much of a spinster. She wasn't too attractive to look at, you know."

He grinned back at me. "I know. I've seen her in the village and over in Walnut Creek. I just thought I'd ask." He shut his notebook and stood up. "I'd like to see the woman's room. It's pretty late, so I'll wait until morning to start questioning the servants."

"All right," I said. "I'll take you up to her room."

We met Mrs. Hill, the nurse, in the upstairs hall. She said Miss Conover had just taken over, and my aunt's condition remained unchanged. Then Atwood and I went on to Parsons' room.

Until we went into Parsons' private domain, I don't think that the entire horror of her death had hit me, but when I saw the order and cleanliness and the things that she would never again use, the impact of what had happened seemed to hit me like a rabbit punch. Until then I suppose my emotions had been dulled into insensibility.

I sat down heavily and pointed to the little blue painted desk. "That's it," I said. "Her papers will be in there."

I started to cry, wretchedly and silently, and Atwood didn't pay any attention to me, and I was very glad. I just let misery take over until I was startled out of my unhappiness by Atwood's holding a paper toward me.

"This is the woman's will," he said. "It might interest you."

I blew my nose and mopped up my face and started to read.

"My lord!" I said when I had finished the short, typewritten document. "Can you imagine that?"

Parsons had willed her worldly goods half to her sister and half to me! I swallowed hard and looked up at Atwood.

His eyes were dead, expressionless, cold. I heard the paper rattling in my hand as I held it out to him.

"You didn't know this?" he said, without any expression at all in his voice.

"No, no," I protested. "The poor old thing. I hadn't any idea in the world." I started to cry again.

Atwood walked back to the desk and picked up three little books. He handed them to me without a word.

They were bank books. The sums in them amazed me. One showed a balance of $3,197, another $578, the third $12,463! "Good sized bank accounts for a servant, aren't they?" Atwood's voice penetrated my astonishment.

I pushed my hair off my forehead. "They certainly are," I breathed.

Atwood went back to the desk. He sat down with his back to me and kept on looking at more papers. He'd read something and then lay it to one side. Then he'd read something else and put it on another little pile. He wrote some things in his notebook. Finally, he stood up and handed me two things—an old, faded snapshot and a yellowed newspaper clipping.

"Recognize the picture?" he asked.

I nodded. It was a poor photograph of Eleanor Rutledge which did her beauty little justice.

"Mrs. Rutledge's daughter, Eleanor, isn't it?" he asked. I nodded again. He pointed to the clipping. "Can you read French?"

"Yes," I said and read the clipping. I looked up when I had finished. "It's the account of the death of a Prince Serge Alexandrovitch Obronsky." I stumbled over the difficult Russian name. "It says he died in an automobile accident in Mentone at the age of twenty-one. He was a cousin of the Romanoffs—distant, though."

Atwood took the clipping away from me. "What do you suppose she kept that for?" he asked.

I sighed. "I don't know. I never heard of the man. Maybe she worked for his family or something. My aunt acquired Parsons in Mentone. How did you recognize the photograph? Of Eleanor Rutledge, I mean."

"I've been in the hospital," he answered. "I've seen the big picture in the hall."

He went back to the desk and fussed around some more. Suddenly he whirled around and pointed his finger at me. I nearly fell off my chair.

"What'd that woman leave her money to you for?" he shouted.

I swallowed hard. "I don't know," I gasped. "I really don't. I guess she just liked me. She knew I didn't have much money of my own."

He got up out of his chair and walked over to me still pointing his pudgy forefinger at me. "And she never told you what she was going to do?"

I shook my head emphatically. I couldn't talk. I was too scared.

"And you can't explain how a servant could have that much money?" He whipped out the words.

I took a deep breath to get my bearings. "How much is it altogether? About $16,000, isn't it?" I said. "Well, she could save that much in twenty-six years. She had her room and board and even most of her clothes. She never even had to pay a doctor bill—only dental bills—and she never spent anything except for presents for her family and us. She could have done it. She could have. It isn't so strange." The words poured out of me.

He snorted. "I can see I'm in the wrong racket. I should have taken up butling."

He went back to the desk and gathered up some of the papers and put them in an envelope. He put the envelope in his pocket.

"You'd better cable the woman's sister," he said, handing me a thin airmail envelope with a name and an English address on it. "I want this room locked up, and I'll take the key. Tomorrow morning I'll question the servants, and as a matter of routine, I want to know where you were last night between ten and twelve."

His voice was thoroughly business-like. There was none of the tone in it that he used when he spoke of Aunt Ella.

I tried to think. So much had happened since last night—all of it awful—that I had difficulty in remembering. I thought back. Then I nodded.

"My mother and I went home to my house pretty early," I said slowly. "About nine-thirty probably. We were all tired." My heart rattled around a little, and I wanted badly to lie about what I had done when I got home, but I didn't dare. I had no assurance that Amelia would back me up. She might easily throw me to the wolves the way I had tried to throw Tony. I gulped, and I heard my voice come out of my throat sounding strained and queer. "When we got home my mother went to bed, but the house was hot, so I walked over to the Hilliards. They weren't home, so I came back and went to bed."

"What time?" Atwood was looking directly at me, and I made my eyes steady with iron self-control.

"I don't know," I said. "I undressed in the dark. It was too hot to pull the blinds. Maybe eleven, maybe later. I was on the terrace for quite a while before I went over to the Hilliards."

He said "huh," just like that. "Your mother? I thought your mother was dead, Miss Brooks." The words were smooth and cold.

"Not at all," I said briskly. "She's very much alive. She's been in South America for a great many years, and—" I was getting a little irritated with Atwood's knowingness—"what would you know about my mother anyway?"

He laughed without joy. "Miss Brooks, this is the most important house in the county. There isn't a thing that goes on here that people don't talk about and wonder about. Everything you people do is of vital interest to the village of Rutledge."

CHAPTER 10

This night will end. This night will end, I kept telling myself.

Morning will come, and other nights and other days will pass, and some time I'll understand all that has happened and is happening. There will be no more fear and horror and doubt, and I'll pick up my life where I left off.

I'll know who killed Parsons and why—and even if it's horrible knowledge, it will be better than not knowing—and Aunt Ella will get well or die, and life will go on somehow.

I turned over for the thousandth time. All my self-preaching was useless. This night would go on forever. I'd go right on suffering forever, unable to understand the deadly violence that had come to Oak Hill. Amelia Ortiz would never speak, never explain her sinister presence. Aunt Ella would lie for years unfeeling, unconscious. Atwood would go on threatening me, loading the burden of his suspicions onto my shoulders.

The sleeping medicine that Miss Conover had given me when Atwood finally left had been wasted. My mind had rolled and tossed and turned in the same futile rhythm as my body. There had been no blessed blotting out of horror in heavily drugged sleep.

I lay flat on my back, muscles of hands and jaw and legs rigid, my eyes clamped tight shut. My skin was hot and my mouth dry and tasting of endless cigarettes. The faint rustle of leaves on the trees outside my window startled me like the clamor of thunder. The sudden, shrill cries of the birds scraped across my raw nerves like fingernails on a blackboard.

I jumped out of bed with a small stifled scream.

I had to get out, to move. Anything was better than this senseless, unending futility of asking myself questions I couldn't answer.

The sky was light. The hideous night had ended, but the day was little better than the dark. I had no hope, no lightening of my fear.

I found the bedraggled clothes I had worn the day before. When I had dressed, I opened my door into the hall and crept stealthily to Aunt Ella's sitting room. I saw Miss Conover dozing in a chair. She looked tired in the half-light.

Aunt Ella lay in her big bed as still as though death had come at last. Only the jagged rasp of her breathing coming from motionless lips indicated that life still clung to her paralyzed body. I walked out of the bedroom and through the sitting room without disturbing Miss Conover.

The long hall was silent, impersonal. Behind the closed doors, the Starrs and the Forresters still slept, I hoped for their sakes. I knew somehow that they would have need of physical vitality before the days of death and uncertainty rolled by.

Outside, the dew-laden grass and flowers and shrubs were fresh and inviting, but as I walked up the driveway to the road, I watched the sun rise in a blaze of angry red and orange streaks that promised more heat, perhaps even worse than that of the days before. Already as the sun poured down the valley, the leaves on the trees had subsided into stillness. The dawn breeze had died.

The Farm House across the creek sent shudders the length of my spine. As if I had been present, I saw the dark and nameless figure trundling its grisly burden to the blackberry vines. I could almost smell the fear and horror that attended that grim task.

I let myself into my house quietly. There was no need to awaken Amelia. She, too, would need sleep. But my care was useless. I smelled the heartening smell of coffee cooking. I called out.

"Amelia, you're up?" I'd decided to call her by her first name. "Mother" was a bit too much.

The kitchen door into the hall swung open. Amelia stood on the threshold wearing a voluminous, beautifully made white robe. Above the handsome robe, I was startled to see her heavy face haggard and gray and frightened. For the first time, I felt that I'd had a little glimpse behind the careful mask that she ordinarily wore.

"Susan!" Her voice quavered. "You frightened me half to death."

I nodded. "I'm sorry. I came in quietly. I thought you'd still be asleep."

She swallowed perceptibly, and then the old mask slid down over her features. "Of course. I see." She smiled a little. "You look as though coffee might do you some good."

"Yes," I said, "I'd like it. I'll take a shower first." I stood hesitantly in the middle of my living room. "What do you think? Shall I close the house up and draw the blinds while it's still cool, or shall I leave it open?"

A little trace of fear crossed her face.

"You'd better close it," she said grimly. "Keep it well locked. Somebody came here in the night."

I whirled around to face her. "What do you mean!"

She shrugged her shoulders in an eloquent Latin gesture. "Just that. I heard someone try the terrace door—very softly—in the night. When I called out, there was no answer. The person went away."

I put my hand up to my forehead, as though my hand could shield my brain against a further influx of mystery or puzzlement. "But why?" I said stupidly. "Why? There's nothing here."

"I don't know," she said flatly. "What did the Sheriff want with you? Bea said you were with him for hours last night."

I looked directly at her. "He says someone at Oak Hill killed her. It wasn't a tramp."

She bit her lips and clutched at the door jamb for support. The objective part of my mind told me that it was interesting to watch her disintegration.

"Why? Why does he say that?" Her voice was a rough whisper.

I told her why Atwood knew that an outsider hadn't been responsible for Parsons' murder. Amelia listened closely until I finished. "My God!" she breathed. Then she turned and went into the kitchen.

I followed her and drank the coffee she poured out for me. When I had gulped the contents of the cup, I set the cup down on the tile sink with a clatter.

"You know something," I said very decisively. "You know a lot. Why don't you tell? There's something dreadful going on. What is it?"

I would have said more, but she interrupted me. "No, no. I know nothing. I came here to see Ella. This has nothing to do with me."

She started to walk out of the room, but I grabbed her by the arm. "Then why are you scared to death?" I snapped.

With a tremendous effort, she pulled herself up to her imposing height. The mask slid down again. It was an admirable performance. "Don't be a fool, Susan. How would I know anything? I haven't even been at Oak Hill for nearly thirty years. I was travelling in this country. It is quite natural that I would wish to see my family, is it not?"

I laughed unnaturally. "At this late date? I think it's very amusing. This belated but touching family feeling."

My physical condition was frightful, and on top of that my nerves were splintered. A wave of futile anger swept over me. It was all I could do to keep the tears out of my voice.

"Atwood thinks I killed Parsons," I quavered. "How do you like that?"

Amelia looked directly at me. She laughed queerly. "That's ridiculous. Why would he think that?"

I was very near hysteria. "She left me her money. Half of it. She had about sixteen thousand."

A strange smile twisted Amelia's heavy features. "Sixteen thousand dollars for twenty-six years of excellent service. Rather special service. That's very little, isn't it?"

Then she got away from me and went into her room and shut the door. I followed after her. "Listen," I said, "you've got to help me. Please." The childish tears had come.

She opened the door. "What is it?" Her voice was very hard.

I gulped. "Friday night I went out. Did you hear me go?"

"Yes, I heard you go on the terrace, but I didn't hear you come in. I must have been asleep." There was almost a shadow of pity in her eyes. Almost, but not quite. "I'm sorry, Susan." Then the fear came back. "I shall leave here. Today."

I shrugged my shoulders and went to my room. You'll leave if Atwood lets you, I thought to myself.

I took a shower and dressed and set out for the Hilliards without seeing Amelia again. I had an idea that Anne or Joe might have been the ones who tried the terrace door. They might have come over to see me and didn't want to waken Amelia. But the idea was a poor, thin one, and I hadn't much hope that it was correct.

The path leading from my house to the Hilliards was shady and cool under the trees, but the unshaded patches were already hot. My clean red and white linen dress and comfortable saddle oxfords that I had put on after my shower had helped, but not much. My head felt like lead and it ached.

Anne's garden, on which she spent so much time and care, looked dusty and bedraggled. The summer flowers were gone, and the fall ones hadn't started to bloom. Even the white-painted furniture on the terrace looked grimy. The September heat had done its work.

I walked around to the back door and was greeted with loud yappings from Sandy, their brindle Scottie, I could see Anne in the kitchen. I rattled the screen door, and she looked up from the stove, her kindly face breaking into a heart-warming smile. "Susan!" she said, opening the door. "Come in, child. I got up early so that I could come up to see you. You poor baby."

Anne Hilliard Watson is like Aunt Ella. Good and kind and fair. She is about ten years older than Joe, and when her husband died, she came out from Ohio to keep house for her brother. Aunt Ella, who liked Joe personally as well as professionally, sold them a couple of acres in our valley, and they built a nice little house on it. Joe did a lot of work at the Rutledge Memorial, and with Aunt Ella's sponsorship, his practice around the village had come along very nicely. Joe and Anne were a fine addition to the life of our neighborhood.

Anne's ready sympathy was too much for me. I started to cry, all the time feeling very ashamed of myself but not able to stop.

Anne took me into the breakfast room and shoved me into a chair. She stood beside me with her arm across my shoulders and kept saying, "There, there, darling. There, there."

After a while I stopped and mopped up my face and apologized. "I didn't sleep," I said. "I'm a wreck."

"And no wonder," she said. "I went up to Oak Hill last night, but Tony told me you were with the Sheriff."

The sun streamed into the cheerful blue and white room. White begonias bloomed in red and blue pots on the window sill, and the white organdy curtains at the window framed a distant view of Mount Diablo, all blue shadows and golden brown curves in the early sunshine. Somehow life didn't seem quite as awful as it had a few minutes earlier. It just didn't seem possible to sit in that room with kindly, sensible Anne and believe that murder and violence had taken place a half a mile away. I smiled up at Anne.

"I wish I'd seen you last night," I said. "Maybe I wouldn't have gone to pieces, but that damned sheriff scared the pants off of me."

I told her about his horrid suspicions of me, and his reasons for believing that someone in Oak Hill had killed Parsons.

Anne, I suppose, is really rather homely. Her eyes are small, and her skin is burned by the sun and lined around her mouth and eyes because she laughs and smiles so readily. Her straight, sunburned brown hair is drawn back into an uncompromisingly tidy bun. Most of the time she forgets about make-up, but she's so nice that it doesn't matter what she looks like.

When I had finished talking about the sheriff, she laughed. "I never heard of such nonsense in my life. The man's a fool." She went into the kitchen and got the coffee and a cup and filled it for me. "He's probably excited because the thing happened at Oak Hill. When he gets up this morning, he may have better sense."

She went off to call Joe. When she came back, she told me to come out in the kitchen and keep her company while she fixed breakfast. She put me to work squeezing oranges, and I felt a whole lot better.

When Joe came in, my heart did a little handstand. Like Anne, he looked nice and sensible and normal.

Anne and I both talked at once and told him about the sheriff's suspicions and Parsons' will. He pooh-poohed the whole business. "Atwood's a good man," he said. "Very intelligent, but naturally he's excited about doings at Oak Hill. He'll get over it."

I smiled happily. Joe's reassurance was welcome, and it was kindly, too, and my heart gave an extra beat in gratitude for two such friends as Joe and Anne. I knew, somehow, that whatever happened, Joe would give me good advice and his strong right arm—for the rest of my life if I gave the slightest indication that I wanted them. And right then I knew that I did want them for the rest of my life.

I bit into a piece of toast in order to hide the wave of sentiment that was threatening to engulf me. A breakfast table is no place for a girl to decide that she's in love with a man and intends to marry him, provided, of course, that the gent is willing.

"Say," I said, "did either of you people come calling last night? At my house, I mean."

Anne and Joe both shook their heads.

"Of course not," Joe said. "We knew you'd been put to bed up at the big house. Why?"

I smiled. "My strange parent is very jittery. She says someone was trying to get into the house last night. Probably imagined it."

They said yes, she probably had. The fears and mental twistings and turnings of the night before were receding from my mind in orderly fashion.

"Joe," I said, "how about Aunt Ella? How did she seem last night?"

"Her condition's all right, Susan. I'm very well satisfied. Bromley'll be over this afternoon."

I gasped and smiled. "You mean she'll get well?"

A doubtful frown creased his forehead. "Well, it's too soon to say."

My spirits dropped about ten degrees from their former high. "Oh," I said.

Then the telephone rang, and we stopped talking to listen for the number of rings. We have rural telephone service in Rutledge, and Joe and I are on the same line. My ring is two, his is four. The two rings jangled from the library. I got up.

"I'd better answer it," I said. "It might be from Oak Hill."

I went into the small pine-panelled library and picked up the telephone. I said hello, and then I stopped. I heard Amelia's voice talking to a man. Then his voice sounded with what seemed a note of urgency and almost hysteria. They spoke in Spanish. I hung up and went back to the breakfast room, wondering who Amelia's friend might be.

"It was for my mother," I said, sitting down at the table. "She was speaking Spanish to some man, and they both sounded excited. But Spanish probably sounds excited to anybody that can't understand it."

Anne gave me a long look. Then she grinned. "Listen, Susan, I'm going to pry. What in heck is your mother doing here?"

I shrugged my shoulders and threw up my hands. "I really don't know, Anne. She says she's just paying us a visit, but she also says she's leaving today."

Joe and Anne nodded solemnly, and I kept still. There seemed no point in telling them of Amelia Ortiz' mysterious behavior and her terror.

We sat in silence for a few minutes. I finally roused myself to light a cigarette and ask for more coffee. I sighed deeply as I exhaled the long plume of smoke. "Joe," I said hesitantly, "did you see Parsons? After, I mean."

He nodded. "Yes, I did. I helped on the autopsy last night." He looked down at his plate, then he looked up as though he'd decided to let me have it. "She was first stunned with something heavy—to knock her out. Then her throat was cut with a knife, probably after she was taken from the house."

My good breakfast did strange things in my stomach. Anne leaned over quickly and took my hand.

"Joe," she said angrily, "you should have better sense."

CHAPTER 11

After promising Anne that I would try to get some sleep during the day, I rode up to Oak Hill with Joe.

Glore let us in, and the poor old man had aged five years over night. He shook his head sadly. "It's a bad business, Miss Susan. The sheriff's questioning the servants in the library—one at a time. He's been here since seven o'clock."

Upstairs I waited in Aunt Ella's sitting room while Joe went in to see her. I caught a glimpse of Miss Quincey's lean figure busy in the bedroom. In a few minutes, Joe came out looking very cheerful and nice.

"She looks pretty good, Susan. She had a good night," he said.

Miss Quincey closed the bedroom door, and Joe walked over and put his arm across my shoulders and gave me a squeeze. I felt swell.

"Now, take a bromide and get some sleep," he said. "I'll be back this afternoon, and I expect you to swim with me, young lady. Also to resemble something human."

I walked down the hall with Joe. As we approached the door of the room where I had spent the night, Selma came out. The strained, puzzled expression on her face stopped me.

"What is it, Selma?" I asked. "What's the matter?"

She started in fright when I spoke to her. Apparently she hadn't noticed me. She licked her lips. "Why, nothing, Miss Brooks."

I walked on to the door of the room. Then I stopped dead in my tracks, my eyes almost leaping from their sockets.

"Good Lord!" I gasped. "What's happened?"

Joe stood close behind me.

There wasn't one thing in that room where it belonged. The bedding and the mattress were on the floor, as were the rose satin padded linings from the drawers. The Savery highboy had been pulled a good two feet away from the wall. The writing paper on the desk was in a muddle, and the blotter had been pulled out of its pad.

"Selma! What is this?" I demanded.

Selma's open young face was drained of its usual high color. Her brown eyes were round in wonder.

"I don't know, Miss Brooks. I thought you did it. I came in to do the room, and that's what I found."

"I? Why would I make a mess like that? I left here at five o'clock this morning. Somebody else did it."

Joe was walking quietly around the room looking at things. He opened the doors to both closets and pointed. The padding on the shelves had been ripped off and thrown on the floor. We looked in the bathroom. The towels had been thrown around and the medicine chest stood open.

Joe whistled. "I hope they found it. They did a good job of looking."

All Anne's careful cheering-up was gone. With a rush, I realized again that we'd had a murder at Oak Hill and that there were a lot of strange things going on.

"Don't touch anything, Selma," I said in a dead voice. "I'd better tell the sheriff."

We locked the door, and I took the key, and with stolidly reluctant steps I followed Joe down the hall and down the stairs. When we were almost down to the lower hall, the door to the service wing was flung back, and Bea burst through like a cannon ball.

Her face was distorted by anger. She ran across the hall with her white pleated skirt flashing behind her like the wake of a fast boat. She banged the library door open, and I ran down the stairs and into the library behind her.

Her tongue flicked over Atwood like a stinging whip.

"What do you mean by coming up here and throwing this house into complete chaos?" she snapped. "You can get out and do your questioning elsewhere. I won't have it."

Atwood got up as she spoke. His face was impassive. Then I noticed that Robert, the chauffeur-gardener, was in the room. His face was white with purple smudges under his eyes.

"The servants are all threatening to leave. How dare you do a thing like this?" Bea's words banged out, but they seemed to make no impression at all on Atwood. He waited until she finished.

"One of your servants has been murdered, Mrs. Forrester. It's my duty to find out who did it, and that involves questioning the other servants."

Bea's jaw set. She was accustomed to having her orders obeyed, but I didn't think she'd have much luck this time. "The maids are all in tears. You've badgered them until they can't think."

Atwood shrugged his shoulders and smiled wryly. "A great tragedy, I'm sure, Mrs. Forrester. So is murder."

He and Bea looked at each other across an abyss of animosity. We waited.

"Now, Mrs. Forrester, if you'd like it better, I can order your servants to come over to my office for questioning."

Bea apparently chose the lesser of two evils.

"Very well," she said. "You may stay here, but I can see little necessity for such brutality. Viola's quite useless."

Atwood snorted. "I imagine she is," he said. "She quarrelled with the

Parsons woman the other day." He gestured toward Robert, whose face got whiter as Atwood spoke. "I'm trying to get this man to tell me the truth about the reasons for the quarrel. I haven't had much luck—so far."

The "so far" was ominous.

"What quarrel?" Bea asked. "What're you talking about?"

Robert would have undoubtedly welcomed a good big hole to jump into at that point.

"Your maid, Katherine, tells me that she overheard Viola and Parsons quarrelling violently last Friday morning. Robert's name was mentioned several times." Atwood seemed very pleased with himself. Bea's eyes narrowed.

"Katherine told you this? Well, I'll fix her. Tattling. Stirring up trouble." Bea started out of the room, and I was very sorry for Katherine.

I walked over to the desk and handed Atwood the key to the bedroom. I swallowed hard before I got up the nerve to speak. "You'd better take a look at this room upstairs," I said slowly. "I slept in it last night. Since I got up at five this morning, somebody's pulled it all to pieces. Looking for something, I think."

Atwood looked at me for a long time without speaking. "Where did you go when you got up?" he asked at last. I told him. He nodded.

"My mother says she thinks somebody tried to get into my house last night, too," I said reluctantly.

Atwood's head jerked back. "Any idea what you have that somebody else might want?"

I shook my head slowly from side to side.

"None in the world," I said.

CHAPTER 12

Atwood told me to get out of the library. He did it politely enough, but he made it clear that I wasn't wanted, so I went. Joe left to make his morning calls.

I wandered around the house looking for someone to talk to without success. Bea was busy bullying the servants, Nanny was busy packing up the children to take them to the Forresters' San Francisco apartment where they would be safe from murderous fiends.

Finally I located the Starrs and Tony down at the pool. The young Starrs were splashing in the cool green water. Will, unlovely in wine satin Lastex trunks and pot-belly, was fuming.

"That man Atwood is overstepping his authority, Tony. I think you're making a great mistake in allowing him to come here and disrupt this house," he said emphatically.

Tony, very beautiful in blue satin Lastex trunks and magnificent tanned male body, shrugged his huge shoulders. "The man has to do his duty, Will," he said from his perch at the edge of the pool where he was dabbling his feet in the water. "It's a rotten business, of course, but poor old Parsons didn't deserve what she got. If somebody around here did it, Atwood's got to find out who."

I told them about the midnight caller at my house and the torn-up bedroom. Will's head jerked back with an almost audible snap. His mousy skin turned blue. "Good God, Susan," he said, "you didn't tell Atwood about it, did you?"

The heat, my lack of sleep, and the worry were too much for me. I snarled at Will.

"Of course I told him. Why not?"

Mabel, who was livid from rigid corseting and the heat, pulled herself erect in her long chair. Her rather dull eyes were round with excitement.

Will pursed his lips. "Are you trying to involve the *family* in this mess, Susan? Use your head."

I gave Will a baleful look. "I'm not trying to involve anyone," I said. "I'm just telling Atwood what happened." I started to walk toward the little colonial dressing house.

"Susan!" I turned back at Tony's call. He smiled at me very pleasantly as he scrambled to his feet. "Listen, my love, I'm a lawyer. Maybe you'd better consult me before you pour out your soul to the good Atwood, huh?"

His tone was light, but the expression in his eyes was definite. He stood up and followed me to the dressing house. I was ready to scream with irritation. I simply could not bear the thought of being alone with Tony after the humiliations of the night before.

I started into the female half of the building, but Tony gently and firmly hung onto me. He swung me around so that I had to face him. He smiled, showing about twenty-six of his perfect teeth—not a filling in his mouth.

"Be careful, darling," he said gently. "This is a nasty mess. I'm going to get dressed and go up there and sit in on Atwood's questioning-bee. I'm sorry about last night."

"What do you mean?" I said angrily, jerking out of his grasp. "What are you sorry for? The note?"

He shook his head patiently from side to side. "No, Susan," he said, "I didn't write the note, but I'm sorry I had to disclaim you so brutally. After all, we don't want Atwood to get any peculiar ideas about us, do we?"

My heart wobbled and fluttered. "No," I sighed, "but somebody's got some peculiar ideas, Tony. Somebody in this house wrote that note, and they knew I'd respond just as I did. It's a stinker."

"I knew it. That's what's so frightening. Servants always know too much." He threw up his hands in a gesture of despair.

He walked off, and I went into the first dressing room I came to and kicked the door shut viciously behind me. I hauled off my clothes and threw them onto a chair and pulled a yellow bathing suit out of a drawer. I had a horrible time getting it on. The more I pulled, the hotter I got, and the more I just plain sweat, the more I had to struggle with the bathing suit. When I was finally wedged into the thing, I sat down limp and panting with heat and humiliation and frustration.

A servant in Aunt Ella's house knew that I'd dance to any tune Tony Forrester played for me. All the chin-keeping-up and hell and heartbreak I'd gone through four years before had been wasted. I probably hadn't fooled anyone.

I was shoving my hair up under a tight yellow cap when Peggy came into the dressing room after a diffident knock.

I pulled myself together sufficiently to smile at her. She was well worth smiling at. Her really beautiful young body *belonged* in a white bathing suit.

"Is it all right for me to come in?" she said shyly.

"Of course. Peggy, you ought to live in a bathing suit. You're a fair treat for these old eyes."

She laughed. She also blushed. "You're no slouch yourself, Susan." Then her young face sobered. "Isn't all this terrible, Susan? I could die." She swallowed. "I just don't know what to do." Her gray eyes were clouded with worry.

"What do you mean?" I said quietly.

She looked nervously about her. "I *heard* the wheelbarrow. I heard the elevator, too. Daddy said for me not to tell that man. The sheriff."

"The elevator! My lord!" I gasped. The elevator explained a lot. The murderer had probably used it to bring Parsons downstairs. The wheelbarrow had provided the rest of the transportation. I sat thinking very hard and not paying any attention at all to Peggy.

Parsons was a little woman—only about ninety-five pounds or so—but by using the lift which was right next to Aunt Ella's rooms and the wheelbarrow for the rest of the grisly trip, a woman could have done the job very nicely.

I was roused from my thoughts by a gentle poke on the arm from Peggy.

"You won't tell, will you, Susan?" she said urgently.

"No," I said, "not yet. It isn't necessary, but you may have to tell some time. Listen, Peggy, what time did you hear this stuff? Do you know?"

She nodded her head soberly. "It was eleven-thirty. I was just going to bed. You see, I wasn't sleepy. I always get excited when we come here, and I'd been taking a bath for hours and messing around with all the bath salts and stuff that are in there. I'd just turned out my light, and I'd looked at the clock." She spoke rapidly as though it were a relief to tell the story.

"But you didn't look to see what it was?"

Her eyes were almost round as she slowly shook her head from side to side.

I sighed. "That'd be too much to hope for." Then I stood up. "The plot thickens, to coin a phrase. There's no sense in my trying to think. I'll just swim instead."

Peggy sighed, too. "I guess I will, too. It's a whole lot cooler than anything else we can do around here. Bill's supposed to report tomorrow morning. Do you suppose the sheriff will let him?"

"Sure," I said. "This is no skin off Bill's nose. Atwood's working out on the hired help."

Mabel and Will were having what looked like a very brisk little family row which they interrupted as I walked past them. Young Bill was floating idly in the middle of the pool, so I dove under him and came up underneath him and acted very playful and kittenish and asinine. The water was sheer heaven.

Peggy joined in our antics, and when we were tired, we got out and lay on canvas mattresses in the shade and didn't talk at all.

I tried to think about what had happened and was happening, but the swimming on top of no sleep did the trick, and a heavy black curtain of weariness came down over my mind and brought me peace.

"Wake up, Miss Brooks. Wake up!"

The command penetrated the blessed oblivion, the blackout of horror and worry. I tried to slide back unsuccessfully.

I sat up and shook my head that was full of an aching buzz. I was dripping wet. As I shoved my hair out of my eyes, I looked up to see Atwood standing over me expectantly. Peggy and Bill Starr no longer lay upon their canvas mattresses. Will and Mabel had gone, too.

"All right," I said thickly. "I'm awake. What now?"

"Sorry to have to wake you. I'm finished here for today, but first I have to ask you a few questions." He sat down on the end of a chaise longue and leaned toward me.

I stood up awkwardly. My legs were stiff and cramped from lying so long on the hard mattress. "Look, what time is it?" I asked.

"Three-thirty."

"I've slept a long time. Do you mind if I get a drink of water? I'm still in a trance."

I went over to the bar in the dressing house and drank three glasses of ice water. I knew enough about Sheriff Atwood by that time to know that it was wise to have one's wits in decent order during questioning. Then I went back and sat down in a chair that faced Atwood. I was looking toward the house which was about fifty yards away up on the knoll. The pool is slightly south and east of the house, but I could see the terrace through the trees very plainly. Atwood had his back to it.

He twisted his mouth to one side as though he were thinking very carefully of what he was about to say.

"Have you found out anything?" I asked.

"Quite a lot," he said quietly, "but nothing definite yet." He paused for a second. "Miss Brooks, I've talked to your mother, Mrs. Ortiz. She tells me that she had no particular purpose in coming here. She was travelling in this country, and she just decided to come and see her family. Is that correct?"

I reached over to get a cigarette from a box on a little white iron table. When I had it burning, I nodded my head and said, "Yes, that's right. At least, that's what she's said to all of us."

"You didn't know she was coming?"

"No. It was quite a surprise." I smiled grimly.

"And you've never seen her before? Since you were born? And she never communicated with your aunt?"

"That's right. As far as I know. Of course, Mrs. Rutledge had her stroke Friday night, and as she was ill in the evening, I didn't tell her Mrs. Ortiz was here, so I don't really know whether my aunt knew she'd be here or not."

Atwood glanced down at his feet, then he looked straight at me out of his cold blank eyes. He fished around in his pockets. He handed me a yellow Western Union blank. It was a copy of the wire which I had sent to Will Starr summoning him to Oak Hill. I could feel myself getting hotter by the second. I was glad to see sweat drip off the end of Atwood's nose.

The wire said: VERY ANXIOUS HAVE YOU, MABEL AND BOTH YOUR CHILDREN AT OAK HILL WEEKEND SEPTEMBER 13. IMPORTANT BUSINESS TO DISCUSS WHICH CONCERNS ALL OF US. PLEASE WIRE IF CONVENIENT.

ELLA RUTLEDGE

I handed back the wire without saying anything. I knew that I could do a lot of protesting and tell Atwood to get after the servants, but I knew, too, that that wasn't the answer to Parsons' death. It was a family affair. Enough had happened to prove that to me, and Atwood was no fool.

"I understand you sent that wire from Walnut Creek. That right?"

I nodded. "That's right. Mrs. Rutledge asked me to send it last Tuesday, so I did, but don't ask me what the business was about. I don't know."

"But as far as you know, Mrs. Rutledge didn't send for Mrs. Ortiz. That right?"

"So Mrs. Ortiz says."

Atwood grunted slightly. "Now to go back to Friday night. You say you and Mrs. Ortiz went home early—around nine-thirty. She went to her room, and you went out on the terrace. After a while you walked over to the Hilliards. That right?"

I nodded.

"When you came back, was your mother's light on or off?"

"Off," I said. "I wondered at the time if she'd been able to sleep. It ... it was so hot." There seemed to be no point in telling Atwood that Amelia's arrival had started a lot of conjecture and excitement among the members of the family. He undoubtedly knew it anyway.

"And you didn't hear anything during the night?"

"No," I said slowly, "I didn't. It took me a long time to get to sleep. Then I slept like the dead until the telephone woke me up in the morning."

Atwood leaned over to help himself to a cigarette, and I looked up toward the house. With incredible self-control, I refrained from gasping aloud with astonishment. Mr. Opal and Bea stood on the terrace talking earnestly. My astonishment came from the fact that Mr. Opal had his arm through Bea's and was holding her hand and patting it with both of his. Bea, who loathes being touched, was practically being pawed by Mr. Opal, of all people, and she was smiling about the whole performance—Bea who hated even to shake hands and who refused to allow Tony to kiss her in the church at the conclusion of the marriage ceremony, because she couldn't stand public demonstrations of affection.

I glanced back at Atwood who was busy lighting the cigarette. When I looked up at the house again, Mr. Opal and Bea were shaking hands, only they were using both their hands to do it.

Finally Bea went into the house, smiling pleasantly, and it wasn't her forced social smile either. Mr. Opal, dressed in bright green slacks and shirt of the type frequently seen in Hollywood, walked down the steps and around the back of the house toward the place where we park cars. Will wonders never cease, I thought dazedly.

I had no more time for Mr. Opal and Bea. Atwood was still full of questions.

"Now, Miss Brooks," he said briskly, "I understand from the children's nurse that Parsons told her that Mrs. Rutledge got a letter in the last week or two that seemed to upset her. What do you know about the letter?"

"Nothing," I said. "Parsons and Nanny both told me about it, but Mrs. Rutledge didn't. Did you ask the Forresters?"

He nodded. "They don't know anything, either."

The time for protest had arrived. "Listen," I said, "are you just curious or have you method in your madness? Why are you fussing around with the family? What about this quarrel Viola and Parsons had? I don't get this, and I really think we've all been pretty patient."

Atwood glared at me. "Patient! That's right. Patient. And not one of you will tell me a thing that might be important. Even the servants won't talk about the family. And Parsons and the other maid quarreled because the maid had been out late with the chauffeur and couldn't do her work right the next day. That's a good motive for a brutal murder, isn't it? In fact, Miss Brooks, you're the only one around here with a decent motive!" His face was flushed and red. He mopped it with a handkerchief that had already seen good mopping service. Then he rapped out another question before I could recover from his accusation. "Have you a key to Oak Hill?"

Stunned, I answered quickly. "Of course I have."

"Where were those keys Friday night?" His voice was urgent.

"With my other keys. In my house. Why?"

"Miss Brooks," he said with exaggerated patience, "the murderer was either in the big house or had to have keys to get into it. The murderer stunned the maid, got the wheelbarrow out of the locked tool house, cut her throat, took her down to the blackberry vines, and put the tool house key back on the board near the back door. The butler swears that the house was locked up, that he's never failed to lock it in the thirty years he's been here. *Why* was that maid murdered? That's what I've got to find out."

Excitement was pounding through my veins. "Listen," I said, "where's the weapon? The knife that was used to cut her throat?"

Atwood shrugged his shoulders. "I don't know. We haven't found it, but the cook says there's a knife missing from the rack in the kitchen. We'll have a fine time trying to find it. There're plenty of places to hide a knife in the house or the grounds between here and the Farm House." He lifted his eyebrows in a gesture of resignation. "And when you're ready to tell me what you have that somebody else wants, I'll be glad to hear that, too."

There was a great big angry lump in my throat. "I don't know," I said vigorously. "I haven't anything that anybody else would want except a little inexpensive jewelry and a few pieces of old silver. And that's that. Did you find any fingerprints in my room?"

"No, ma'am, but we found plenty of glove prints and smudges."

"Well, I think this pussy-footing around outside my house and tearing up my room is the well-known red herring, just as that note was." I leaned back hot and exhausted, also hungry.

"Red herrings or not, somebody in this house who knows plenty about the family habits is doing all this. Everybody was asleep in separate rooms all during the whole time, and nobody knows anything, and if they do, they won't tell. Might get their names in the paper and not on the society page, either." He stood up, disgusted and hot and disagreeable-looking.

He turned on me abruptly. "You don't like your mother, do you, Miss Brooks?"

I gaped in astonishment. "I don't know her very well," I said weakly. "I don't either like or dislike her."

A combination of fear and excitement welled up in me after Atwood's next speech. His eyes were blank, but something distinctly like a sneer curled his mouth.

"You and Forrester are a pair of smooth articles, too. I'd give a lot to know just what you two are up to with your notes and your dears and your darlings."

Angry tears smarted in my eyes. "You're a fool," I said stupidly, my voice trembling. "That's just Tony's way. After all, he's my cousin's husband."

"That's just it," Atwood snapped. "Your cousin's husband. A fine mess, isn't it?"

He turned on his heel and walked off briskly with long, emphatic steps.

If I had been beaten with a knotted rope in Atwood's pudgy, ugly hands, I couldn't have felt more shorn of dignity or decency.

CHAPTER 13

Filled with an aching depression, I dressed and dragged myself into the house. It took resolution and stern self-preaching for me to convince myself that Atwood was bluffing, that he couldn't really believe the accusations that he'd hurled at me. He was only trying to pry information out of me, scare me. That must be it. In any case, there was nothing I could do except put the whole mess out of my mind and find out how Aunt Ella was.

I met no one in the halls, which, upstairs, are thickly carpeted in rich crimson broadloom. The well-oiled lock on the door to Aunt Ella's sitting room made no sound when I opened it so that my arrival was unannounced.

At first glance, I thought the room was empty. It wasn't. A startled intake of breath made me swing around on my heels. Amelia Ortiz straightened up quickly and confusedly from her position at my great-aunt's handsome secretarial desk. Her black eyes flashed a message of fear.

"Susan, you frightened me. I didn't hear you coming." Her voice was calm, but the expression on her face belied her calm.

My mind and body were so filled with animosity that I could scarcely speak. I had to wait until I found words suitable to deliver the stinging reprimand the woman deserved.

"What are you doing prying in my aunt's desk?" The pulse that roared in my ears was so loud that I could scarcely hear my own voice.

Amelia's poise slid down over her visibly.

"Really, Susan, aren't you being a little ridiculous? You're very touchy, I think. I hardly feel called upon to explain my actions to you, but I'm looking for a piece of paper on which to write a note." Her heavy eyebrows drooped in disapproval. "You have an unfortunate habit, my dear, of sneaking up on people. I don't like that characteristic in you. Openness is much more desirable in a young girl."

I could feel my own jaw jutting angrily. Once again this incredible woman had put me on the defensive. My voice came out shrill and childish.

"Then what is that letter you have in your hand?"

Amelia sat down at the desk with her back turned to me. I wanted to hit her.

"My correspondence is no concern of yours, Susan. It is a letter to which I shall now write a reply."

She drew a sheet of Aunt Ella's note paper toward her and picked up a pen and started to write, but I wasn't finished yet.

"It's customary for guests in this house to write their letters in the library or the guest rooms on the paper provided for them, not at the hostess' desk." When I had finished speaking, I heard a faint murmur of voices coming from the bedroom.

Amelia sighed irritably. "It's more convenient to do it here, Susan. I've been waiting for the two doctors to finish their examination of our aunt. I shall write my letter. There's no need for further discussion."

And that was that.

I flung myself onto the love seat and snatched a cigarette and lit it and nervously flicked ashes into one of the big crystal ash trays that are used throughout Oak Hill. Amelia's imperturbable black back moved slightly in motion with her pen. When she had finished her note, she sealed it and put it and her other letter in her big black bag and snapped the catch decisively. She got up and came over to help herself to a cigarette. I punched the lighter for her, and she sat down in a chair opposite me, smiling and poised as you please.

Then we made polite conversation just as though we didn't dislike each other intensely and as though life at Oak Hill were pursuing its usual calm, gracious pace without murders or serious illness or mysterious goings-on.

"Ella has done a good deal of remodelling and modernizing in the house, has she not?" Amelia said in a social voice.

"Yes," I said. I could feel myself smiling reluctantly. "The modernizing was my first job when I came back from school. We had an architect, of course, but we did over all the service parts of the house and bathrooms and stuff. Curtains and upholstery, too."

"I congratulate you on your good work, Susan. It is really very elegant." She leaned over just in time to dump a half inch of ash into the ash tray. "This house must have given you a good send-off in your work. You are doing well?"

I nodded. "Yes, thanks to Aunt Ella." I could feel myself blushing. "Please, I'm not trying to be nasty. I'm not trying to make a point of what she's done for me. You understand."

Amelia raised her thick eyebrows and laughed lightly. Her eyes were deeply amused. "Of course, my dear. I am very cognizant of my own position in your life. It has been quite negligible, but Ella wanted it that way." She sighed, and I wished that she'd talk less like a pretentiously written book and more like a human being. "Of course," she continued, "living in South America for so long makes the customs of this country seem strange to me. In the Argentine, it would be quite unthinkable for a girl of good family to work in a shop and live alone. Tell me, Susan—if you will forgive my impertinence—why have you not married? Because you have no money to speak of? You are really very attractive and well connected."

I was irritated, but after all the woman's curiosity was understandable. I had plenty of the same about her.

I laughed. "Something like that. One man asked me, but I didn't like him. The man I liked would have none of me." I hoped that my phony voice and expression would pass. I smiled inwardly at the thought of what Amelia would say if she knew of my plans for Joe, but I spared her the shock.

"And Ella never gave you a dot? That seems strange." Amelia's voice was quiet and uncritical.

The words shot out of me. "Look, Amelia, you weren't a child when you went to South America. We don't have dots in America. Aunt Ella gave me a good business so that I wouldn't have to take the first man that came along. I'm not exactly senile anyway. I may still be able to hook some poor man. My Lord!"

It was impossible for me to remain on civil terms with my mother for more than three minutes at a time. I was delighted when the door of the bedroom was opened, and Joe and Doctor Bromley came out.

Introductions were performed, and Doctor Bromley's warm handclasp and crinkling blue eyes filled with kindly friendliness seemed to lift a big load off my mind in two seconds flat. He was a big man with a big voice.

"Well, Miss Brooks, I know you'll be glad to hear that our prognosis is positive. I think Mrs. Rutledge is going to get well." He laughed as he spoke, filling the room with good news, dispelling the animosity and fear and worry. Even Amelia's smile and words of joy seemed sincere. Joe's wide, flexible mouth had lost the signs of tension it had worn for so many days.

"Oh," I said in a squeaky, tear-filled voice. "Oh, how wonderful."

I ran into Aunt Ella's room and stood by the bed looking down at her. She still couldn't talk or move, and the right side of her face sagged grotesquely, but she did look better. I poured out words of affection and relief and thanksgiving and hoped and hoped that she heard them and understood.

"Come on, Miss Brooks, you mustn't tire Mrs. Rutledge." The nurse pulled me gently away from the bed and sent me out of the room.

When I suggested a swim for Joe and Doctor Bromley, they both accepted.

"I'll have to get back to the city for dinner, but I'll be glad to cool off first," Doctor Bromley said eagerly. "It's still hot there. I don't understand it. Five days now. I've never known the heat to last more than three before."

I nodded, understanding. Three days of heat in San Francisco. Then fog to cool it off. I went off to round up the rest of the family and to tell them the good news.

When we were all settled near the pool with big glasses full of cold things, Doctor Bromley told us about Aunt Ella's condition.

"You see," he said, waving his glass in emphasis, "a clot formed on the left side of her brain. That, in a right-handed person, causes paralysis of the right side and of the speech centers. I think the clot is dissolving."

I looked around the group as the plump doctor spoke. There was interest on every face, and each face indicated it in characteristic fashion. Amelia's raised eyebrows and slow nod were her only concession to expression. Will Starr's emphatic nod and tightly pursed lips and impatient, "Yes, yes, I see," conveyed the impression that the doctor was wasting valuable time. Any fool knew the mechanics of a stroke.

Mabel's face was bland, flat, dull; Bea's interested but petulant; Tony's was creased with an automatic smile. Bill and Peggy were round-eyed and concerned and perhaps a little bored. Joe and I alone, I felt, were jubilant.

Will interrupted the doctor's further explanation of his patient's condition.

"How long will it be before she can talk?" he asked.

Doctor Bromley shrugged his big ruddy shoulders.

"I can't tell accurately. Maybe a few days. Maybe a few weeks, but unless she has another stroke, she should recover." He set down his drink and stood up, yanking at the blue flannel trunks Tony had loaned him. They were too tight. "I'm going to get busy with my swim."

He dived into the pool and splashed and made a lot of noise and seemed to enjoy himself thoroughly. I followed his with a quick dive from the side of the pool. When I came up, I turned on my back and floated lazily, looking up at the sky and the branches of the oaks that laced it with their thick, dark green leaves. My cap was tight so that I couldn't hear. I seemed to float on a sea of peace and relief. Occasionally I turned my head to wet my face. I was even cool.

When Aunt Ella could talk again, she'd tell us about the business, and, I was sure, she would be able to tell us what had happened to Parsons, too. Whoever killed Parsons would be punished, and then life would return to its old, easy, accustomed pace. Bea and Tony would go back to their apartment on Nob Hill, and I would spend the winter with Aunt Ella.

The fall would come with its soft rains that touched the surrounding brown hills with green. The leaves would turn yellow and drop, and if we got a little frost some of them would even turn red which is unusual for a California fall in the Bay region. The nights would be sharply chilly and the days bright with sun. Big oak fires would blaze on the hearths, and Magruder would pick hundreds of bronze and yellow and white and dark red chrysanthemums for the house. Friends would come to drink tea out of delicate Spode cups. We'd see a lot of Joe and Anne, and after a good day of hard, interesting work, I'd dine with friends or read new novels in my comfortable bed or go to the movies or play Russian Bank with Aunt Ella. And Joe and I ... There would be no more heat or fruit flies or suspicion or sorrow or fear.

When the skin on my hands was puckered and white from my long stay in the water, I swam slowly to the edge of the blue-tiled pool and pulled myself out of the water. Joe and Doctor Bromley had gone. Bea had dressed and was walking up the path toward the terrace. Will and Tony were talking.

"Tony, I don't think that doctor knows his business," Will said petulantly. "A few days or a few weeks. What am I supposed to do? Spend my life driving up and down California waiting to talk business to Ella. I don't know whether to stay or go home." Will's mousy, ill-natured face was tight with annoyance.

Tony laughed easily. "Well, you might as well go, Will. I imagine it'll be some time before Ella can talk to you."

Amelia opened her mouth to speak. Then she shut it. I wanted definitely to hit Will. He and his fussing about business as though Aunt Ella had had a stroke to spite him and keep him from affairs of importance.

I was right back in the midst of the trouble and all the lovely, calm thoughts I'd had in the pool were childish dreams, wishful thinking, fantasy.

Amelia stood up, her well-made black sheer dress falling in graceful folds around her straight legs. "Susan, you are going down to your house?" she asked.

I nodded. "Yes," I said. "We can take the station wagon. I'll dress down there."

I didn't even bother to collect my clothes from the dressing house. It was too hot, and I was bored and angry with Will. I wanted to get away from him.

As I swung the station wagon from the driveway into the road, I bumped toward the ditch. A thick cloud of heat-laden dust swirled around us, and I turned toward Amelia to apologize for jouncing her. Her face was set, emotionless, but her hands clasped in her lap were white where the skin was drawn taut across her knuckles. I had a distinct feeling that Amelia might keep emotional expressions off her face, but that her hands would not be so easy to control. The tension might have been caused by my poor driving, but I thought not.

I heard the barking and snarling as soon as I turned in my driveway. I parked the car in the shade and hopped out quickly without waiting to assist my parent.

"Bonnie! Bonnie!" I called. "Stop it. What's the matter?" There is a small dooryard in front of my house bordered with a white picket fence. The gate swung open, and just below the two brick steps that lead to my front door, the dog jumped and leaped and barked.

The object of her attentions was a fragile young man of medium height. His hair was dark and shiny and sleek, his little moustache neatly waxed. His eyes were large and brown and filled with an expression of hysterical terror as he endeavored to beat off the dog with a thin Malacca cane. His too carefully fitted black suit reminded me of the clothes that Frenchmen wear on Sunday.

I grabbed the dog's collar and picked her up and held her dusty little black body in my arms. She continued to growl half-heartedly.

"I'm sorry," I said. "She's a watchdog. Your hitting at her with the cane made her worse."

The fragile young man's eyes trailed off to a point behind me, and I watched an ecstatic smile break over his pale, almost girlish face.

"Mama!" he screamed and dashed around me toward Amelia. I turned to watch.

So I had a brother, a half-brother to be exact.

He and Amelia performed a rather elaborate embrace which involved both cheeks and the shifting of their arms. Amelia's expression was veiled, but I knew very definitely that she did not join in the hysterical joy of her son. They spoke in Spanish so of course I couldn't understand what they said.

I put the dog down with an admonition not to bite our relative and pulled my white terrycloth robe tighter about me. For some wild, unaccountable reason, I wished that I looked better upon the occasion of my first meeting with an unexpected brother.

Amelia forced a reluctant smile across her face and introduced me to my half-brother, Carlos Ortiz.

He bowed, and he kissed my hand, and I actually heard the click of his heels. The meaning of Amelia's early morning Spanish telephone conversation was clear.

Then I said, inadequately, that this was all very interesting and perhaps we'd better go inside.

CHAPTER 14

My half-brother's manners were impeccable. Not so his English. He turned frequently to his mama for assistance in conveying apologies, explanations, and compliments. He said "ee-smokeen" when he meant "smoking." It was very amusing and very hard to understand, but I finally got the idea that he'd needed to consult with his mama on a matter of important business and had, with difficulty, found his way via bus and taxi to my house.

I went off to dress and left my relations to their consultation. In the few moments I had spent with them, I had seen a strange softening process take place in Amelia's iron exterior. She loved her son devotedly. He seemed to be extraordinarily dependent upon her. He was also a weak little fop, and quite patently I was an outsider and of no consequence to either of them, and I didn't care at all.

The problem of what to do with Amelia and Carlos was solved for me by a knock on the door. As I was fully clothed, I said, "Come in."

It was Amelia, her face once again veiled and hard. But her right hand was a tight fist. She sighed as she sat down in my blue and yellow striped slipper chair.

"Susan," she said firmly, "this is most embarrassing and most difficult." She hesitated for only a second, and then she went on as though there was no time to be wasted in false delicacy. "Carlos came here to tell me that our funds have not come from South America. It is very serious—about the hotel, I mean. I don't like to ask it, but if you could lend us two hundred dollars for a few days, I should be most grateful."

I wanted violently to laugh, but I controlled myself. My mother was simply incredible, but perhaps not so incredible after all. Because she loved her dandified little son, I suppose that borrowing money from an abandoned daughter was a small enough matter.

I smiled a trifle maliciously. "All right," I said. "It'll have to be a check, but I want to make a bargain with you. Tell me why you came here. That's fair enough, isn't it?"

Her jaw set firmly, and wrinkled little pouches formed at the corners of her mouth. "I have told you, on numerous occasions, that I came to see my aunt as I was travelling in this country."

I smiled again. "All right, you win, but tell me something else. What was Lawrence Brooks like? Have I any family in England? Stuff like that. Aunt Ella said she never knew anything about him." Naturally I'd wondered about my father and his family ever since I was old enough to know I had one. My heart was tight with anticipation as I realized, quite clearly, that at last I was going to get some information.

Amelia gave me a long look. "You'd be much better off not knowing, Susan. Do you insist?"

I nodded and reached for a piece of Kleenex to wipe off my face. My bedroom was insufferably hot.

"He was a complete and absolute rotter. Unfaithful, spendthrift, dishonest about money. His father was an Episcopal clergyman, and he had disowned Lawrence before I married him." Amelia stood up. "Will that do?"

It is not nice for a girl to know that her background, her parents, are not straight, but I'd asked for it. In a way I was almost relieved. It's much better to know than to guess. Undoubtedly Aunt Ella had known all this, but she'd pretended ignorance to spare me. I couldn't decide just then whether she'd been right or not.

Amelia had started to leave the room.

"Wait, please," I said. "Let's finish this. Tell me the rest of it."

She turned slowly and raised her eyebrows and smiled thinly. "I believe Lawrence's parents have been dead a great many years. They were decent, well-bred people but poor. What little they had I imagine went to Lawrence's sister. He never knew anything about you. I had already divorced him when I discovered I was pregnant. When I found that out, I managed to get out of England—it was during the war and not at all easy to do—and I went to Mentone where Aunt Ella and Eleanor had a villa. They'd been there at the start of the war, and Eleanor was too ill to be moved. I stayed there until after you were born, and then I went to South America." The words had been coming rather fast, but finally she paused for a minute. "I know what you think of me, Susan, but try to understand my position, won't you?"

I caught a glimpse of my face in the dressing table mirror. It could have been called "A Study in Harrowing Emotions."

"Understand what?" I said in a husky voice.

Amelia came back and sat down. She leaned toward me and spoke with more warmth in her voice than I had ever heard before.

"Susan, I had a horrible life with Lawrence Brooks. I met Ortiz—he was in the Argentinian Legation in London—and he was the most fascinating man I have ever met in my life. I loved him deeply until the day he died." Her black eyes got blacker with emotion. She was frightening, and I could easily imagine that to be loved by a woman like Amelia might be rather a burden. "I wanted to marry him, and I would have done anything on earth to do it. I couldn't take Lawrence Brooks' child to South America—Ortiz was jealous. Anyway, Lawrence was dead and his people couldn't have done anything for you. I *had* to turn you over to Ella. Do you understand?"

"Yes," I said slowly. "Yes. I think I do." I'm a pushover for a sad story. I was almost sorry for poor Amelia and her great love, and I quite understood that turning me over to Ella to rear was an act of good sense if not especially maternal. I laughed jerkily.

"All right," I said. "Thanks for the information. I'll make you a check, and let's take Carlos up to Oak Hill for dinner. I like to see the relations gape."

Amelia shrugged her shoulders noncommittally. "Very well. He can take a late bus back to the hotel." She left the room and went down the hall to her room to dress.

Depressed and uncomfortable, I finished my hair and went into the living room. Brother Carlos leaped to his feet and bowed prettily. He said something which, I gathered, meant that my dusty rose dinner dress was becoming and that he was delighted to have such a pretty sister. He rolled his big brown eyes wildly as he spoke, and I laughed at him good humoredly.

The living room felt like a steam bath, so I opened the French doors leading to the terrace on the east side. It didn't help much as the air that came in from outside was as hot and still as that in the room. But it was fresher.

"Carlos, would you like a drink?" I said very distinctly and a little too loudly as though shouting would make English more understandable.

"A dreenk?" he said, smiling and showing a lot of teeth that needed the attentions of the dentist.

This sparkling repartee went on for some time, but Carlos and I finally got together on a Tom Collins. He came out in the kitchen with me while I made it. He admired the kitchen and all its appointments very extravagantly.

"Reech. Reech," he said, running his tapering fingers over the white enamel stove and icebox.

Of all the fool things, I thought to myself. A brother I've never seen until the last hour, and we can't even talk to each other.

We took the drinks back to the living room, and I asked Carlos to excuse me while I wrote out a check. I subtracted the two hundred dollars from my balance and was left with the staggering sum of $23.62 in my personal checking account which is separate from the shop account.

Amelia's bag lay upon the edge of the desk. I decided to be tactful and put the check in it and say nothing to Carlos. Even if he knew that his mother had borrowed money from me, there was no point in talking about it.

Carlos stood in the French door looking up toward Oak Hill undoubtedly thinking about how "reech" it looked. He didn't see me unsnap the catch on his mother's bag. I don't think he even heard the sharp intake of my breath as I saw what was in the bag.

An airmail envelope addressed to Mrs. Henry Rutledge, Oak Hill, Rutledge, California, stood out sharp and clear against the black lining.

The return address in the upper left-hand corner said Ortiz, Hotel Pierre, New York City.

The surge of excitement and anger and blinding knowledge that welled up in me made me brave if foolhardy. I tore the letter out of the bag and out of its envelope, and I read it, not caring a hoot whether Amelia caught me or not. I knew that this was the letter that had upset Aunt Ella a week ago Saturday—the date told me that—and I knew, too, that Amelia had stolen it out of my Aunt's desk.

It was written on a single sheet of thin, airmail paper, and the reading of it contributed little to my knowledge, but a great deal to my feeling of apprehension. It said:

DEAR AUNT ELLA–
In a few days I am leaving for California. My husband died a few months ago, leaving me and my son badly situated financially. For this reason, I shall come to see you in an effort to make some change in the arrangement which we made when Susan was born.
With all affectionate good wishes, I am
Your niece,
AMELIA ORTIZ.

For a few seconds, I debated what to do with the letter. Keep it and show it to the sheriff? Or confront Amelia with it? No, I'd put it back. If necessary I could tell Atwood about it, but Amelia was sure to discover its loss before I could get hold of him, and if I talked to her about it, she'd only put me in the wrong. I could imagine a long stream of snappish remarks anent the reading of other peoples' letters.

With shaking hands, I put the letter back in its envelope and replaced it in the bag and laid my folded check on top of the bag. Carlos paid no attention to me. Amelia was still in her room. I sighed heavily. Funds from South America, my eye. The Ortiz family was broke and had come to California to get something out of Aunt Ella. I smiled to myself. Perhaps they even had some idea of moving in on Sister Susan. No wonder Amelia was interested in my success in the decorating business or the possibility of a dot.

But why had she gone to the trouble of stealing back the letter? And what was there about Amelia and her "arrangement" which caused Aunt Ella to summon her family? And most important of all, what had this to do with Parsons' death? After all, Parsons had almost fainted when she heard that Amelia had arrived at Oak Hill, and Parsons had been at the villa in Mentone when I was born. She must have known what the arrangement was.

The completely baffling array of questions poured through my brain with such speed that it took Carlos quite some time, apparently, to get my attention.

I shook myself mentally. He was pointing at the dog who stood on the terrace looking hungry. Hungry, doubtless, for a chunk off Carlos' leg as well as her dinner.

I fed the dog, and all the time I was in the kitchen, I kept thinking about Amelia's letter and its possible connection with Parsons' death. Slowly and reluctantly, I admitted to myself the possibility that my mother was a murderer. It was not an easy admission. I had just been told that my father was a rotter, and I bitterly resented my shoddy, off-color background, but there was no denying Amelia's potentialities as a murderer.

She had had access to the keys for Oak Hill, and while she had not been there in nearly thirty years, she might easily have remembered the arrangements about the tool house and the keys to the outbuildings. Perhaps it was wildly, remotely possible that she knew of Parsons' will in my favor and had some hare-brained idea of getting the money for herself and Carlos. The thing that stumped me completely was the lift. How could she have known about that? It had been installed in the house only four years ago, and no one used it except Aunt Ella.

And there was absolutely no way she could have known about me and Tony and his method of signing notes "af." And she could not have ransacked my room at Oak Hill after I left it at five o'clock in the morning.

No, definitely, Amelia, if she was in this game, was not in it alone.

Dinner at Oak Hill was another strange, tense gathering of the clan. We all carefully skirted any mention of Parsons' murder. Silences fell frequently, and our efforts to fill them were half-hearted. Will and Mabel announced that they would leave for Long Beach in the morning and would drop young Bill off at Fort Ord on the way. I wondered if Atwood knew of their plans, but said nothing.

Bea said that there had been a steady stream of people telephoning and calling all day to inquire about Aunt Ella. "We've got enough flowers and jelly and fancy fruit for a hospital," she said.

Tony, when he had recovered from the shock of learning that I had a little South American brother, was very nice to Carlos. He spoke fair Spanish, and I think Carlos was very grateful to him. Anyway, he smiled a lot and showed his unattractive teeth. Occasionally Amelia joined in their conversation, but most of the time she was silent and preoccupied. With good reason, too, I thought.

Coffee on the terrace was drunk hastily as though all of us would prefer to get the forced social amenities over with and be free to sit quietly and puzzle over the days' doings. Mabel and Will and their children went upstairs to pack and get to bed early.

Tony offered to drive Carlos back to town, but Amelia, almost diffidently, asked me if Carlos could stay at my house for the night. "We have a good deal to talk about," she explained. I said Carlos could stay and that I would sleep at Oak Hill, and my mother and brother trailed off toward the library for their talk.

Bea said she thought she'd cope with her bills, and she looked very depressed as she said it.

Tony and I were left standing in the hall alone. He grinned at me, and against all reason and good sense, I felt warm inside and faintly excited.

"Let's you and me go into town and have a drink, huh?" he said.

I rationalized. I needed somebody to talk to. I needed somebody to tell about Amelia's letter. That's the excuse I made to myself for agreeing to go in to the hotel in Berkeley with Tony. Actually, I just wanted to go, and I didn't care what Atwood or anyone else might think. I wanted to get away from Oak Hill and the knowledge of my own nasty background and my fears and suspicions, and I wanted perversely to be with Tony.

"Okay," I said, grinning back. "I'll borrow a wrap from Bea." I knocked at Bea's door and was told to come in. She was sitting at her small white and gold kidney desk with as big a heap of bills in front of her as I had ever seen outside of a contractor's office.

"You have quite a chore, my girl," I said. "Writing out checks for those."

She laughed dryly. "It isn't the check writing that bothers me. It's paying the damned things." She sighed.

Well, if Bea was in debt, it was no skin off my nose. "I'm going into town with your husband. Will you lend me a wrap?" I asked.

She smiled. "Such nerve. Going out with my husband and in my clothes. Sure. Take the white wool one in the right-hand closet in the dressing room. It'll look very well with that dress."

I went in and found the wrap and put it on and admired the effect. I didn't really need the coat on account of the heat, but my arms were bare, and my dress had what is known as a "plunging" neckline, and I didn't think it looked too well for a bar on Sunday night.

As I stood before the mirror, I heard Bea's telephone ring. I went back to the bedroom, and as I crossed the threshold, I heard her say softly, "All right. In an hour."

She hung up, and I said, "Thanks pal," and went downstairs, wondering mildly what Bea was going to do in an hour.

I was glad that I had come with Tony. The rush of wind on my face felt fine. The top of Tony's car was down, and I leaned back and looked up at the sky. It was inky black, and suddenly I realized that there were no stars in it. As we approached the Orinda cross road about five miles from Rutledge, a quick, brief flash of light blinked in the sky. It was pink for a second, then blue-white.

"Tony," I yelled against the rush of wind, "did you see that? Heat lightning!"

He nodded and yelled back. "That's right, baby. I've never seen it around here before. Have you?"

"No, I haven't."

We actually talked about the weather until we got through the tunnel. We agreed that we had never known heat of such intensity or duration in the Bay Area, and that we were undoubtedly having the well-known heat wave.

The bar in the hotel was a welcome sight. Pale blue-green lights shone through glass brick, giving the effect of glacial ice. The lamps in the glass-enclosed lounge were low, as were also the music and the chairs and sofas and the voices of the occupants. The view of the Bay Bridge and the lights of San Francisco was beautiful and richly impersonal and just what I needed.

I ordered my favorite drink of fizz water, limes, lots of cracked ice, and no alcohol. Tony ordered a planter's punch, and when the pretty little Chinese waitress had brought them, we sat quietly without talking. There was a good old tune coming softly and nostalgically out of the muted loudspeaker on the wall. The tune was called "Soon," and I remembered it very well, and my insides felt melted.

Tony reached over and took my hand, and I didn't pull it away immediately. A fine kind of a fool I was to let myself in for this kind of thing. Until this morning, really, I'd had a good strong armor of resentment against Tony that had protected me for a long time. Tony, in the dressing house, had managed somehow to find the rent in that armor, and here I sat in a thoroughly romantic setting mooning like a school-girl over the past.

But that's what being alone with Tony did to most women. He just had too much charm or magnetism or what you will for a girl to keep her head. Good, kind, dependable men were apt to be forgotten in Tony's presence. I suddenly jerked my hand away.

"Tony, I came in here to talk to you about my mother," I said in a very forced, brisk voice. "That woman is up to absolutely no good. She loves that little half-brother of mine—loved his pa like mad, too, it seems—and I think she'd do anything for him. But anything." I looked at Tony very significantly, and he winked broadly.

"If this is the well-known brushoff, my love, have it your own way. What's the dope?" He shifted his handsome big body so that he sat sideways on the sofa and could look directly at me.

I told him about the letter which I had read without even a guilty conscience to taunt me. Tony whistled.

"What do you make of it?" I said.

We discussed the letter for some time, and Tony's conclusions were the same as mine. Amelia was undoubtedly at Oak Hill for a purpose, probably money, and she could have murdered Parsons, but she couldn't have known about Tony's customary signature on notes to me nor could she have ransacked my room. A thought kept nagging at the back of my mind, a question I wanted to ask, but I kept losing the thing just as I almost had it.

"Listen, darling," Tony said slowly, "here's an idea. Maybe somebody else in the house knew that Amelia had done in Parsons and wanted the body found. After all, the murderer went to a lot of trouble to hide it. So the note to you."

The idea certainly carried weight. "A very good idea, too, but who's looking for what?"

"Herrings. Bright red. Scaring Amelia, maybe."

The question I'd wanted to ask finally became clear. "Listen," I said excitedly, "you slept out by the pool the other night. Did you hear anything? Or see anything? I've been trying for days to remember to ask you."

Tony shook his head mournfully. "Not a thing. I'm an exceptional sleeper—especially after eight highballs." He sighed. "Of course, the wheelbarrow was trundled off in the opposite direction from where the pool is, but they could have run the thing right by the couch, and I wouldn't have heard it. In other words, darling, I must confess to you that I'd got myself drunk and passed out."

"Shame on you," I said.

We lapsed back into silence again. I watched the heat lightning flicker over the black sky, and I listened to another old, old tune whine out its sad tale of love that was lost, and I wondered why cheap, undistinguished popular music always has such power to dig up the past and bring unwelcome memories.

Because I was tired and because my emotions were raw from overwork, I let myself slip back without a struggle. I remembered how it felt to be very young and in love and eager for the future, and I let myself wonder a little about what that future might have been if Tony'd gone on wanting to marry me instead of deciding that he wanted Bea.

Tony's words stabbed painfully as their meaning sank into my brain, but I made him say them again.

"I wonder how things would have turned out," he repeated, "if I'd had sense enough to recognize the difference between love and being excited."

I shook my head and said "Shut up," between clenched teeth. He'd done his old trick of reading my mind, almost.

"If it's any comfort to you, darling," he said quietly, "I've known for a long time that I'm the world's prize fool." He paused for a second. "Are you going to marry Hilliard?"

"Maybe," I sighed, "if I'm asked."

Joe seemed a little remote at the moment.

Tony put his lean, brown hand over mine and gave it a hard squeeze. "Don't, please. For a while. I can't say any more now." If we'd been any place but in the hotel, I would have cried the tears that clamored for release at the back of my eyes.

"Shut up," I said shakily. "You're a cad, and you have two nice children. You've done enough to me."

"How right you are," Tony said, his mouth twisted in a heartbreaking little grin.

Seeing Mrs. Ronald, Rutledge's leading purveyor of gossip, sitting on a sofa within hearing distance of Tony's and mine didn't help matters much, either. She bowed politely as we walked past her on our way out, and, I thought, rather pointedly sent her love to Bea.

There have been a good many times in my life, I am proud to say, when dignity and good sense have triumphed over the yearnings of my emotions. When Tony told me, very reluctantly to be sure, that he honestly felt that we were not suited and that he and Bea were, I had plenty of dignity and good sense. And that was all I did have on the positive side. I had a broken heart or mind or whatever you want to call it, and I hurt all over.

That Sunday night under one of the big trees at Oak Hill, I didn't have any dignity and not an ounce of good sense. If I had had, I would have struggled away from Tony, called him a cad, and run very fast for the house.

Instead, after listening all the way home to the sound of his voice saying things I'd wanted for years to hear, I let him put his big hands on my shoulders and draw me to him, and I frankly and unashamedly enjoyed the kisses that followed. Tony's charm wasn't phony then, even if my brain had turned to water and my knees to pulsating jelly. It was wonderful, and in those few minutes I got back quite a lot of confidence that I'd been without for a long time.

I loved being loved again, and I was far away in a beautiful, childish little dream world of my own. That's why I didn't hear the sound of a car or see its headlights as they flashed full upon us.

Tony pushed me from him with a muttered, "Sorry, darling," and dragged out his handkerchief and mopped the lipstick off his face. I did likewise.

When I finally saw it, the inopportune automobile was parked at Oak Hill's front entrance. Two men got out, and my heart plunged abysmally. If I had combed Contra Costa County, I couldn't have made a more unfortunate choice of people to see me kissing Tony under the oaks. The two men were Joe and Sheriff Atwood.

Tony laughed unconvincingly. I just gritted my teeth and groaned and walked over to where the bright porch light shone down on the doctor and the sheriff.

To this day I blush painfully and hideously at the bare thought of the looks Atwood and Joe gave me that night on the great porch of Oak Hill. The aching embarrassment even now can make my heart race and cold sweat leap from my pores.

Atwood's devilish countenance twisted in a sickening sneer. Joe's eyes had real pain in them, but his mouth was blank and entirely unfriendly. Neither of the men made any comment on what they had seen. Not then, that is. Tony alone was poised and his usual friendly self.

"What's up, Atwood? Kind of a late call, isn't it?" he said, unlocking the front door.

The men stood back to let me go ahead, and I wondered wildly if I could faint or just fall down in a heap. Instead I walked unsteadily into the house and stood in the hall and listened without opening my mouth.

Atwood snapped out his words. "I want to see everyone in this house who was down at the swimming pool when Doctor Hilliard was this afternoon. Get them up and have them come down, will you?" He flung his hat on a console and walked briskly toward the library, opened the door, and closed it after him. I heard Amelia's and Carlos' voices raised in excitement.

Tony's smile, as he spoke to Joe, was decidedly feeble. "What's up, Joe?

Something serious?"

Joe nodded, his face stony and unrelenting.

"Very serious, Forrester. Somebody stole a phial of morphine out of my coat in the dressing house. There was enough there to kill four or five people."

Tony had become Forrester.

I sank down on the Chippendale settee. The excitement and satisfaction to my pride that I'd had from Tony's about-face had become thoroughly cheap and childish and tenth-rate.

CHAPTER 15

For hours and hours, I sat in the hall, each passing minute adding to my apprehension and to the disgust I felt for myself. Joe went in to sit with Atwood, and I watched the members of the household file in and out of the library.

Will's sparse hair stood on end above his sleepy and rather stupid face as he went in. When he came out, he glowered at me and tramped off upstairs without a word.

Mabel's head was encased in a hideous brown hairnet that would assure the tight rigidity of her wave upon the morrow. She, too, went in blank and sleepy and came out angry. Amelia and Carlos had drifted off to the blue drawing room shortly after Atwood's arrival. Peggy and Bill were round-eyed with fright and sodden with youthful sleep. Glore and Jane were fully clothed, but they looked unutterably weary. I remembered dimly that they had come down to the pool to serve drinks and canapes.

Tony had vanished after he went upstairs to wake up the family, and Bea had not appeared.

Morphine! I kept saying the word over and over and over. Morphine. What did anyone in our house want with a lot of morphine? I tried to tell myself that Joe was mistaken, that the morphine had been stolen somewhere else, but I couldn't. I knew very well, too well, that Joe would think long and carefully before he told Atwood that morphine had been stolen from him at Oak Hill. I knew, too, that Joe was always careful to carry his drugs in his coat and not in his bag which was frequently left in his car or around his patients' halls where it was accessible to too many potential thieves.

He'd thought it safe in his coat in the dressing house, and it hadn't been.

As young Bill passed me in the hall with a bleak, embarrassed nod, I realized that Atwood had undoubtedly given all of the family instructions not to speak to me. The realization, of course, only increased the already loud jangling of my nerves.

Atwood came to the door of the library. His blank blue eyes glinted angrily.

"Is the dressing house locked at night, Miss Brooks?" he asked coldly.

I nodded. "You want the key?"

"Yes."

I got it for him from the board by the back entrance. He took it and told me to wait in the library.

Joe looked up as I came into the room, but he didn't get out of his chair. His lean face seemed to have aged fifteen years in an hour. His eyes were dark with tragedy. He leaned forward with his elbows on his knees, his hands clutching his forehead. And I knew when I looked at him that the lost morphine was only part of his troubles. Lost faith in Susan Brooks was the other part. And there was nothing I could say, no excuse for my own cheap, weak actions. At that moment I *hated* Tony, and at the same time I knew I was unjust.

"My God, Susan," Joe said thickly. "How could I have been so careless? How could I?"

My own voice was heavy with emotion as I spoke. "Are you sure it was here, Joe? Are you sure?"

He nodded dismally. "I thought and thought and thought for hours, and it couldn't have happened anywhere else. It just couldn't. I even came back here and searched the dressing house and your aunt's rooms and the part of the grounds where I was. I looked everywhere before I told Atwood, but I had it just before I came here this afternoon, and I needed it for a patient right after I left here. This is the only place I had my coat off." He patted the pocket where the phials should have been and weren't.

Atwood called softly from the direction of the pool. "Come on down here, will you, Hilliard? I want you to show me where the coat was."

Joe stood up, and I followed him through the French door to the terrace and down the steps and around the pool to the dressing house.

The little building has a room about ten by twelve at one end which houses the bar, icebox and sink. This room can be closed off with louvered folding doors on the side facing the pool, but during the day in summer, the doors are left open. From the bar section of the dressing house, there is a door leading to a small hall. Two doors in the hall lead to what we call the male and female halves of the house. In each half, there are four small dressing rooms with showers between. Anyone going into the dressing house proper can, therefore, enter either the male or female half without being seen from outside.

I watched Joe point out the place where he had hung his coat in the first male dressing room.

"Made it kind of easy, didn't it, Hilliard?" Atwood said with what I thought unnecessary sarcasm. Any fool could see that Joe was half insane with regret.

"That's right, Atwood, very easy."

"And everybody in this house was down here this afternoon—the family, that is, and as you were the first to undress, any of them could have taken it." Atwood rocked slowly back and forth on his heels, his head shoved down tight on his shoulders. He turned to me. "Where'd you put your clothes, Miss Brooks?"

I led him into the little dressing room where I'd changed. My red and white printed linen dress was still there on a hanger. My underwear and shoes were neatly arranged on a shelf. Apparently one of the maids had been down to tidy up before the place was locked for the night. "Those are my clothes," I said.

Atwood walked over and pawed at the pockets of my dress. Then, to my intense annoyance, he pawed, with his ugly, pudgy hands, at my slip, pants, bra, garter belt, and stockings. He even put his fat fingers inside my brown and white saddle oxfords. An expression of resentment on Joe's face was the only cheering sight in the place.

"Why didn't you dress, Miss Brooks? Why'd you leave the clothes here?" Atwood's lowering expression made me half sick with fear.

"I had to dress for dinner anyway, so I wore my bathing suit home and took my shower there," I said, a little too sharply.

"You walked down to your house in a bathing suit?" he asked.

"No. I had a terry cloth robe over my bathing suit, and I rode in the station wagon. With my mother."

He bit ruminatively at his heavy lower lip. Then he snorted. His next speech caused me to grope at Joe for support.

"Well, if you stole it, you've had plenty of time to hide it, haven't you?"

I couldn't answer. There were no words to answer that kind of question.

Back at the house, Atwood made me describe my actions at the pool at least four times. He also made me describe my actions in detail since then, and when I told him how I had spent the evening with Tony, the expression on Atwood's face made me long to dissolve into thin air, to die, anything to be released from his contempt. He fired question after question at me, and if I hadn't known that he was trying to trap me in some sort of damning admission, I would have thought him exceedingly stupid.

"Yes," I said for the fourth time, "I think I was the first woman to undress. That's right.... Mrs. Forrester and Miss Starr went in afterwards.... No, neither Mrs. Ortiz nor Mrs. Starr swam.... They may have gone in the dressing house. I didn't notice.... No, I never went back. I went home almost immediately after I got out of the pool."

Quite obviously Atwood had convinced himself that I had stolen Joe's morphine, secreted it in the pocket of my terry cloth robe and made a dash for home as soon as I got out of the pool.

So angry that tears were not far off, I shouted at Atwood. "Why don't you go down and search my house if you think I've stolen the morphine? Why don't you?"

Atwood's face flushed beet-red, the broken veins in his cheeks a deep purple. "I didn't say you'd stolen it, Miss Brooks. You could have—just like all the rest of these people. But I'm not accusing anyone. Where's Mrs. Forrester?" he snapped.

But he had accused me. I leaned back, breathless. "I don't know," I said.

"Well, suppose you hunt her up for me, and don't tell her what's happened, either." He gave his orders as though he expected them to be obeyed, and strangely enough I thought I'd better obey them.

I walked wearily over to the door to the hall and pulled it open. Bea, her dark eyes enormous in a perfectly white face, stood at the foot of the stairs. I had a fleeting impression of movement as though she might have been listening at the library door and had just got away in time.

"Inside, sister," I said bitterly. "Atwood's at it again." I hoped he heard me.

Bea gulped and walked into the library and shut the door. She was still wearing the dress she'd worn at dinner and had a short red tweed wrap slung over her shoulders.

Tony came down the stairs, his face troubled and unhappy.

He swore softly and fluently. "Bea get home?" he whispered.

I nodded and pointed to the library. "She's getting hers now."

"I had quite a time finding her," he said. He squeezed my arm just above the elbow, and I yanked it away from him. "Did you pinch Joe's morphine, honey lamb?" He grinned unconvincingly.

I wrinkled my nose as though I smelled something bad. "Of course," I said. "I'm going to use it on Atwood the first chance I get. *Who* and *why* the morphine, Tony?"

He sighed loud and long. "It's good for either murder or suicide, Susan. Also nice for doping people, I believe, if you don't want to do them in completely."

At that point a white-faced Amelia and Carlos full of flutters came out of the drawing room.

"Susan, that Atwood. He refuses to allow Carlos and me to return to Berkeley," she said breathlessly. "I will not stay in that little house of yours. It isn't safe. We must be put up here at Oak Hill."

I swallowed with difficulty. "I don't think there's room here, Amelia. All the nurses and everything. Nothing will happen to you in my house."

"Very well," she said, "Carlos and I can sleep on the sofas in the drawing room, but we are staying right here, and I am going to insist to Bea that the doors to the service wing be locked. A murderer with morphine! It's frightful."

There was no point in telling her that there were no murderers with morphine down at my little house.

At two o'clock Monday morning Atwood, his men and a husky policewoman had finished their search of Oak Hill and the inhabitants thereof. They left in a body with Atwood muttering something about needles in haystacks.

Amelia and Carlos, to Bea's intense irritation, were installed in the nursery, as the children and Nanny had been sent to San Francisco. Amelia was given Nanny's bed in the night nursery; Carlos the sofa in the day nursery.

Bea, white and shaken and fearful, readily agreed to the locking of the doors into the service wing. I wanted to ask her where she had been that Tony had such difficulty finding her, but my own sense of guilt about my actions with her husband was so great that I could scarcely look at her, let alone speak to her.

My room had been restored to its usual order. The bed was turned down invitingly with a sheer pink summer nightgown thrown across the foot. Only a tiny smudge of grayish powder on the edge of the bathroom mirror was left to bear witness that someone had torn the room apart and that Atwood had examined the room for fingerprints.

I undressed slowly and turned out the light and got into bed. My door was securely locked, and I was safe from the morphine thief, but not from the horror of my own thoughts.

Why had Parsons been killed? If I knew that, there might be some possibility of knowing who had done it. I knew that I hadn't killed her, but Atwood didn't know that, and I was the only one in the house with what was, seemingly, a decent motive. Atwood's statement shortly before he left that he wanted to see the books for my shop showed me very clearly that he thought I had a good motive for killing poor old Parsons.

My stomach was knotted and tight with fear. My heart seemed to have crept up into my throat to pound and beat with a violence that was nauseating.

Amelia, Carlos, the Starrs, Bea and Tony paraded before my aching eyes with monotonous regularity. Each time I passed them in crazy, whirling mental review, my failure to ascribe motives to them left me more hopeless.

The net that Parsons' death had strung around Oak Hill was pulling tighter and tighter until the pressure almost made me scream aloud. And behind the murder, my mind throbbed with shame for my behavior with Tony. Joe Hilliard had seen me performing a guilty, dishonorable action. And Atwood had seen, too! God alone knew what Atwood would do to me when daylight came.

After an hour and a half of this mental flagellation, the tears came. Great tearing, retching sobs pulled and jerked my body until my nerves were sore and raw.

I struggled out of bed, gasping for breath. The room itself seemed to press in on me with the weight of my own hysteria.

I fumbled with the door until I got it open. My last remnant of good sense told me that I'd have to stop this performance somehow. That I'd have to get some dope from the nurse and get some sleep so that I'd be able to cope with the police questioning that Monday was sure to bring.

The hall was dark. Completely and thoroughly dark. And we had left the lights burning as a safeguard outside our locked doors.

The skin on the back of my neck tingled with primitive fear. I clutched the door jamb for support. The sobs that rose in my throat were suffocating. The heavy carpet prickled my feet. As I groped for the wall I felt cold drops of moisture slide down my back.

Every nerve in my body told me to scream. To scream out my fear and horror. To demand sanctuary from my loneliness. Somehow I beat down the waves of hysteria that threatened to engulf me.

I stumbled and plunged down the black, silent hall like some terror-stricken animal fleeing from a predator in a black wood.

With my hand on the cold crystal knob of Aunt Ella's sitting room, I stopped, my knees melting beneath me. There was a soft whish of sound somewhere behind me in the black hall.

Suddenly I yanked open the heavy door. I thought I'd find light and the comforting presence of the red-headed and sensible Miss Conover.

But the sitting room was dark. Dark like the hall. And it had no business to be dark.

I rammed my foot against a small table. A sharp stab of pain brought my screams almost to the surface, but not quite. There was still the door to the bedroom to be opened. Then I'd be safe.

The door *was* open. A sudden flash of heat lightning showed me that it was. And the bedroom was dark, too. And completely and entirely silent.

My eyes found the big bed, its white sheets and blanket cover shining faintly gray in the black dark.

There was no sound at all except a strange, rather pitiful whimpering. In the paralysis of my fear, I realized that I was making the whimpering noise.

There was no light. No nurse. No sound of Aunt Ella's heavy breathing coming from the bed.

I backed up a few steps and found the light switch and pushed it. Quickly I put my hand over my eyes to shield them from the sudden glare.

Then I walked over to the bed like an automaton. I leaned over the sleeping figure of my aunt. My dear good aunt whom I loved with all my heart. And I *knew* as soon as I looked closely that she was too still to be merely asleep.

I saw the ugly round welt on her blue-veined arm. A voice in my mind screamed out at me that Joe's morphine had found its use.

CHAPTER 16

The tenuous thread that held me to consciousness threatened to snap with each passing second. Only a sibilant rush of sound held me back from the dark blankness for which I would have been so grateful.

I looked up. The swish of Bea's taffeta negligee subsided into stillness as she stood on the opposite side of the bed.

Her eyes almost leapt from their sockets.

"What's the matter with you?" She rasped out the words.

I had no power of speech. I could only point with an arm that jerked involuntarily.

I don't remember anything clearly after that. I only know that Bea understood that Aunt Ella was dead and that the nurse was gone.

Joe came, and after a while Atwood. Before that, though, Bea aroused the other members of the family, but she kept us all out of Aunt Ella's room, and she kept the service wing locked off until Atwood arrived.

A strange thing happened to me. It was a manifestation of hysteria, of course. But after I had been shoved into the wing chair in Aunt Ella's sitting room, I seemed to lose all power of speech or movement. I knew that there were exclamations of horror and waves of terror emanating from all the other members of the family. I knew, too, that one of them was a murderer. I did not care at all. I was simply cut off from the rest of the world in an icy, remote vacuum of my own.

I believe it was Mabel Starr who got me a robe and shoved my arms into it without any help at all from me. I just sat still for a long, long time, not paying any attention to the strange men who walked through the room and out again.

When Atwood tried to talk to me, I didn't answer. I couldn't. His voice had no reality and his words no meaning. I have learned since that Joe Hilliard understood what was wrong with me and insisted on my being given a sedative and put to bed.

When I woke up at last, it was dark, except for a little pool of light near the chair where Mrs. Hill sat knitting on the other side of my room.

I closed my eyes quickly, trying to shut out the memories of the night before. I thought that perhaps I might go to sleep again, drift back into the good darkness that held no grief or terror. But it was no use.

Ella Rutledge was dead. Murdered. I had to acknowledge that appalling fact, to admit its reality.

My voice was shaky and weak. "Mrs. Hill," I said, "I'm awake. Did they find out who did it?"

She started violently and blinked. Then she stood up. "No, they didn't, Miss Brooks. Would you like something to eat now? You've slept about sixteen hours."

I shook my head from side to side on the hot, sticky pillow. "No thanks. Ask Mrs. Forrester to come in, will you?"

She gave me a long, strange look as she lit the lamp on the bedside table. Then she went out and closed the door softly behind her.

In a few minutes, Mrs. Hill came back and silently handed me a bedjacket. I put it on, and she arranged the pillows behind me so that I could sit up. Then she went to the door and said, "You may come in now."

It wasn't Bea who came in. It was Atwood.

Mrs. Hill left the room, and the sheriff sat down in a slipper chair by the bed. Neither of us said anything for a few minutes. The silence was ominously heavy. Finally he broke it. His voice was low and even and sure, his eyes colder than I had ever seen them. My mouth was dry.

"I'm glad you can talk again, Miss Brooks. I want you to tell me about last night."

I took a deep breath. Then I told him.

He made a noise that was a cross between a snort and a sigh. "So you went to Mrs. Rutledge's room to get a sleeping pill? That's very interesting...." He leaned toward me with a quick, jerky movement. "What'd you do with the hypodermic needle?"

I could feel my face twisted in puzzlement.

"What needle?" I said.

"The needle you stole from the nurse after you knocked her out with the ash tray. The needle you used to kill Mrs. Rutledge."

I struggled up in bed until I was completely erect.

"You fool," I cried. "You filthy fool! How dare you say that?"

"Because it's the truth." He rapped out his words until they beat upon my mind like a hail of painful stones. "The maid caught you trying to kill Mrs. Rutledge last Friday night, didn't she? So you killed the maid, and you had to kill Mrs. Rutledge before she recovered from her stroke. You stole the doctor's morphine—you knew where he carried it—and you used it. And you knocked out the nurse with an ash tray the same way you did the maid. We found the two ash trays in the little elevator, right where you left them. They make good weapons, don't they? Good heavy crystal."

I can't be hearing this, I thought frantically. I'm dreaming. I'm still asleep. This can't be real.

"No, no!" I screamed. "You're crazy. I loved my aunt. She's the best friend I ever had. I couldn't kill her. I *loved* her."

Atwood leaned toward me, his head hunched down onto his shoulders.

"*But not as much as you loved Forrester!* You loved him more than the woman who took care of you and raised you and did everything in the world for you when your own mother didn't want you. Didn't you?" A sneer had twisted his face almost beyond recognition as he spoke.

My heart roared and pounded. My breath came in agonizing, sharp gasps. "You can't believe that. You *can't*. You're insane!"

"So I'm insane, am I?" He was close to shouting. "I know all about how Forrester jilted you and married your cousin, and you've been trying to break up the marriage ever since, haven't you? I saw you and Forrester under the trees last night. I wasn't insane then, was I?"

I leaned back exhausted and weak. "I know what you saw. I don't deny that. But I don't love Tony. I don't want to marry him ... I...." Then I stopped. There was no sense in dragging Joe into my own particular hellish mess. "I didn't kill my aunt. I *didn't*."

Then I started to cry. I didn't care what Atwood said anymore. He couldn't really believe such nonsense, but Aunt Ella who was good and kind to everyone had been hideously murdered, and that was all I cared about.

Atwood's voice intruded on my grief.

"We'll go back to the beginning," he said firmly, his voice quiet and controlled once more. "Last Friday night. You came up here and tried to kill your aunt. You tried to smother her with a pillow, and the maid caught you, didn't she?" He motioned for silence when I tried to interrupt with denials. "So you picked up one of those big ash trays and hit the maid over the head. Then you took her downstairs in the elevator—you were careful to wipe off all your prints—and you got the knife and the wheelbarrow and finished up the job. Didn't you?"

"No, no, no," I moaned.

"And yesterday morning," he snapped, "you got up at five o'clock and sneaked into your aunt's room to try the job again, but you got cold feet, didn't you?"

My mouth hung open in terrified surprise. I could only shake my head from side to side.

"The nurse saw you sneak in there, but it was light, so you didn't dare take a chance. She saw you—the same nurse you knocked out this morning. And then you put her in the elevator, but you didn't get a chance to kill her, did you? Your cousin caught you too soon."

I found my voice. "That nurse did see me go into my aunt's room Sunday morning. I went in to see how she was. That was all." My speech was incoherent with tears. "I didn't kill anybody. I didn't knock anybody out. The nurse couldn't have seen me, because I didn't do it."

"No, she didn't see you," he said in an ugly snarl, "because you were careful to sneak up on her."

I kept silent for a few minutes, and slowly and thoroughly I pulled myself together. A good strong sense of self-preservation told me very definitely that my ragged nerves would have to be quickly and magically mended so that I could think intelligently.

"I didn't do any of these things. And why do you think I tried to kill my aunt. What's the motive?"

Atwood's laugh was grisly. "All right, I'll tell you. You wanted to kill your aunt before she changed her will. You knew you'd never get Forrester unless you had money, didn't you? He jilted you in the first place because you were a poor relation and not the Rutledge heiress, didn't he? And this time you weren't going to take any chances. You had your house and your business—the maid's will made her killing better, too—and you were going to make sure of the fifty-thousand-dollar bequest, weren't you?"

Very slowly and deliberately I got a cigarette out of the box on the bed-table. I lit it and inhaled deeply.

"All right, Sheriff Atwood," I said through a cloud of pale gray smoke. "Am I under arrest?"

Atwood hesitated, and I hung suspended in a vacuum of fear. "Not yet," he said shortly.

"That's fine," I said. "I'm not going to answer any more questions. In the meantime, if you care to look in Mrs. Ortiz's black handbag, you'll find a very interesting letter she wrote Mrs. Rutledge from New York a couple of weeks ago. She mentions financial difficulties. You'll also find that Mrs. Forrester is in debt and that the Starrs always need money." I smiled dryly. "In fact, every member of this family has a motive right in the class with mine."

Atwood stood up, his almost chronic sneer distorting his face.

"You're a nice girl, aren't you, Miss Brooks?" he said levelly. "Throwing suspicion on your whole family. Even your mother."

"Somebody's thrown plenty on me, and I'm innocent," I snapped. "I didn't even know that my aunt had the faintest intention of changing her will, and I'd give quite a lot to know who told you all this lovely stuff about me and Tony Forrester."

"Mrs. Forrester told me, Miss Brooks. She's been perfectly aware of your tactics ever since she married Forrester. She thought they were funny—until murder came into the picture, that is."

I was so angry at Bea's perfidy that I could scarcely speak, but I managed.

"Did she tell you why she came into Mrs. Rutledge's room this morning?" I asked.

Atwood nodded grimly. "She did, Miss Brooks. She was worried about her aunt, and she tried to find you. She found you, all right."

Bea. Bea doing all this to me. I couldn't understand it. She wasn't especially fond of me. I knew that, but I simply couldn't believe that she'd deliberately tell Atwood all these damning things—some of them lies.

I swallowed. "And what's this business about my aunt changing her will?"

Atwood laughed without joy or humor.

"That's where the joke comes in, Miss Brooks. Your aunt died intestate. She destroyed her old will last week, so you don't get your fifty thousand dollars after all. Mrs. Forrester is still the Rutledge heiress."

He chuckled maliciously and left the room.

CHAPTER 17

No member of the family came near me after Atwood's visit. I was left alone except for Mrs. Hill who brought me a tray with soup and toast on it. When I tried to talk to her, she said quietly but firmly that she really couldn't bear to talk about the awful thing that had happened. She was genuinely moved. Like all the nurses from the Rutledge Memorial, she had known my aunt for a long time. Mrs. Hill's reluctance to discuss the monstrous crime was understandable.

I asked her how Miss Conover, the nurse, was, and she said that Miss Conover was all right, that she had been sent to the hospital with a slight concussion but would be up and around in a day or so. Of course, she had not seen her assailant.

When I finished the soup, the nurse gave me a pill which, she said, Doctor Hilliard had prescribed, and in a surprisingly short space of time I had once more drifted off into heavy, untroubled sleep.

In the morning my mental depression was as heavy and agonizing as ever, but I was so far recovered physically as to be able to attend a family gathering in the library which John Leonard, Aunt Ella's lawyer, had requested.

Uncle John—uncle by courtesy—my aunt's old, old friend, greeted us quietly as we filed in. His beautiful white hair glinted in the sunlight that streamed through the windows at his back. His kindly, well-bred face was weary and sad. I could easily imagine the intensity of his grief for the loss of his good friend. Since childhood, I had seen the close relationship that existed between Aunt Ella and her lawyer. He, perhaps more than anyone else, had known the full extent of her generosity to all with whom she came in contact. There had been, too, a delightful element of gaiety and comradeship between them. It had been a meeting of two good minds born in the same period and of the same background. In fact, someone once told me that there had been considerable surprise at Aunt Ella's failure to marry John Leonard after Henry Rutledge's death.

As we took our seats in the mellow, wood-panelled room, there was no conversation, not even a desire for it. The fear and horror we had endured in the last thirty hours made normality impossible.

Bea's white face was haggard. Mabel looked sixty instead of her actual forty-five. Even Will's pomposity was subdued. Amelia and Carlos, who huddled together as though asking protection, were like sharp black and white drawings. Peggy and Bill gave the impression of two small children lost in a terrifying world. Even Tony, who had scarcely troubled to look at me as I came in, was shorn of his poise and his charm. He acted as though he had discarded them as something inappropriate to the occasion.

And as John Leonard quietly and slowly unfolded the astonishing story of my aunt's affairs, I could feel the heavy ice of fear beginning to coat the room and the people who sat in it. There was no question in my mind that fear of gigantic proportions oozed from everyone in the room—from the guilty murderer whose fear was undoubtedly greatest of all, as well as from the rest of us.

There was nightmarish hostility, too, and futility and insecurity.

I listened to John Leonard's words with every ounce of concentration my mind could muster. I had an unreasoning hope that he could tell us why this dreadful thing had happened.

He cleared his throat gently and folded his beautiful frail old hands on a neat pile of papers that lay on the desk in front of him.

"I don't think it's necessary for me to say," he began shakily, "how shocking, how cruel, how unspeakable this crime is." He shook his head from side to side as though he might with movement force the dreadful reality of Ella Rutledge's murder out of his mind. "My loss of an old and dear friend in such a manner.... I'm afraid I can't speak of it further. I'll go on to the business which I must discuss with you. As I told the sheriff yesterday, Ella Rutledge died intestate."

Bea interrupted him with a quick, sharp gesture. "You're sure of that, Uncle John?"

He nodded emphatically. "Yes, Bea, I'm very sure. I've discussed the matter with Tony, and he assures me that she didn't ask him to make a new will, and examination of her papers reveals no holographic will which she might have made herself."

Tony was a partner, a very junior partner to be sure, in the firm of Leonard, Bellini, Leonard, Witherspoon, and Forrester—Aunt Ella had bought the partnership for him as a wedding present—but he did not ordinarily have much to do with Aunt Ella's affairs.

"But, Uncle John," Bea said nervously, "I'm not criticizing you, but I don't understand how you let this happen. I mean, why didn't you make sure that she made a new will before she destroyed the old one?"

Will Starr, who sat on the other sofa protectively holding Mabel's plump little hand, put in his two cents worth. "Yes, Mr. Leonard," he said pompously, "I quite agree with Bea. I don't see how you could allow such carelessness in the affairs of a client as important as Ella Rutledge." I wanted very much to hit the little mouse.

Uncle John Leonard smiled patiently. "I know, Mr. Starr, but if you'll all give me a chance, I'll explain the matter to you fully." He breathed deeply and then went on. "For some time I had urged Ella Rutledge to make a new will as it was impossible for her executor to carry out the terms of the old one. To be explicit, there was not enough money." He paused, and every one sat up abruptly. There were sounds of astonishment all over the room.

"That's quite right," he continued seriously. "The long list of bequests to friends, to relatives, to charities was greater than the amount of the total estate, so I urged Ella to allow me to prepare a new will." Bea started to interrupt again. He gestured for silence. "Please, Bea, let me continue in my own way. I know it's a shock to all of you—" He even managed a wry smile. "—but Ella Rutledge was not nearly as wealthy a woman as the world thought. You see, she gave away so much money."

I could very definitely hear Bea's breathing from clear across the room.

"She gave millions to the Rutledge Memorial, as you all know. She gave money to all of you and to many others. She gave money to all of her old servants—trust accounts to be turned over to them on her death. She loaned money, without interest, to nearly every tradesman in the village. Some of it has been repaid—more has not." The old man's voice had a strange, triumphant quality as he talked on. It sounded almost as though he were chanting an ode in tribute to great, good deeds, as though he were proud to recount this story of foolish generosity. I was proud to hear it.

He smiled gently. "On top of her generosity, she suffered several financial losses. For some time now, she has been living on her capital, and there is not a great deal of that left."

Will leaned forward eagerly. "How much capital is there?"

I was sick with anger when I realized that most of the people in the room were not really grieving relatives but vultures. John Leonard's face flushed a faint pink as he answered Will's question. He was angry, too.

"In the neighborhood of sixty to seventy thousand in cash and securities. That will probably largely go to pay the inheritance taxes on Oak Hill," he said with quiet asperity.

Bea got up out of her chair and walked stiffly over to the desk and leaned toward John Leonard. I was deeply and painfully ashamed of the expression on her face. "Do you mean to tell me that I'll get nothing but this white elephant of a house that nobody'd buy and that I can't afford to keep up?" she snapped.

Uncle John sighed. "That's right, Bea, but you can sell off the eastern four fifths of the valley—over a period of time. The real estate people are anxious to get it for subdivisions. There are 2500-odd acres back there. The pears never even paid the taxes anyway."

For some time an inscrutable smile had twisted Amelia's large mouth.

"And the jewels, Bea?" she said quietly. "They are much too valuable to be worn, and the price of diamonds is away up, I'm told. They should bring you a nice amount." She leaned back against the red leather sofa that made a dramatic foil for her black clothes and her black and white face.

John Leonard laughed. "My dear Amelia, Ella sold her jewels in 1928. She got a lot of money for them—boom times, you know—and the Rutledge Memorial got the proceeds."

Amelia shrugged her shoulders and said, "So? That's interesting."

"But, Uncle John," Bea said insistently, "I need money *now*. Right now!"

He said patiently that it would take at least a year to wind up the estate, but that he might be able to arrange a loan, after all the claims were in. She said, impatiently, that anything that meant money would be agreeable, and I did a lot of mental gaping as I could not understand what had happened to the really sizeable fortune Bea had inherited from her parents. But that was none of my business anyway.

"But what about the rest of us?" Mabel said urgently. "What about Will and me and our children?"

Amelia sat up and took notice, too, as Mabel asked her question. Carlos said something in Spanish to his mother, but she motioned for silence. Tony, who knew all the answers anyway, looked down at his hands, his eyes quiet, impervious.

John Leonard licked his pale, dry lips. "You and your children, or rather, your husband and your children, Mrs. Starr, have no claim on Ella Rutledge's estate. Beatrice Forrester is the only heir."

Mabel's plump, undistinguished face had turned a dark, unhealthy red. "We're relatives, aren't we? Will's mother and Ella's husband were brother and sister. Why haven't we any claim?"

A deeply amused smile had spread over Tony's face. He had the grace to try to suppress it.

"Mrs. Starr, when Henry Rutledge died, his widow legally adopted her stepson, Albert Rutledge, to insure his share of the remainder of his father's estate. Albert was left one third, Eleanor received one third, which at her death reverted to her mother, and Ella Rutledge the remaining third. If Albert had lived, he would be Ella's heir, but as he died in 1924, his daughter naturally succeeds to her step-grandmother's estate. There are no other heirs. Is that clear?"

The expression of blank dismay on the Starr family's faces would have been funny if it hadn't also been greedy. Will's horrid little eyes glinted savagely.

"Mr. Leonard," he said, "will you answer me this? Were my wife and I mentioned in the will that was destroyed?"

"You were," John Leonard said quietly. "You were left the sum of $50,000, Mr. Starr."

Mabel gasped. Peggy and young Bill looked at each other in astonishment.

"All right, Mr. Leonard," Will snarled. "How do you know Ella Rutledge destroyed that will and not somebody else trying to do us out of our rightful inheritance?"

Mr. Leonard's poise and patience were infinite. "I have here a letter which I received from Ella Rutledge on Wednesday of last week, Mr. Starr. It is in her handwriting. I had previously sent her all copies of her old will. I'll read it to you. It says: 'Dear John—Thank you for sending me the will so promptly. I have removed my signature and those of the witnesses from all copies. I am keeping the remainder until our next conference which should take place the beginning of next week. I have sent for the Starrs as there is important business which I must discuss with the entire family. The old will, even if it were possible to carry out its terms, is grossly unfair to Susan, and I must make it right for the dear child before it is too late.'" He put down the letter and folded his hands and sat back.

Every mouth in the room, including my own, hung wide open.

"But I don't understand," I said. "What did she mean? She's always been more than fair to me." I was completely and thoroughly puzzled.

Uncle John smiled quizzically and shook his head. "I don't know any more about it than you do, Susan."

Bea's great dark eyes sparked dangerously. She flung out her hand in a violent gesture. "What rot! She did everything in the world for Susan, who hadn't an ounce of claim on her. The shop, her house, everything. How much was Susan supposed to have in the old will?"

Bea's anger and animosity made me wince. She really did think I'd tried to break up her marriage, apparently. Only that could account for her hostility.

"Ella's will said—here it is," he said, picking up a legal document. "It reads: 'and to my beloved grandniece, Susan Brooks, I do give and bequeath the sum of $50,000 cash to be paid to her immediately upon my death, secure in the knowledge that she has otherwise been well provided for.'"

"Yes," I said with a good deal of rancor, "I have been very well provided for. Aunt Ella made it possible for me to earn my own living at work I like, and I don't need fifty-thousand-dollar bequests or anything else."

I was sick and tired of the atmosphere of grabbing. I had to let the rest of them know that it was possible to *work* for money, not just to inherit it.

Bea snorted in disgust. "What rot! You sound like Horatio Alger," she said snappily. "Did she deed you the house and the shop?"

I nodded smugly. "She certainly did, Bea. Isn't that tough?" I was behaving like a brat, and I didn't care.

John Leonard's eyebrows were raised and a trace of a smile quivered around his mouth. He probably was quite accustomed to the bickerings of the survivors concerning the estates of their rich relations.

"And when did you record the deed, Susan?" he asked quietly.

I could feel the blood pouring into my face. I was badly scared for the next two minutes.

"I never did," I said hesitantly. "It was all notarized and everything more than two years ago, but Aunt Ella said not to record it until after her death."

Bea laughed, victoriously and without mirth.

"That's swell, Susan. It probably isn't worth anything, and you'll have to pay me rent."

"No, Bea," John Leonard said firmly and a little too loudly. "You're very much mistaken. If that deed's been signed and delivered, that's all it needs. The recording isn't important. Susan owns her house and shop just as much now as if the deed had been recorded over in the County Courthouse the day it was drawn."

I greatly enjoyed the sagging of Bea's petulant face. I enjoyed the discomfiture of the Starrs, too. In fact, the only people in the room who were taking their licking at all well were Amelia and myself. I alone, of course, knew that she had come to Ella Rutledge in desperation, and now her hope of help from that quarter was entirely gone, but her face was as blank and casual as though this whole matter meant nothing to her.

Tony, too, seemed to be more amused than concerned.

Bea, the heiress, was more upset than anyone else as her next words strongly indicated. "How much did she leave the servants?" she said through a cloud of briskly exhaled smoke.

"Ummm," John Leonard said hesitantly. "Well, let's see now, Bea. She must have set aside close to eighty thousand dollars. She gave twenty-five to Parsons alone."

We were all gaping and groaning again.

Bea leapt out of her chair.

"I won't have it!" she shrieked. "You've got to give me that money. That's ridiculous. I never heard of such nonsense."

The interview was beginning to tell on John Leonard. His paper-thin eyelids closed wearily over his tired gray eyes. He shook his head sadly. "Bea, those servants gave your grandmother loyal service for many, many years. Besides, there's no way you can get the money. That money is all in individual trusts in a bank. It'll be paid to the servants immediately. It's in their names. Has been for years."

She swung around on me. "And isn't that lovely for you, ducky? You'll get half of Parsons' twenty-five thousand, won't you? But that probably isn't news to you, is it?" Her last words were spoken so viciously, so threateningly that I was breathless, suffocating.

The old lawyer put out his hand in a gesture for silence. "Bea, Bea, please stop it." His voice quavered and shook. "How can you behave like this with your poor grandmother's body still in the house? Her murderer still unfound? How can you?"

His old eyes were bright with thin, unshed tears. My own ran over. I got up and went over to the window and stood with my back to the rest of the room.

Bea's next words swung me around on my heels. Her voice was choked with dry sobs. "All right," she shouted, "we'll find the murderer, and we won't have far to look, either! I can't stand any more of this. I can't stand it!"

She flung herself at the door and pulled it open. Tony followed her with deep concern etching his face.

The door banged violently behind them, and I turned back to the window. Outside the heat lay heavy over Oak Hill's gardens. I looked sadly at the pool, the scene of so much fun in my lifetime—the scene, too, of the theft of the morphine.

A rasping noise from Will Starr's throat caused me to turn back to the room. "Mr. Leonard, I must confess," he said slowly, "that I cannot understand how a lawyer of your ability and prominence allowed a client to dissipate a fortune such as Mrs. Rutledge had when her husband died. Can you explain that?"

Uncle John raised his head which he had rested wearily on the back of the high leather chair. "Mr. Starr," he said softly, "Mrs. Rutledge was a very strong-willed woman to begin with. She was also mistress of her own fortune, and when she remonstrated with me and told me time and again that she felt money should be spent to benefit numbers of people rather than a few heirs, there wasn't much I could do. She knew that young girls who had tuberculosis needed help. She gave it to them." He smiled wryly. "She gave you over a hundred thousand dollars, too, Mr. Starr. You know that very well, don't you?"

Will's mousy face turned from pale gray to pale purple. He summoned his family to him like a belligerent little rooster and shepherded them out of the room.

Uncle John turned the swivel chair slightly and took my hand. He smiled up at me kindly.

"You and I are all alone in our grief, aren't we, Susan?" he said softly.

I nodded, unable to speak, and squeezed his slender old hand.

He sighed. "She must have had some other lawyer draw up your deed," he said thoughtfully. "I wonder why she didn't want you to record it."

"She said she didn't want me to have to pay the taxes," I said. "Just another instance of her generosity."

"Well, record it, child, and stay out of this mess, won't you?"

I gulped. "I'm afraid I'm pretty far in it already," I said. "Bea's told the sheriff a lot of nasty things. He thinks I murdered...." I couldn't say it. I started to cry again.

He stood up and put an arm around me and drew me to him. "There, there, child. You know that's nonsense. These policemen have to try everybody. He doesn't really mean anything as foolish as that. Why," he said, laughing a little, "we know all about the devotion you and Ella felt for each other."

"But, Uncle John," I mumbled incoherently against his immaculate stiff shirt front, "somebody did it. Somebody right in this house."

He squeezed my shoulder so hard that it hurt.

"I know it, Susan. I know it. It frightens me."

"Who do you think did it?" I asked, hoping the legal mind might help. "Who?"

He shook his head violently. "Susan, I don't know." He swallowed. "I can't accuse anyone of such a hideous thing without proof, and yet when I listened to those parasites this morning...." His voice trailed off weakly.

The door to the hall was banged back. Bea, still angry, still childish, stood in the doorway.

"Susan," she said viciously, "as you know, Oak Hill is now my house. I'll be very glad if you and your family will get out—except for the funeral, of course. We have to keep up appearances—and stay out."

She turned on her heel and strode off rapidly.

Amelia and Carlos who had been carrying on a low-voiced Spanish conversation for some time both stood up. Amelia raised her hands in a gesture of helplessness.

"Shall we go, Susan?" she said, a queer smile twisting her mouth.

Fighting back tears of despair, I turned to John Leonard.

"Good-bye," I said. "Please come and see me. I need you. Oak Hill is the best place I've ever been thrown out of."

I've had my share of good and bad moments in my life. I still think that the worst one was the time I walked across the great black and white marble-paved hall to the front door.

My beloved aunt lay murdered in her bed upstairs. I was no longer welcome in my old home. I was going out into the scorching September day with my mother and half-brother who were total strangers, and strangers I didn't even like.

I felt so *alone*.

> *"I, a stranger and afraid,*
> *In a world I never made."*

CHAPTER 18

Carlos, Amelia, and I straggled down the road. Amelia was dignified, quiet, thoughtful. Carlos, always polite, endeavored to make conversation for which I had no heart. I suppose that the sight of the three of us, two very dark and dressed in black, one very blonde and dressed in white, trailing through the dust at the edge of the macadam road would have been pathetic, if it hadn't also been ridiculous.

I wondered what my mother and brother intended to do next—stay with me or go back into town until the two hundred dollars were gone. But I didn't ask, and I had a pretty good idea that Amelia would make plans, effective ones, when the time came. Carlos would do as he was told.

We turned in my driveway which is about one hundred feet long, and I whistled for the dog. I hadn't seen her since Sunday, but I wasn't worried about her. She had learned in her puppyhood to scramble through the orchard and go around to the Oak Hill kitchen when she was not fed at home. In fact, she often didn't wait to find out if I were going to feed her, but instead went up to Mrs. Griggs' well-stocked kitchen and said politely enough that her mistress wouldn't be home and that she would welcome a handout from Mrs. Griggs. As a result, she was a pretty fat dog.

I whistled again but no Bonnie.

"The dog is gone?" Carlos asked, his brown eyes round. He seemed pleased.

I grinned a little. "You aren't afraid of that little dog, are you, Carlos?"

"No. But he try to bite me, yes?"

"She wouldn't bite you now," I said, "because you're with me."

Amelia had paid no attention to our conversation.

As I unlocked the front door, I thought grimly that I'd have to find a cleaning woman down in the village. There would be no more maids coming down from Oak Hill to make my house an orderly, shining little gem.

I flung back the front door. Then I stopped—abruptly and completely.

"Good Lord! What now?" I exclaimed.

Amelia and Carlos crowded behind me. Carlos said something in Spanish that sounded like swearing. Amelia said, "My God!"

My living room was a wreck, just as the bedroom up at Oak Hill had been. The carpets were rolled up, pictures awry on the walls, sofa and chair cushions and books and papers from the desk dumped on the floor.

Phonograph records had been pulled out of their albums and dumped in a careless heap. Some of them were broken. My lovely Bach *Chaconne*—all three records—cracked right across the middle.

I could feel my blood rushing like a torrent. I was so angry I was suffocating. A lot of ugly words spilled into my mind as I grabbed the telephone and demanded the sheriff's office in Martinez.

Amelia's face was chalky. Carlos' was sheer puzzlement.

I was almost unable to speak when I finally got Atwood on the telephone.

"This is Susan Brooks," I snapped. "I know I told you to search my house for morphine, but I didn't tell you to wreck it. You're a vandal! How dare you do a thing like this?" The words tumbled out in an incoherent stream. It took Atwood quite some time even to understand who I was.

"What are you talking about, Miss Brooks? Explain yourself," he said testily.

"I'm talking about what you did to my house. You broke some of my best records. I'll sue the County for this and you, too."

Amelia had gone off to her bedroom when I started to talk to the sheriff. She came back and made a gesture with her hand indicating that the whole house was in the same condition.

"My mother says you've done the same thing in every room in the house. What are you going to do about it?" I demanded.

I finally gave Atwood a chance to talk. He said, very emphatically, that he had not messed up my house, and that none of his men had either.

I swallowed hard.

"Well, somebody has," I said when I finally got my breath. "You ought to see it."

"Don't touch anything," he said decisively. "Not a thing! I'll be right over."

I hung up and walked slowly through the rest of the house. Even the kitchen was a mess. All the glasses and dishes and groceries had been taken off the shelves and the red oil-cloth that lined the cupboards and drawers ripped up.

"Can you beat it?" I said to my mother, who had trailed along after me. "Can you beat it? I simply don't understand it."

Amelia pursed her heavy lips. She gestured with her head. "Come and look at the guest room," she said.

I looked. There wasn't one thing in the room that hadn't been moved. Amelia pointed dramatically at her small suitcase. It had been literally carved up with a kitchen knife that lay beside it on the dismantled bed.

I ran quickly into the big storage closet that opened off my bedroom.

My own handsome luggage, a recent gift from Aunt Ella, had also been ripped to shreds. The lock on my big Malm trunk had been smashed with a hammer and the inside of the trunk hacked to pieces, so that the moire lining hung in ribbons on the metal and wood frames.

Carlos, the idiot, picked up the hammer.

"With this?" he said, smiling cheerfully.

"Carlos! Put that down. There might be fingerprints on it," I said with irritation.

He looked very injured. His mama explained his idiocy to him, and I walked wearily back to the living room.

Amelia and Carlos came in. We all just stood in the middle of the room, gaping stupidly. I flashed Amelia a quick glance as I saw her knot her right hand in a tight fist and then stretch out the long fingers stiffly.

She was frightened. I knew it. I was, too, of course, but Amelia, I felt, had an idea of what this was about.

"What do you think?" I said. "What does it mean?"

She shook her head and tried hard to make her expression dispassionate. "I cannot understand," she said. Then she pointed to the floor in front of the French door.

A few pieces of broken glass lay on the waxed oak floor. I walked over quickly with an idea of pulling up the venetian blind. I knew what the broken glass meant. The searcher had got into the house by breaking the pane of glass near the lock. Then I remembered Atwood's admonition not to touch anything.

The telephone rang, and I answered it. It was Wilda in my shop, full of very sincere sympathy.

"Miss Brooks," she continued, "I hated to bother you—I know you can't think about the shop now—but Mr. Opal's called three times to ask if you're coming in."

I could feel my eyebrows shoot up. I had, of course, done Mr. Opal's house some eighteen months ago, but surely he wouldn't want to talk to me about decorating at a time when everybody in the village knew of my aunt's frightful death.

"That's all right, Wilda. I'll call him later and see what he wants. Can you manage all right without me?" I asked.

"Yes, of course, Miss Brooks. Oh, dear, you don't know how awful we all feel about Mrs. Rutledge. It's just terrible!" Her voice was heavy with tears. "After they cured my sister in the Rutledge Hospital...."

"I know, Wilda. It's ghastly."

Between her sobs and the oppression in my own heart, I had difficulty understanding her.

"What did you say, Wilda?" I asked, puzzled. I was sure I couldn't have understood her.

"Miss Brooks, it's just awful. All the men are hanging around the bar getting drunk. They say that as soon as Atwood makes an arrest, they'll lynch whoever did it."

I was profoundly shocked. I knew what a loss my aunt's death was, Lord knows, but the vision of the good villagers in a lynching mood was a little too much.

"Now, Wilda," I said with a great deal of false assurance, "that's just silly. Everybody's shocked, of course, but the men'll sober up. They're decent people. They'll let justice take its course. Besides, Atwood hasn't even caught the murderer yet."

"He says he'll make an arrest within twenty-four hours," she howled disconsolately.

"That's just newspaper talk," I said.

I finally calmed the fears of my assistant and promised to look in the next day. I explained the telephone conversation to Amelia. Her mouth twitched in horror.

Then she did a very strange thing. She put her hand on my shoulder and squeezed it gently. The implication of her action was nauseating.

I pulled away from her. "You, too?" I asked. "You think I did it?"

She stared at me without blinking. "Of course not," she said clearly. "But Atwood thinks so."

I jerked my shoulders with annoyance. "But he can't prove it, and he can't arrest me until he does."

A car's wheels sputtered over the gravel of the driveway and skidded to a stop. Atwood and three other men got out of a black sedan and walked rapidly into the house. "All right, Miss Brooks," he said briskly. "Anything missing?"

My living room seemed crowded with the four men in it. One of them quickly got his camera out of a case and prepared it for picture-taking. Another unpacked a fingerprinting kit. The third just walked around looking at things.

I shook my head. "I don't know. I never thought of that. As I told you the other day, there isn't much to take."

I went into the dining room and was reassured by the sight of my Georgian tea service in its accustomed place on the sideboard. "Well, I guess the silver's all here." My very simple jewelry was all present and accounted for in the bedroom.

"All right," Atwood said. "We'll take your prints—your mother's and brother's, too—and then see what we can find. When we get through, you can look over the papers in the desk to see if everything's there."

Much against my will and better judgment, I smiled. "Look, if somebody was looking for a paper in this house, the first place to look would be the desk, wouldn't it?" I paused to enjoy Atwood's discomfiture. "Then why bother to hack up an expensive trunk if something was taken from the desk?"

Atwood snorted his irritation, and my mother and brother and I were fingerprinted. Carlos was very reluctant until his mother did a lot of explaining in Spanish.

When the tall, sandy-haired fingerprint expert had cleaned the black ink off our fingers, I beckoned to Amelia and Carlos. "We can sit on the terrace," I said.

We sat in torrid silence. Amelia suspected me, and I suspected her, if not of murder, at least of guilty knowledge. That letter had meant too much to be passed off lightly. I had a question on the tip of my tongue, but I bit it back. No point in showing my hand yet. I wanted to ask her what arrangement she and Aunt Ella had made when I was born. Certainly it had been something about money, and everybody connected with Aunt Ella had needed money.

Carlos, subdued for once, resisted impulses to talk, either to his mother or me. He chain-smoked and between drags hit his cigarette incessantly on the edge of the ash tray. I wanted to scream with annoyance.

Instead, I got up and walked around my little garden which sadly needed attention. Magruder, of course, would not be coming down to take care of it any more.

The lawn was dry and hard, and I was about to get the long handle to turn on the sprinklers when I noticed a faint stirring under one of the shrubs. Every other leaf in the garden hung still and quiet under the oppressive heat. I knelt on the grass and peered into the shrub.

"Why, Bonnie," I said fatuously, "won't you even speak to me?"

The little black dog lay on her side, her tail twitching faintly. I couldn't see her very well.

"Come on out, you lazy dope," I said.

She didn't move from her reclining position, so I reached in and tried to pull her out by her collar. I stopped quickly.

She yelped pathetically, and I distinctly heard the click of her teeth.

"Carlos," I called, "come here and hold this shrub out of the way." It was a thickly leaved English laurel.

Carlos finally got the idea, and I crawled across the hard-baked earth until I could get a good look at the dog.

She looked up at me with pleading in her black eyes. Her tongue, ordinarily a good healthy pink, was swollen and white. As I knelt closer, I saw the ugly cut on her head. I ran my hands gently along her ribs. They were swollen and lumpy, and she winced when I touched her. Only the ardent wagging of her tail reassured me.

"The poor thing," I said, "she's hurt."

"So?" Carlos said, interestedly. "An auto?"

"No," I said, shaking my head vigorously. "I don't think so. She never goes in the road. She got hit once a long time ago. She's scared of the road."

With great difficulty and a lot of conversation directed at the dog, I got her out from under the shrub and into her basket which I brought from the back porch. "I'll have to get the vet. I can't imagine what's happened to her."

She managed to lap a little water from the bowl which I held for her as Amelia and Carlos stood over me.

"I think an auto," Carlos said.

My eyes had strayed back to the shrub near the house. I jumped quickly to my feet.

"An auto!" I shouted viciously. I ran over to the shrub and reached in and pulled out Carlos' Malacca stick. I brandished it in his face. He backed away from me in the direction of his mother, his eyes wide and frightened. "An auto! Here's your auto. You beat that dog, didn't you? And went off and left her to die. You little brute, you!"

I almost hit him with his cane, but not quite. I shouted, Amelia remonstrated with me, Carlos shrieked a chorus of "no's," the dog yelped feebly.

I advanced once more on Carlos as a flash of knowledge streaked into my mind. "You came down here, you little rat, and beat the dog and broke into my house and tore it to pieces, didn't you? Didn't you?"

"Susan, stop it!" Amelia grabbed my arm. "Stop it! Carlos did nothing of the sort. Are you crazy? Why would he break into your house when I have a key? After all, he wouldn't cut up my suitcase, would he?"

"Oh, wouldn't he?" I squealed, my throat parched with angry emotion. "Wouldn't he? That'd make a fine red herring—tearing up your suitcase."

Atwood appeared in the midst of this dignified family row, and I wished with all my heart that Amelia Ortiz and her offspring had stayed in Buenos Aires where they belonged.

"What's the trouble, Miss Brooks?" Atwood said, glowering at all three of us.

I told him. "I think Carlos beat my dog. There's his cane. It was under the shrub where I found the dog. I think it was he who searched the house."

Atwood examined the dog and the cane. Amelia looked as though strangling was much too good for me.

"Did you do it, Mr. Ortiz?" Atwood asked.

"No, no, no," Carlos wailed, almost ready to weep. "I have not been here since Sunday. I left the stick here. I did not do this."

Amelia darted a malevolent glance at me as she spoke to Atwood. "My daughter is upset because her dog has been mistreated, sheriff. She's jumping to conclusions. My son has been with me constantly since he came out from town."

Atwood grunted, took the cane gingerly with a handkerchief wrapped around his hand, and started into the house. "This place was searched last night, Miss Brooks. It seems Mrs. Ortiz sent one of the maids down here late yesterday afternoon to get some things and the house was all right then." He turned to my mother. "Just for the record, Mrs. Ortiz, you're willing to swear that neither you nor your son came down here last night?"

Her face was tight and white with annoyance. "I'm perfectly willing to swear to that statement. My son and I did not leave Oak Hill."

Amelia looked at me as though she'd like to use the stick on me. "Really, Susan. This is in rather bad taste, don't you think?"

I muttered ungraciously and followed Atwood into the house. I asked to use the telephone to call the vet, and he said it would be all right as I had already smeared the thing hopelessly with my own fingerprints.

The vet, a very nice man who loved the animals he cared for, finally came and took the dog away. He was properly shocked at her condition, but said that she would recover. I sat around hating Amelia and Carlos and laying all our troubles at their door.

Atwood and his men finished their work without much success. There were no prints on the stick—naturally—and the prints in my house were fairly well identified as those of the Oak Hill maids—they had all been fingerprinted on Sunday—my own, and Amelia's. I explained why the maids' prints had a right to be there. There were a lot of prints coming from the well-known gloves without which the modern criminal does not operate. When one of Atwood's men found Carlos' prints on the hammer in the storeroom, I explained, much against my will, how they'd got there. Then Atwood settled down to question me.

We put the cushions back in my blue loveseats and sat opposite each other to talk, the glass-topped coffee table between us well smeared with gray powder.

"Miss Brooks," Atwood said, "surely you must have some idea why your house was searched, haven't you?"

"No, really. I haven't. I haven't a thing in the world that I can think of that somebody else might want." I was very serious.

"How about legal documents?"

I paused to make a mental inventory of my legal documents. "I have a passport, a bank book, the pink slip for my car, some insurance policies, and a deed to my house and shop. They're all in the bank in Berkeley."

"How about letters?"

I sighed. "My correspondence isn't very extensive. I write to a couple of school friends in the east. The rest is mostly invitations and thank-you notes and stuff like that." I pointed to my mahogany knee-hole desk. "As you can see, my desk is small, so I never keep letters after I answer them."

Atwood was leaning forward with his elbows on his widespread knees.

"And you're sure you burned the typewritten note that you thought Forrester had sent you?"

"In the incinerator of my kitchen stove Saturday afternoon—worse luck!" I said bitterly.

"Miss Brooks, did you keep Forrester's letters? The ones he wrote you before he was married?"

I smiled grimly. "No, Sheriff Atwood, I did not. I got rid of those long ago. Tony gave me the ones I'd written to him, too. And they went into the same bonfire." I remembered that bonfire very well indeed, too, and the dull, leaden feeling in my chest as I watched all my young dreams go up in smoke in the orchard back of Oak Hill. "Why do you ask?"

"Sometimes old letters can be made to look like recent ones."

"But who'd want to do that?" I was amazed.

"I don't know, Miss Brooks. It was just an idea. We have to try everything." He sighed. "Did your aunt ever give you anything to keep for her? Or did anybody else ever give anything into your care?"

I wracked my brain without result. "No. I'm sure they didn't. Aunt Ella, too." I smiled grimly. "You see, we never had any mysterious goings-on around here until last week."

One of the sheriff's men poked his head in the door to say that he had asked the neighbors—Anne and Joe, of course—if they had seen any prowlers the night before. They hadn't. Inquiries at Oak Hill were equally blank.

I got a cigarette out of the box on the table. To my undying astonishment, the sheriff sprang to his feet and lit it for me with a large kitchen match which he ignited on the seat of his pants. I nodded my thanks, and he sat down again.

He bit his lower lip in thought. "That maid, Parsons. I'll bet she knew plenty. I think she not only caught the murderer trying to smother Mrs.

Rutledge—the doctor told me about the pillow on the floor—but I have an idea she had to be silenced for other reasons." His eyes glinted behind narrowed lids. "Tell me the truth about you and Forrester, Miss Brooks. I've had the story from people that are hostile to you. It'll be better for you if I have your version."

I hesitated for several minutes. Then I decided that I had nothing to lose. The affair seemed to be common property anyway, and Atwood, for the first time in our acquaintance, seemed to be willing to believe what I told him. I wondered what had brought about the change in his attitude and decided that the search of my house might have turned the trick.

I wet my lips nervously. "It's just about what you've been told. I was in love with him and he with me—I thought. We were engaged, but it hadn't been announced. Then out of a clear blue sky, he—well—he told me he didn't love me anymore, and he did love my cousin. And that was that."

Atwood shook his head slowly from side to side. "That was nice. He give you any reason for his change of heart?"

My face was hot. "Listen," I said, "it wasn't because I didn't have any money if that's what you're thinking. Tony's anything but mercenary. He couldn't help it if Bea was more attractive than I was." I didn't like Tony anymore, and I didn't want to have anything to do with him ever again, but I had to be fair.

"And you took this lying down?"

"Yes," I said quietly, "I guess I did. What else could I do? I told my aunt about it, and she felt badly for me, but there was nothing we could do. People can't force themselves to love one person and not another. I certainly didn't want him to marry me out of a sense of duty when he was in love with my cousin."

"So you and your aunt accepted the new arrangement, and she bought Forrester a partnership in one of the biggest law firms in town and gave them her blessing and never told a soul that Forrester had behaved like a rat to you!" He exhaled with violence.

I interrupted. "He hadn't behaved like a rat. He couldn't help it. He felt awful."

"Yeah? And how did your cousin feel?"

I let out what is known as a hollow laugh. "I thought she didn't know a thing about it. I was mistaken, I've learned.... You see, she'd been in Honolulu for about six months, and I'd met Tony while she was gone. I hadn't told her anything about my engagement—I wanted to surprise her—and she just hit Tony like a bolt from the blue. Curtains for Susan."

"Then what?"

"They got married. I stayed here until after the wedding—Aunt Ella made me stay. She said I didn't have much left but my pride and my dignity, and I'd have to keep that. Then I went to decorating school in New York for two years. When I finished school, Aunt Ella set me up in business. As far as I was concerned, Tony Forrester was a closed incident." I gestured for Atwood's attention. "He still is—in spite of what you saw the other night. You'll have to believe that."

He stood up and walked restlessly around the room. He came back and stood in front of me. "Look at me, Miss Brooks." I looked up. "I'm trying to believe you. You're very popular around here—people liked you and your aunt a lot better than they did Mrs. Forrester—and I talked to that old lawyer, Mr. Leonard. He thinks very highly of you."

My heart was pounding with leaden intensity.

"I know, too," he continued, "that every one of Mrs. Rutledge's relatives—with the exception of yourself—needed money. I looked at the books in your shop last night. You're making a good living, and you seem to have what you need. *But I don't want you to lie to me about Forrester, understand?*"

"I'm not lying!" I said vehemently. "I behaved like a damned fool the other night, I'll admit. But Tony caught me in a weak moment, and it did help my battered pride a little to listen to what he had to say." I paused for a second as the full implications of my speech hit me. "Listen, I'm going to trust you to keep quiet about this. Please, do. We have too much trouble as it is, so don't go running to my cousin to tell her her husband...." My voice trailed off into silence.

"Her husband what?" Atwood spat out the words.

I put out my cigarette as my hands were shaking too hard for me to continue to hold it. I looked at Atwood and met his glare without wincing.

"Regretted his bargain is a polite way of putting it," I said softly. "You've seen my cousin. She's exceedingly attractive, but she isn't exactly easy to live with. This disloyalty is no pleasure to me, either."

Atwood let out a long, slow whistle. "My God, Miss Brooks. Give me a Mexican Saturday night stabbing any day. You ladies and gentlemen!" He jammed his hands deep into his pockets. "And I'm to understand that you are no longer in love with Forrester and don't want to break up his marriage and marry him yourself."

"That's absolutely right," I said. "I don't think that any marriage based on a wrecked home in which there are two little children would have the slightest basis for success. I don't like messy situations of any kind, particularly marital ones." I was glad to hear that my voice sounded as sincere as I wanted it to. "Good grief, can you imagine what Aunt Ella would have felt if I'd contemplated marriage to Tony?"

Atwood sat down on the loveseat again.

"Yeah.... As I understand it, Forrester had no money of his own, and even now, his income isn't great. Is that right?"

I nodded slowly. "His father was a country doctor in a small town in Ohio—Gates Mills. His mother died of cancer when Tony was in high school. The father died when Tony was a junior at Stanford. The father's insurance lasted until Tony got through law school. He was working as a claim adjuster for an insurance company when I met him. Aunt Ella was going to give him the partnership when we were married. She did the same thing when he married Bea."

Atwood gazed off into space as though digesting the information I had given him. Finally he spoke. "Did your aunt like Forrester, Miss Brooks?"

I hesitated for only a second. "Yes," I said firmly, "she liked him very much for himself. I think she was disappointed about what he'd done to me, but she was very fair. Very just, if you like."

We lapsed into silence, and I could hear a low murmur of voices coming from the terrace. Amelia and Carlos having one of their interminable Spanish conversations. How I wished I knew the language.

I coughed lightly. "Did you ask Mrs. Ortiz about the letter she took out of Mrs. Rutledge's desk?"

Atwood nodded. "Yeah, and she said it was none of my business and had nothing to do with the killings. How do you like that?"

"I didn't expect anything else, to tell you the truth."

I wanted to tell Atwood how strange life had become. I wanted to explain to him that up until the week before when Aunt Ella had me send for the Starrs, our lives had been simple and open and exactly what they seemed to be. But I couldn't seem to find the right words. Nothing dramatic had ever happened to me in my whole life—with the exception of Tony—in spite of my outlandish birth and parentage.

Atwood's rasping voice interrupted my train of thought. "This William Starr, Miss Brooks. I've had a brief report on him from Long Beach. He's in the real estate business, and it's rumored that his affairs are in bad shape. What do you know about that?"

"They usually are," I said smiling. "My aunt was very good to Will and helped him out of jams on many occasions, but she was very impatient with him. You see, he put his father's money into oil wells that weren't on Signal Hill, and when that was gone, he got caught short in real estate. He never would go out and get a salaried job. His fortune was always just around the corner—if Aunt Ella would lend him a little more money."

"She *loaned* him money, you say?"

I nodded. "But I'm sure she never expected to get it back. She did it for Mabel and the children more than for Will. She was, well, sorry for them, I guess. Will's such a windbag."

Atwood seemed intent upon an examination of his stubby fingers. "Mr. Leonard tells me he can't find Starr's notes. Do you know anything about them?"

I shook my head. "Not a thing."

The sheriff laughed lightly. "Starr says Mrs. Rutledge sent them back to him marked paid, and he destroyed them. A hundred thousand dollars' worth."

"That sounds just like her. Anyway, I noticed that Mr. Leonard said this morning that Aunt Ella had *given* him a hundred thousand dollars."

Atwood gave me a long, lingering look. "Did you ever hear of Starr being mixed up with another woman?"

I nearly fell off the couch. Then I laughed. "Good Lord, no. I never even thought of Will in a romantic role. Why?"

"I just wondered. How about Forrester? Any woman besides yourself, that is." He smiled with his eyes as he spoke.

I smiled back. "Nope. I think Tony's been a good and faithful husband."

"And Mrs. Forrester has been a good and faithful wife, has she?"

I nodded. "Yes, I'm sure she has. She's very conventional." I looked down at the table quickly in an effort to hide my eyes. Bea's telephone conversation last Friday when she was in bed, her antics with Mr. Opal on the terrace, and her Sunday evening absence from the house crashed into my mind like a bolt of thunder. But I could see nothing to be gained by reporting my suspicions to the sheriff. I'd let Bea carry all the nasty tales for the family.

"Tell me about the letter you saw in your mother's pocketbook, Miss Brooks."

I told him as nearly as I could remember what the letter said, how I'd seen Amelia take it out of Aunt Ella's desk, what Parsons and Nanny had told me about how it upset my aunt, and how I'd happened to read it.

"I don't like throwing her to the wolves," I finished. "I'll admit I don't feel particularly filial about her, but all our troubles started after she arrived, and I'm very sure that she could tell a lot if she wanted to."

Atwood stood up. "I agree with you," he said emphatically, "and I can't do a thing with her. She says she and her son arrived in Berkeley last Thursday, stayed in the hotel Thursday night, and she came out here Friday. She swears the son didn't come until Sunday, and the hotel people back him up. And she's flat broke." He sighed heavily. "Well, I'll tackle her again."

As Atwood went off to the terrace to talk to my mother, the telephone rang. It was Glore who said that Mrs. Forrester had asked him to call and remind me that Parsons' funeral would be held that afternoon at the little Episcopal Church in the village. I thanked him and hung up, wondering what the servants must think of all this gore and horror and the family divided into warring camps.

I had the books back on the shelves and the records in the albums and the pictures straightened when the telephone rang again. This time it was Mr. Opal.

"Oh, yes," I said not too cordially, "the shop told me you'd called. What's up?"

He made a long, elaborate speech of sympathy, and I had a catty feeling that he'd consulted a thesaurus shortly before telephoning. I knew very little about the man, actually, except that his bank had given him a good credit rating and that he had come from Los Angeles, but I always had a very definite feeling that Mr. Opal's gentlemanly behavior was a comparatively recent acquisition rather than congenital.

I thanked him for his kindness and said that, yes, it was simply unbelievable. His next speech was practically unbelievable, too. He said, "You know, Sue, I think you ought to have a little respite from all that mess, get away from it for a while."

The amazing thing was that he'd called me by my Christian name for the first time—I loathe people who call me "Sue" instead of the proper "Susan"—and that he should display such solicitude for my welfare.

"I'm afraid that's impossible," I said, waiting for him to get on with it so that I could finish fixing my house.

"Sue, why don't you come over here and have a drink with me late this afternoon? Alma Van Tuyl's coming, and I think it would do you good to get out of that atmosphere. Please say you'll come."

I was amused at the chaperonage. That's the kind of thing Opal would think of. So very punctilious. But I was about to refuse anyway when I quickly changed my mind. There was something very strange about his calling me, and I had to find out what.

"All right," I said. "I'll be over about five-thirty or six. Thanks for asking me."

Now what? Bea's beau, as I had mentally tagged him, wanted to see me, and he didn't want to come to my house to do it.

Atwood and his men finally left, and Amelia came into the house. I asked her if she wanted to go to Parsons' funeral, and she said she supposed she ought to. I didn't ask her why, but I wondered.

"All right," I said, "I'll drive you and Carlos into town afterwards."

She smiled faintly and did her eyebrow trick. "The sheriff has said that we must stay here," she said quietly.

I was furious. "But there isn't room for Carlos," I said, trying to keep the anger out of my voice. The last thing in the world that I wanted was more of the company of my mother and brother. I was quite willing to provide them with money if they'd just get out and leave me in peace.

Amelia thrust out her hand, palm up. "He can sleep on that large sofa, Susan. I know very well that we are not welcome, but unfortunately, we must stay."

Carlos on the sofa! That was really too much. Messing up my house.

Amelia had started for the guest room, but she turned back. "There are other reasons why we must stay, Susan. We must all protect our interests, you know, and I can't do that in Berkeley."

"Interests!" I cried. "What do you mean?"

She walked off without answering, and I had learned better than to try to question her when she didn't feel like talking.

The back door bell jangled, and I went to answer it. It was a delegation from Oak Hill consisting of Glore, Mrs. Griggs, and Jane, all of them looking old and tired and heart-sick. I welcomed them warmly and took them into the living room where we could all sit down. We talked for some time about our great loss. Finally, they got to the point.

Glore was spokesman. "We wanted to tell you, Miss Susan, that we've all given notice—all the servants in the house, that is. We're leaving right after the funeral—Mrs. Rutledge's, that is." The old man's voice was tired and shaky.

"Well, Glore," I said slowly, "of course I know most of you are ready to retire anyway, but don't you think maybe you should stay as long as Mrs. Forrester needs you? There'll be a lot to do, you know."

Mrs. Griggs edged her plump body a little forward. Her face was flushed and red. "No, Miss Susan, we're not going to stay in that house a minute longer than we have to. We love Oak Hill, but we're none of us going to work for Mrs. Forrester. It's too much. Even Katherine and Nanny are going to quit."

I forced a smile to crawl over my face. "Oh, now, Mrs. Griggs, I'm sure you wouldn't want to let the family down."

"Miss Susan, we know Mrs. Forrester's your cousin," Jane interrupted, "but we've all of us said all along that we'd never work for Mrs. Forrester. We'd decided to leave even before she told us she'd have to cut our wages in half."

Why didn't they just quit, I thought, instead of dragging me into this?

"Well, Jane, it's your decision of course. You're free to do what you like, but I'm sure that you want to do the right thing. Don't leave Mrs.

Forrester in a mess, please." I stood up as I finished speaking.

Then Jane started to cry. Her wrinkled old face got red, and the muscles twitched agonizingly. I patted her thin bony shoulders. "Oh, Miss Susan," she wailed, "if only you'd got the house instead of Mrs. Forrester...."

"Now, now, Jane," I said briskly. "You must pull yourself together. This is silly."

Both Glore and Mrs. Griggs looked as though they'd like to join Jane in a good cry, but they didn't.

I finally herded them out of the house and on the way to their duties. Jane, as a parting shot, pulled her nose out of the huge handkerchief she'd been wailing into.

"That Opal," she moaned. "In Oak Hill. I couldn't stand it."

The three old servants were up at the road before I recovered from my amazement. I couldn't have asked them what they meant about Opal in any case, but I knew, definitely, that I'd go to Opal's house for a drink even if I contracted two broken legs and a case of smallpox in the meantime.

CHAPTER 19

The chunks of earth thudded onto the casket as the undertaker's men lowered it into the grave. The dry, brassy heat pressed down on the bare hillside studded with granite tombstones and scrawny shrubs and the iron fence that enclosed the Rutledge cemetery.

The minister's words rolled sonorously across the open grave.

"Forasmuch as it hath pleased Almighty God, in his wise providence, to take out of this world the soul of our deceased sister, we therefore commit her body to the ground...."

I paid no further attention to the surplice-clad minister. Instead I looked at the faces of the Rutledge family standing in the foreground. How much did one of those faces conceal? And how much did the murderer think that Almighty God, in his wise providence, had had to do with taking out of this world the soul of Elizabeth Parsons, a hard-working, reticent old woman?

I wanted to laugh, or at least make a noise like laughing. All the fine, upstanding Rutledges there in the heat paying their last respects to a faithful servant. Amelia, black and calm; Bea, beautifully dressed in white and Aunt Ella's pearls; Will, his eyes red-rimmed, a black armband sewn neatly on the left sleeve of his oxford-gray coat; Tony, yellowish under his deep tan; Mabel, dull and dumpy and visibly sweating through her white rayon dress from which she'd removed the red pockets.

I started and in spite of the heat shivered. There was something significant about Mabel in white.

All around me there was a murmur of voices. My own voice slid into tune with the others. "And lead us not into temptation; But deliver us from evil. Amen."

Deliver us from evil but how? Deliver us from the evil that had wantonly killed two old women. Helpless old women.

Mabel in white! Of course. I remembered. Mabel had been a nurse before Will married her. Mabel knew all about hypodermic needles and how to fill them with lethal doses of morphine.

The stirring of movement around me dragged me back to the present. The services had ended. We walked over to our cars, and my mother and brother got into mine. I was about to follow them when Tony came over to me.

"I'll be down to see you tonight," he said urgently. "Late. Midnight." His lips scarcely moved as he spoke. I was sure no one else heard him.

As we passed through the cemetery gates, newspapermen clicked their cameras. I saw Atwood's stumpy, neckless figure at the side of the road, too. I glanced at my mother's impervious face. Only her black eyes betrayed the emotion she was feeling.

"Those crowds," she said, as we drove slowly along the road lined on both sides with people from the village. State police had kept them out of the church and the cemetery. "They're so curious. So morbid."

"Yes," I sighed, "I guess they are. And why not?"

I turned left into the highway. As I made the turn, Holz, the butcher, stepped back out of the road. He gave me a long, straight look as though searching my face for signs of guilt. I nodded to him, but he didn't return my nod. His action was disquieting when I thought of Wilda's wild story of a threatened lynching.

Tony's little speech in the cemetery pushed thoughts of Holz out of my mind. So he was coming to see me. Perhaps he was going to try a repeat performance of Sunday night, but I'd soon fix that. Bea might have ideas about Opal—and I'd know pretty soon, I felt—but there would be no more nonsense about me and Tony. Ever.

Bored, hot, depressed, I drove Amelia and Carlos into town for their luggage. My heart dropped another three feet when my mother told me that their trunks would be delivered the next day. Trunks! Were they planning to stay with me indefinitely? I wondered helplessly how I'd ever get rid of them.

Amelia calmly chattered at my side about the charms of Berkeley, its winding streets and trees and gardens. She also talked a lot about the exodus to the country that had taken place in the last three or four years, and I made a lot of perfunctory replies.

I stopped at the market at Orinda to buy food. Somehow I had no desire to face the tradespeople in Rutledge just yet. The look on Holz's face was still too vivid.

When we got home, my mother and brother busied themselves in the guest room stowing their clothes. I put away the food in the kitchen and was washing my hands at the sink when I heard my name called from the garden. I hastily dried my hands and went outside with a broad smile on my face. Anne Watson had come to see me.

"I'm so glad to see you, Anne," I said. "I needed you."

She grinned and sat down on the terrace and lit a cigarette. Her kindly face was wet from the exertion of her walk.

"You poor baby," she said. "I was up at Oak Hill three times yesterday, but you were asleep every time." The grin had left her face. "Susan, I still can't believe this dreadful thing. Joe says it's true, but such wanton cruelty just doesn't seem possible."

"I know," I said shakily. "I know."

We talked for a long time, getting nowhere. Anne asked me to come over to dinner, but I told her I couldn't. I nodded toward the guest room. "My mother and brother are staying here," I said.

Her eyes were round with wonder. "They're not staying at Oak Hill?" she asked.

I shook my head. "No," I said hesitantly, "there's too much for the servants to do. Carlos has to sleep on the couch, but it can't be helped."

"Well, bring them to dinner. You shouldn't have to bother with guests."

I said I would and that my relatives were no bother, which was arrant falsehood.

"But I'm going out for a drink around five-thirty. Will that make it too late?"

"No, that's all right. It's too hot to have dinner before eight anyway. Where are you going for a drink?" Her curiosity was not as impertinent as it sounded. Anne was genuinely interested in my rather mild social activity.

I watched her face carefully as I answered. "Mr. Opal's," I said, "chaperoned by Alma Van Tuyl."

"Good Lord, Susan. What next?" She was laughing wildly.

I nodded solemnly. "Mr. Opal is just like you. He thinks I ought to get away from it all—have a little relaxation."

Anne opened her mouth to speak. Then she shut it.

"You were going to say something, Anne. What?"

She shook her head. "No. Nothing important. The sheriff's man was asking me if I'd seen anyone around your house the last couple of days, but he wouldn't say why. Do you know?"

I told her about the house being searched and my room at Oak Hill. I could feel my heart beginning to hammer sickeningly again. "It's so ghastly, Anne. There's something strange and dreadful going on, and I haven't the slightest notion of what it is. It's so frightening."

She whistled. "I think Atwood ought to give you some protection. I think it's dreadful for you to be in this little house with just another woman and a boy."

I snorted. "Oh, I'm safe enough, but I wish I knew what was going on."

We sat in silence for a minute. The silence was broken by the blare of my phonograph playing *The Dance of King Kastchei* from Stravinsky's "Firebird Suite." Carlos apparently was entertaining himself.

Anne pulled her chair nearer to mine to make herself heard. "Joe told me last night that he'd been very thoroughly investigated—by Atwood. The sheriff seemed to have some idea that Joe might have stolen his own morphine, and you can imagine how Joe felt when he found how it had been used. The poor devil." Anne's eyes were compassionate. She reached over and took my hand. "What did you do to him, Susan? He made a couple of rather bitter remarks about you."

My face was so hot it hurt. I knew exactly what I'd done to Joe, but I couldn't tell Anne that he'd caught me kissing Bea Forrester's husband. I stood up and walked about nervously. I stuck my head in the French door. "Turn the volume down, Carlos. That's too loud." He was sitting happily almost in the phonograph. He leapt to his feet, grinned, and shouted back at me.

"What you say, Susan?" He smiled helplessly.

"Oh, my Lord," I said with irritation. *"Trop de bruit!"*

"Vraiment?" His smiled increased.

Well, at least he could speak French, and although mine was no great shakes, we probably stood a better chance of making ourselves understood in that language than in English.

I showed him how to fix the phonograph and came back to sit by Anne. "It speaks French," I said. "My brother. You want to meet him?"

She grinned. "Do I not? And your mother, too."

Amelia and Carlos came out to meet Anne. Everybody was very well-mannered and charming, and I explained about Anne's dinner invitation. Everything was just dandy. Just as though we didn't have murders and lies and guilty secrets and dog-beatings in our midst.

Anne got up to go, and I walked across the garden with her and down to the bridge across the creek. I looked over toward the Farm House, thinking of my other trip. Only five days ago. It didn't seem possible. I wanted so much to confide in Anne, to tell her everything that had happened—all the things that hadn't got into the papers, such as Bea's throwing me out of Oak Hill—but I couldn't. There was no reason why Anne should be the receptacle for my troubles and anguish, and I still didn't feel that I could discuss family troubles with outsiders.

She patted my shoulder as she was about to leave me at the bridge. "You be nice to Joe, Susan," she said very seriously. "Please don't hurt him. I hate to be an interfering, doting sister, but he really is crazy about you. And I know you like him. Hang onto his friendship. You need each other—now more than ever."

Her face was flushed, and I was sorry for her as well as for myself. I knew she hated to make the speech she'd just made, and only a strong desire to keep both Joe and me happy would have prompted it.

I smiled wanly. "Sure, Anne. I know."

I turned and walked back to the house. Carlos was busy at the phonograph. Amelia was in the kitchen making her everlasting coffee.

At five-fifteen, dressed in my very nicest white summer dress, I drove through the village and over to the little valley where Mr. Opal lived. I had to give him credit for having a nice house, whatever else I thought of him. It was a low, white-shingled rambling affair set in a grove of old, old walnut trees. The landscaping, though of recent date, was attractive, and the stables and kennels perfectly in keeping with the ideal of a gentleman's country house.

I parked my car and walked through the garden to the terrace which looked cool and inviting under the shade of a big walnut tree. Alma Van Tuyl, a svelte, stupid, blonde woman of forty, was taking her ease in a white-iron, green-upholstered long chair.

Mr. Opal, wearing flawless white flannels with lots of pleats, gay brown and white oxfords, and a navy blue jacket, hopped to his feet and greeted me very cordially. A quick expression of sympathy wiped out his smile.

"Dear Sue," he said, leading me to a chair as though I wouldn't be able to get there under my own power, "this is all so ghastly for you. I'm so sorry. We all adored Mrs. Rutledge so."

To my knowledge, he had met my aunt just once—at a big garden party thing at Oak Hill for the benefit of the Episcopal Church to which the whole world was free to come, provided it had the price of a ticket.

"Yes," I said, "it's ghastly. Let's not talk about it if you don't mind. How are you, Mrs. Van Tuyl?" I asked, sitting down comfortably and looking around for cigarettes.

Mr. Opal whisked out his elaborate gold cigarette case, sparked his lighter into flame, pushed a small table nearer by a fraction of an inch, and rang a bell. All in the wink of an eye.

"Oh, Miss Brooks," she said, "I'm just fine, but won't you talk about the murders? I'm dying to hear. I thought surely you'd tell me all about it. Everybody in Rutledge is dying of curiosity."

Aunt Ella taught me in early childhood that I mustn't go about hitting people who annoyed me. I wondered if she'd mind my giving Mrs. Van Tuyl a really good poke just this once.

Mr. Opal saved Mrs. Van Tuyl's jaw, although she knew it not. "Sue, what would you like to drink? A cocktail, tea, or a long, tall cold one?" he asked. His negro houseman stood waiting for orders.

I had trouble making up my mind. I leaned back and looked seriously at Mr. Opal and thought irrelevantly that if you had to have shiny black hair, a heavy jaw, and a moustache, it was better to have a big one like Mr. Opal's rather than the ridiculous thing Carlos had on his upper lip.

"I'll have a daiquiri," I said. "A huge one like those you get at Trader

Vic's." I grinned at the houseman who grinned back.

"Yes, ma'am," he said happily. "In a champagne glass. I know."

Mrs. Van Tuyl and Mr. Opal said they'd have the same thing, and we all settled down again. Mrs. Van T. had on a baby blue georgette dress trimmed with blue hand-run Alençon. It undoubtedly cost a lot of money and it looked faintly reminiscent of a nightgown. I wondered why middle-aged blondes clung so grimly to the styles and colors which had been becoming in early youth. I hoped I'd have better sense at forty.

"Your garden looks very well indeed," I said, foiling the disappointed Mrs. Van Tuyl. "That man Azivido's good, isn't he? I like that espaliered fruit on the wall around the pool." I turned to dear Alma. "Are you interested in gardening, Mrs. Van Tuyl?"

She smiled, her face looking like a disappointed baby's. "Well, yes, I guess I am. I don't pay much attention. Harry tells the men what to do. But we have a lot of nice begonias now. At least I think they're begonias."

Harry had a whacking big job in one of the steel companies, and it was the wonder of the countryside that he'd got himself married, late in life when he should have had better sense, to his moronic Alma.

We drank our drinks. We talked about nothing. And I was beginning to think that I'd wasted good time coming over to Mr. Opal's as there was no mention of my cousin Bea. In fact, I had a feeling that she was rather pointedly being not mentioned. And Opal was so very chummy and attentive to me. Almost protective, in fact.

The houseman brought another round of daiquiris at six o'clock and more handsome and delectable canapes. I was really enjoying myself. I was cool and relaxed and in pleasant surroundings which were untouched by the nightmares that had gone on in our valley. The voices of my companions droned on, and I made necessary replies to conversation that required no intelligence. The sun disappeared behind the hill and dusk crept through the heavily foliaged grove of English walnuts.

I looked lazily at my watch. Six-fifteen. Dark was coming earlier now, and it always came a little earlier in the valley where Mr. Opal's house was on account of the ring of hills that were so close at the back of his place.

"It's quarter after six," I said in answer to Mrs. Van Tuyl's anguished question.

"Oh, dear," she cried. "Harry will be wild. I'm supposed to be home at six."

She got up in a flurry and gathered up her belongings. Then I got it. This little meeting had been arranged for Mrs. Van Tuyl's benefit. Mr. Opal, knowing her wagging tongue, had invited me so that Mrs. Van T.

could spread the news around Rutledge that I was Mr. Opal's own true love, not Bea.

Mr. Opal turned to me when Mrs. Van Tuyl had resisted his urgings to remain. "But you stay for a few minutes, will you, Sue? I've been given some rather good hunting prints. I don't want to spoil all your good work by hanging them in the wrong place." His teeth flashed a message of cordiality.

"All right," I said. I was in no hurry anyway, and I'd made money enough decorating Mr. Opal's house without cavilling at fifteen minutes of free advice.

When Alma Van Tuyl was safely deposited in her chauffeur-driven car—she couldn't drive herself as she ran into too many things, such as children and cows—Mr. Opal came back and sat down. It had turned quite dark so that it was impossible for me to see the expression on his face.

His voice was easy and pleasant. "Why don't you call me Clare?" he said. "I've taken the liberty of calling you by your first name. I thought we knew each other pretty well."

"Yes," I said. "Clare for Clarence?"

"No," he laughed. "Clare's really my name. Silly, isn't it?"

"All right, Clare," I said, trying to sound very pleasant. "If you'll promise to call me Susan—not Sue, I'll call you Clare, not Clarence."

"I'm sorry," he said. "I didn't want to offend you, but Susan's so prim, and you're not—really."

I refrained from snorting with irritation.

"Susan was good enough for my grandmother, so it's good enough for me," I said standing up. "Let's go look at the pictures."

We went into his library of which I am arrogantly proud. It doesn't look like the usual library in a man's house, and it is still absolutely right. The inside of Clare-not-Clarence's house is dark on account of the big trees and the hills which surround it, so I did the walls and woodwork of the library in a light cream. The big desk is cream-enameled over golden oak—and some of those old golden oak desks have very good lines indeed—with bottle-green linoleum set into the top. The hangings are chintz with a cream ground and big bold red geraniums and green leaves. The chairs and sofa are *not* leather. They are slipcovered for easy cleaning in red and cream and dark green.

I stood in the doorway gloating over my work.

"I still think this is the best room I've ever done," I said immodestly.

Clare Opal smiled with delight. "Everybody likes it," he said.

His hunting prints—if you like that sort of thing—were good, but not for this room. They were too light in line, and I tactfully persuaded him not to hang them. I recommended a handsome portfolio to stand on one of the shelves designed for the accommodation of large books. "You keep them there, and then occasionally you can take them out and gloat."

He winked broadly. "Right as always, Susan. Right as always. I'll do just as you say."

He offered me another drink, and I refused. Then he offered me a cigarette which I took. I had a strong feeling that he didn't want me to go. That he was leading up to something.

When I had sat down on the sofa, he went over to his desk, took out a sealed envelope, and handed it to me. It bore the simple inscription, "Bea."

I could feel my mouth getting hard and tight. So this was it.

I handed the letter back to him.

"Well, what?" I said.

His mouth beneath his Guardsman's moustache was full and red. His jaw jutted slightly.

"Will you deliver it to Bea?" he asked.

"Certainly not," I said snippily.

"Why not?" He sat down in a straight chair and leaned toward me, his face set and hard.

I sighed. "If you can't use the post office, you certainly can't use me. I'm not having any part of this. I'm sorry." I stood up and turned to go.

"Wait!"

I turned around. Clare Opal's cordiality, his easy good nature, his superficial breeding had disappeared.

"Why?" I said, anger pounding in my ears. "Why should I wait? I don't know what you're up to, but I'm certainly not delivering notes to Bea for you."

Opal got up from his chair and walked around me to close the door. I was so angry I couldn't move.

"Servants have long ears," he said with a forced smile twisting his mouth. "Sit down, Susan Brooks. I have quite a lot to say to you. You may as well be comfortable."

Threats! The air crackled with them.

I walked slowly back to the sofa and dropped onto it. Opal turned the straight chair and straddled it with his long arms across its back. My eyes focused on his big hands. They looked like cruel hands, heavy, black-haired, well-muscled. His highly polished nails were unpleasant and somehow frightening, and I thought irrelevantly that Bea should tell him that gentlemen don't have their nails polished. The hands were like the man—brutal and strong with a small proportion of superficial polish.

He laughed maliciously and loudly, and I pulled my eyes away from his hands and looked at his face. The ruddy color in his cheeks was gone, leaving only heavy tan and black hair and blank, unfriendly dark eyes set deep under heavy brows.

"What's funny?" I said blankly. I was steeling myself to sit quietly, to betray none of the emotion that raced through my mind and body.

"You are, Susan Brooks. You and all your kind. All you little ladies and gentlemen who won't carry notes for your friends or commit other clandestine acts that don't affect you." He threw back his head and laughed some more, revealing a lot of gold-crowned molars behind the red mouth and black moustache. "You have your funny little code, don't you. And actually you're just like the ill-bred, boorish men and women for whom you have such contempt. Predatory little animals looking for the same satisfactions without enough honesty to admit it."

His speech had the ring of truth like all clichés. There was no need to comment.

"Is that what you wanted to tell me?" I said quietly.

"No," he said, standing up. "That's only part of what I have to say to you." He started walking around the room, aimlessly, as though giving himself time to think of the words he wanted to use. As I watched him, I remembered a beautiful black puma I had seen in the Fleishhacker Zoo.

He turned swiftly and smoothly and pointed his long right hand at me. "You'd murder an old woman to get what you want, but you won't carry a letter for me!"

I struggled to my feet with tears of blinding rage pouring into my eyes. Before I was erect, Opal darted at me and shoved me back onto the couch.

"Stay where you are," he snapped, "unless you want a good healthy slap."

Amazed at my own helpless acquiescence, I slumped back on the couch. For a few minutes I was the victim of some atavism which told me very surely that the man was a larger animal than I and that I had better do his bidding. I even felt a perverse, uncivilized pleasure in being terrorized. I had lived so long in a world in which men didn't use physical means to subdue a woman that it took me a few minutes to realize that a man like Opal would think very little of handing me a black eye or a broken jaw.

Clare Opal straddled the straight chair again and leaned toward me.

"Now, let's cut the nonsense and get down to business," he said incisively, intently. "I'm going to marry your cousin, do you understand?"

I nodded dumbly. But I didn't understand how the fastidious and elegant Bea could be contemplating marriage with this male animal, this boor.

"And you want Forrester, don't you?" He spat the words at me.

I shook my head slowly from side to side. "No," I breathed, "no, I don't."

He made a queer, sneering, snarling noise. "For God's sake, quit your kidding," he snapped. "You've been mooning around that guy for years. Here's your chance. You can have him."

"No," I mumbled. "No, I don't want him. They have children. They should stay together." I was beginning to come to life again, to lose my fear of Opal's threatened slap. "Besides, I don't believe Bea has any intention of marrying you. You're not her type."

Clare Opal scowled at me. "That shows how much you know about your cousin, my girl. Bea Forrester's in love—for the first time in her life—and with a man, not a pretty clothes horse. Get it?" He leaned toward me. "She'd do anything for me, including marry me. Understand?"

I did a little thinking about Bea's actions of the last few days. She'd risen swiftly to Opal's defense the night he telephoned to ask us to tennis, and she had certainly seemed enthusiastic about the man on the terrace Sunday afternoon. Maybe Opal was right. Maybe this extreme masculinity touched some spark in Bea that the other men she'd known had left dormant.

"All right," I said. "So what? What's this got to do with me?"

Opal smiled triumphantly, coldly, "You're beginning to learn, aren't you?"

I hoped that my face looked as contemptuous as it felt. I kept silent.

"You're going to do two things, Susan Brooks." He spoke very slowly and clearly. "You're going after Forrester and convince him that he wants a divorce. He's already half interested in the idea from what Bea tells me. And then you're going to do something else."

My throat had a strange, uncomfortable lump in it, why I didn't know. I had to struggle to make myself understood. "And what else am I supposed to do?"

Opal's words beat out in carefully spaced rhythm.

"You're going to turn over every cent you can lay your hands on to Bea. The money you'll inherit from the maid, the cash you have now, the proceeds from the sale of your shop and your house and your car and your furniture."

I gaped with genuine astonishment. "What!" I squealed. "And *why?*"

"Because Bea will need cash, lots of it, and you'll have it." He stood up, and his face flushed with sudden emotion. "She and I had bad luck in a business venture."

My breath came painfully from crowded lungs that felt as though my pounding heart had expanded to three times its normal size. I knew so much now. Too much. I knew what had happened to Bea's money. I knew that she was infatuated, blindly in love with this violently male Clare Opal, so much so that she was willing to divorce her presentable husband and deprive her two little children of their own father's care and take into Oak Hill as her husband a man who didn't belong there. She was willing, too, to endure publicity of a highly scandalous nature that would undoubtedly alienate the conservative friends of a lifetime.

She was willing to do all these things, so alien to her background and usual behavior. Naturally, I wondered if she had been willing to murder her grandmother to fulfill her urgent need for money on which the consummation of her love for Opal seemed to hang.

I was so busy thinking about Bea's fantastic behavior that I missed, for a few minutes, the point of Opal's statement to me about my own money.

The silence that hung between us was surcharged with a tension of reckless animosity.

I laughed wildly. "Good Lord," I cried. "You and Bea must be out of your minds. You should be locked up. I never heard of anything so fantastic in my life." I paused for breath as the torrent of words spilled from my mouth. "You seem to think that I want Tony and would be willing to buy him from Bea. Are you crazy? *Are you crazy?*"

I got up and walked toward Opal. I wanted overwhelmingly to seize his lapels and shake him until some faint grain of sense sank into his head.

"No," he said evenly, "I'm not at all crazy. I need money, and I want to marry Bea Forrester, and you're going to help me. It's really quite simple." He stood up and waved his right hand to indicate the attractive room in which our incredible conversation was taking place. "This is a very nice house—mortgaged to the hilt. Oak Hill's a whole lot nicer." His mouth was stretched taut with emotion. "I'm ambitious, Susan Brooks. My father was a driller in the oil fields around Taft, and I was, too, until I got my chance. For a while I made a lot of money. I built this place, and I lived like a civilized human being. I like living this way, and I'm going to continue. And I like the idea of marrying into the Rutledge family, too." He lifted his shoulders noncommittally. "Bea and I were very unlucky. We lost three tankers full of oil for the Japs, so we're broke. You can help us get started again."

Selling oil to the Japs! That was of a piece with all the other shoddy, shabby things I'd learned in the last hour. Selling oil to the Japs in the last days of peace that our country would know for a long time. I shook my head to force my brain back to the business at hand.

"I've told you," I said patiently, "that I don't want to marry Tony

Forrester, so I guess you and Bea are out of luck." I sighed deeply and started to walk toward the door. I felt soiled and weary.

Opal's angry words made me turn back.

"I don't care whether you marry him or not. All you have to do is make him willing for Bea to divorce him and pay up."

"And if I won't?" I snapped.

"You will!"

"Why?"

We both whipped out our words.

"Because I'll give Atwood some evidence that'll land you in the San Quentin death house so fast your head'll spin. That's why!"

I snorted in anger and derision.

"You mean you'll *frame* me?" I asked.

He nodded briskly. "Not exactly, though. I'll just be helping things along. You did murder the old lady, didn't you?"

"No, I didn't. I think Bea did."

His face was suffused with dark red blood that glowed under his tan.

"You're lying, and you know it." He walked toward me menacingly. "But I'll fix you." His eyes were crafty and cruel. "You'll suffocate, Susan Brooks, in the gas house—just like the woman gangster. You'll be a very unpopular murderer. Women who murder old ladies for their money aren't liked."

Part of my mind said that he was blustering. The other half was terrified. I swallowed. "What'll you tell Atwood?" I murmured.

"I'll tell him I was at Oak Hill Friday night and saw you at the berry vines. Bea'll tell him that you offered to buy her husband." His eyes glinted evilly. "With all the rest, that ought to be enough, oughtn't it? And, of course, I'll deny this conversation completely."

My heart ached dully. There was a cold, demoniacal logic issuing from the hideous fantasy of the evening's interview. Opal and Bea, between them, had me in a fiendish position. If I didn't serve their evil ends, help to further their selfish plans, they could make me pay with my life, unless ... *unless* the real murderer was found.

The cunning of self-preservation began to work in my head. I looked at Opal with exaggerated dejection on my face. "I'll let you know," I said. I mopped up my face and fixed my make-up and walked out of the room.

Opal took perverse pleasure in quickly donning his company manners for the benefit of his servants. He walked through the house and out to the car with me, chatting calmly and pleasantly of something that I didn't even hear. He even patted my hand like a solicitous friend as I started the car. He smiled pleasantly and said quietly so that only I could hear, "Cyanide gas is powerful stuff, Susan Brooks."

CHAPTER 20

After my slowed-up reflexes caused me to come close to running into the back end of a truck, I pulled over to the side of the road. I had to rest, to think, to try to make some sense out of the incredible situation in which I found myself.

I realized as I sat in the dark that my mind had tried to reject the actual accusing of any member of the family of the two frightful crimes. I had toyed with the idea that my mother was guilty because I liked and knew her least of all the Rutledge connections, but I had pretty well rationalized her guilt away.

For the first time since I'd found Parsons' hideously mutilated body in the berry vines, I was willing to make a mental accusation.

My fastidious cousin Beatrice Forrester seemed to be amply supplied with motive. She wanted to marry the unscrupulous Mr. Opal so badly that she was willing to railroad me into prison, or worse yet, the death house, if I refused to help her. She had, of course, been wild with anger when John Leonard told her that she was not the great heiress she had thought she was. It seemed to me thoroughly logical to suspect her of having murdered her step-grandmother. Opal's hold on her, his attraction, were so strong as to contain a touch of insanity.

And I, Susan Brooks, was to be another victim, just as surely as Parsons and Ella Rutledge had been victims.

I pressed trembling, clammy hands to my forehead. This crazy business, these wild threats couldn't be real. Surely there was some way I could escape the maniacal demands of Clare Opal and Bea. I had no faith in their continued silence after I turned over my money to them.

Perhaps I could go to Atwood and tell him what they were threatening to do. Surely my story'd have the ring of truth that theirs would lack. But I was terrified, afraid to tell him. He already suspected me so strongly that I was afraid to hand him, on a theoretical silver platter, two more facts—Opal's seeing me at the berry vines and my offer to buy Tony from Bea—that might only serve to clinch his case against me.

Perhaps Tony could help me or John Leonard or a private detective whom I could hire. Surely an innocent woman couldn't be convicted on manufactured evidence. Or possibly I myself could learn some fact that would indicate the true criminal and thus free me. If I could somehow discover what it was that the criminal had been seeking in my house, that might throw some light on the dark, ugly problem that confronted me.

My mind went round and round in an aimless, hopeless circle. Cars flashed by me on the road, and the hands on the dashboard clock crept close to eight, the hour for dinner at Anne's.

Suddenly I didn't care about dinner or my obligations to my friends or my family. My mind had gone back to the idea about the search of my room at Oak Hill and my house. There was the shop.

If that had been searched, I would have heard of it.

I could go to the shop and stay there and wait until the searcher came, as surely he must, and when I turned on the lights, I'd catch him red-handed. It was as simple as that. Desperation made it seem simple. Other places that I inhabited had been searched. Logically, the shop would come next.

I stepped on the starter and drove quickly down to the village. There was still a good-sized crowd in the bar which I could see through the open doors. I drove around to a side street and parked my car and started to walk to the back entrance of my shop.

The night was black and warm and quiet on the side street under the heavily leaved elms. The three small houses that I passed were dark, but I saw the glow of a cigarette on the front porch of one of them which I recognized as the Holz house. My footsteps on the gravel path were blotted out in the whine of tires speeding along the highway half a block away.

I opened the gate in the picket fence that surrounds the little garden in back of my shop and closed it carefully. I walked on the grass to muffle my footsteps. I had no fear of being discovered this early in the evening, and I expected a long wait in the dark, but my trap, as I had mentally dubbed it, seemed to call for caution.

Quietly and carefully I unlocked the back door. Before I entered I bent down and took off my shoes and left them on the step. The linoleum floor in the workroom would resound under the click of high heels.

Then I stepped in quickly and shut the door. The workroom, as always, smelled clothy, and I could see bolts of material for curtains and hangings looming bulkily on the big padded tables where the girls worked. It smelled of stuffy heat and steam, too.

I stood perfectly still, listening. There were no creaks such as buildings usually make at night. The shop was too new. The panelled door leading to the front of the shop gleamed dully. I turned the knob quietly and opened the door and went through. I started to close it, but thought better of my action. I might want to get out in a hurry.

The shop was very dark, and it took me a few minutes to get my bearings. The venetian blinds in the front windows had been lowered and tipped, and the light that ordinarily illuminated my sign was unlighted. Apparently Wilda had put the shop into what she thought was correct mourning.

Once more I stood still. The shop was hot and stuffy, and it, too, smelled of new cloth and rug samples and furniture polish.

There was another smell. I shut my eyes in an effort to place it. It didn't belong there. I was frightened by that alien smell. So frightened that I tried again to place it, but I couldn't, even with my eyes shut. Leather was all I could think of, and that didn't seem right.

I shook myself futilely. A smell didn't matter. It was too early for anyone to be in the shop. The family'd be at dinner at Oak Hill, and Amelia and Carlos would be waiting at my house if they hadn't had sense enough to walk over to Anne and Joe's.

I walked to the left toward my office with an idea of waiting in there where the searcher would be sure to come. Then I changed my mind. The office was too small and too light. An arc light on the highway cast a shaft of light across the blotter on my desk. I reached over and picked up a bunch of papers on which Wilda had written telephone messages— there was enough light to see them. Then I let them fall slowly to the floor. Most of them were from Opal. Opal with his nasty social ambitions and blackmailing and masculinity.

I picked up a fat manila folder which contained unopened mail. I glanced quickly at each envelope. There was nothing interesting, so with my ears pricked for unusual sounds I put the envelopes back in the folder and started to lay it on the desk.

My stomach gave a painful wrench. I dropped the folder, and the letters tumbled to the floor in disorder.

Somewhere behind me in the shop, something had moved. I turned quickly on my heel and walked into the shop and stood listening.

I could see the furniture and the sample shelves and the fireplace in the gray blur. The alien smell seemed stronger. But there was no further sound.

Clammy sweat salted my lips and stung my eyes. I waited, the blood surging in and out of my heart with suffocating intensity. My trap was a fine idea, but terrifying, too. I started across the floor to a hiding place behind the shelves. Then I turned back. I'd be much wiser to stand near the front door and the light switch, as I'd certainly need help some time. Nor did I relish the idea of being sneaked at from behind with one of the Oak Hill ash trays. I felt sure, somehow, that the searcher would come in at the back door as I had. After all, an ordinary skeleton key would open it.

With my hands outstretched, I groped my way toward the front door. Halfway across I ran into a little tilt-top table piled high with samples.

It fell onto the carpet with a muffled thud. My own indrawn breath rang in my ears.

I kicked the samples away from my feet and shoved the table aside and kept on to the door.

Suddenly my heart turned into a hard, hot lump in my throat. I was held in a vise of stark, rigid terror.

My extended right hand touched something made of leather with something warm inside it.

I screamed and tried to force my leaden legs to carry me back, away from the hand that grasped my own.

The lights blazed. The room whirled and tipped and swayed before me.

Through the fog of my terror, Atwood, dressed in a leather jacket, stood before me.

CHAPTER 21

Mute from the reaction of terror, I slumped into a chair. Atwood! What was he doing in the shop? I'd expected almost anyone on earth except Atwood.

I watched him look at the untidy, strewn samples, the overturned table. He glanced from me to the mess and back again. Then he walked quickly to the office. He came back rapidly, his face lowering and ominous.

"So!" he said firmly. "Just as I suspected. We caught you red-handed this time, Miss Brooks."

I swallowed and licked my lips and tried to speak. My voice was slow in coming. Atwood leaned toward me.

"What do you mean?" I gasped.

He roared with anger. "You thought you'd mess up your shop the same way you did the house and your room at Oak Hill, didn't you? Didn't you?"

I could only shake my head, dumb, inarticulate, incredulous. "You even wore gloves!" He pointed dramatically at the white doeskin gloves still on my hands.

I brushed my hair back from my forehead. Then I tried to tell him what I'd been doing, that the papers in the office and the table and samples were accidents.

I tried hard to tell him that I'd been setting a trap, even as he had been. My voice rang hollow and insincere. My throat was parched, burned out with emotion and fear. After a while nothing I said made any sense at all. I leaned back, trembling.

Atwood kept at me. He talked, he stormed, he raged. He outlined his case against me. He elaborated on my motive—my desire to marry Tony. He talked and pounded and threatened. I had motive, I had means, I had opportunity. Everything I had done or said for days was suspicious, twisted with desperate implications. My presence in the shop was the climax, the summing up, the red herring which I was futilely dragging in an effort to cast suspicion away from my guilty actions.

And as he talked, I could feel the net growing tighter around me. If Opal and Bea carried out their threats, that would be the end. My face was soaked in salty water. Acrid, bitter drops formed on my upper lip, and I licked them off with a tongue that felt swollen and dry.

I had murdered Parsons for two reasons—to get her money and because she caught me trying to kill Ella. I had murdered Ella because

I wanted the fifty-thousand-dollar bequest. I had easy access to both the knife and the morphine. I had no alibis. I had found both Parsons' and Ella Rutledge's bodies. I had slipped up badly when I destroyed the note that Tony was supposed to have sent me. I had searched my own room, house, and shop, in an effort to cast suspicion elsewhere.

There it was. Atwood's case against me, neat and pat and complete. And I didn't dare to mention Bea or Opal. With the lies they were prepared to tell Atwood, I could almost smell the fumes of cyanide.

Then he started in on the weapons. Where had I hidden the knife and the hypodermic needle? Where? *Where?* WHERE? My head throbbed under the beating of his voice, the thundering of his questions. I seemed to have been sitting there in the hot, stuffy shop for all of eternity with Atwood's devilish face looming before me and streams of terrifying statements pouring from his mouth.

The weapons! He wanted the weapons.

And all I could do was shake my head and say "No," over and over again until the word lost all meaning.

At last he dragged me out of the shop and put me in his car. The sidewalk was rough and cold under my stocking feet, and I had no words with which to demand my sandals left on the back porch. Shivering with fear and nausea, I was driven up to Oak Hill and again hauled roughly out of the car and up to the house.

Atwood lifted the great brass knocker and pounded it with sufficient violence to shake the thick door. It was opened by Glore whose eyes became round with horror when he looked at us.

The rest of that interview is a nightmare of confusion and pain and fear. I remember dimly that Atwood dragged me upstairs to my aunt's bedroom and shouted and pointed at the bed and that some time Tony stepped in and rescued me. He said he was my lawyer and that Atwood could either arrest me or leave me alone.

Bea, her face drawn and weary, came to the door and looked at me lying on the chaise longue and went out again. I remember hearing Will Starr discussing my possible arrest and Tony answering him.

After a long time, Atwood disappeared, and Mrs. Hill, the nurse, came in and gave me something to drink—a bromide, I think. I sat up quickly when I saw her.

"Listen, Mrs. Hill," I said with a strong overtone of hysteria in my voice, "you know I didn't leave Oak Hill last night, don't you? You gave me that pill, and I went to sleep. You know that, don't you? Please tell Atwood."

She looked away quickly. "I can't do that, Miss Brooks. You see, I went to bed as soon as you were asleep."

No hope. No hope anywhere, at all.

Mrs. Hill told me that Robert, the chauffeur, was waiting to take me home, and with her help I got downstairs and into the car. There was no one in the halls, not even Glore. The family had disappeared. Even Tony my lawyer. I thought platitudinously of rats and sinking ships. But Atwood, too, had gone. I was not yet being taken over to Martinez to the county jail.

My small living room seemed crowded with people. Anne, Joe, Amelia, Carlos. They all jumped to their feet as I came in and closed the door and leaned against it.

"Good God, Susan! We've been nearly crazy. What happened to you?" Joe shoved me into a chair and reached automatically for my pulse.

I had a hard time making a coherent story of my trip to the shop and Atwood's part in it. Finally, they understood, Amelia translating swiftly and impatiently for Carlos. They were all shocked and sympathetic and totally unable to make helpful suggestions. I was too tired to think or care, and when Tony came in, followed by Will Starr, I could only glare and move restlessly in my chair.

The six people in the room talked around and over me, as though I were an inanimate object to be arranged or disposed of as efficiently as possible.

Will Starr tried to conceal his animosity without success. I could see very clearly that he thought me guilty of all the crimes Atwood was trying to pin on me. Only a latent sense of family loyalty accounted for his presence there at all.

"I think she should get out of town. Go away until this thing blows over," he said, interrupting Joe Hilliard's tirade concerning the stupidity of county police.

"Perhaps that might be wisest," Tony said, his good-looking face unsmiling and serious. "That'd give us a chance to do some investigating and get her a good criminal lawyer. That's what she needs now."

Will nodded sagely. "Do you think she'd have any chance of making a good insanity defense, Tony?"

Joe Hilliard leapt to his feet. He was so angry he could scarcely speak, "Why, you damned fool," he shouted, leaning menacingly over Will, "do you mean to sit there and tell me you think Susan's guilty!"

Will pulled away cautiously. "Now, Hilliard, no need to get excited. We're only trying to do our best for Susan. You know as well as I do that Atwood's got a good case against her."

When Joe finished his tirade, there was not much left of Will Starr's character or antecedents, but Tony managed to make him shut up and sit down.

"Really, Hilliard, I think the best thing for us to do is to retain somebody like Dwight Murdock who's had a lot of criminal law experience. He'll know what to do. In the meantime, Susan's had all she can stand." He flashed me a kindly, sympathetic smile. "She needs rest. I think she ought to get out of town for a while until we have a chance to straighten things out."

"You're absolutely right, Tony. Absolutely." Will puffed contentedly on an evil-smelling cigar. I wished mightily that I could faint.

Joe let out a long groan. "What makes you think Atwood will let her go?"

Will's mousy eyebrows shot up. A sly, ironical smile twisted his mouth. "Those things can be arranged, Hilliard. I don't think we'll bother to ask for Atwood's permission."

Amelia, who had sat silent and thoughtful, gestured to Will to be quiet. There was sarcasm in her voice as she spoke. "You mean that you want Susan to run away, Will? That will be nice. That would confirm Atwood's suspicions of her guilt very thoroughly, wouldn't it? And his case would be complete." She got to her feet and came over to me. I took the hand she held out to me. "Come, Susan. You must go to bed. Doctor Hilliard can give you something to make you sleep. In the morning we'll be able to make some intelligent plans for you." Her voice accented the word "intelligent" very strongly.

Amelia and I walked out of the room on a flood of angry exclamations and protests.

She helped me to undress, and when I was in bed, she patted my hand with a gesture that was almost maternal. She smiled steadily. "Poor child," she said quietly. "You're in a frightful situation, but don't worry. It will be all right. I hope you will trust me."

I looked up at her speechless and wide-eyed. So Amelia was getting ready to talk. I had, of course, felt all along that she could do a lot toward clearing up our mystery, and now it looked as though she might do something.

With a quick change back to her usual impersonality, she straightened her shoulders. "I shall fix you something to eat. You must be hungry, and when you have eaten, I'll have Doctor Hilliard give you something."

She left the room, and as I lit a cigarette, the bedroom door opened to admit Tony. He sat down in the slipper chair near my bed.

I protested. "Really, Tony. I can't talk anymore tonight. I'm too tired. I've had too much."

He nodded. "I know. I know. But, Susan, we've got to do something for you. We can't just sit here and hope for the best." He pounded his right fist in the palm of his left hand in emphasis. "Do you realize that if we let Atwood arrest you now, you'll be brought to trial and possibly convicted?"

I swallowed. "And if I run away, he'll find me, and then I'll be worse off than ever." Tears of weakness and self-pity welled up in my eyes. "Besides," I wailed, "it's all on account of you that Atwood thinks I'm guilty."

"Darling, I know it. I feel guilty as hell. And I've explained and explained until I was blue in the face." Tony leaned forward to take my hand, and I jerked it out of reach angrily, childishly. "All right," he said. "Susan, Will Starr has a little hunting shack up in the mountains near Jackson. The sheriff'd never find you there. And then that'd give us time to make investigations—a breathing space, if you like." His tan had taken on a yellowish cast. He looked as tired as I felt. "You could be there before daylight if you'd start now."

I shook my head with emphasis. "Thanks, pal. I'm not running away. And I'd be followed, anyway. If Atwood's going to arrest me, why didn't he do it tonight?"

Tony made the effort to smile. "I said I'd be responsible for you until after the funeral tomorrow."

"All right," I said, "I'll stay right where I am. Amelia told me not to worry. You know as well as I do that when Amelia talks, this whole thing will be cleared up."

Tony looked quickly at the door and then back to me. He spoke barely above a whisper. "Susan, for the love of God, you don't trust that woman, do you?"

I shrugged my shoulders.

"Why ..." Tony said. Then he stopped and refused to complete his sentence.

I shut my eyes. Of course, there was no reason for me to trust Amelia, but on the other hand, I didn't trust anybody. I decided to change the subject.

"Tony, I hear via the grapevine that Bea wants a divorce. Are you going to let her have it?" I spoke quickly before I lost the courage to pry into affairs that didn't concern me.

Tony flushed a deep red. He looked at me long and hard. "Yes," he said slowly, "I'll let her divorce me provided she gives me custody of the children and a trust fund on which to bring them up."

I could feel my eyes bulge in their sockets.

"Really?" I gasped.

He nodded. "That's right. But I'm certainly not turning my children over to a crook like Opal to rear." His voice was sharp and angry, and I didn't blame him.

So that's why Opal was willing to blackmail me. Bea would need cash for the trust fund, because it would take too long to sell the land around Oak Hill.

Amelia came in carrying a tray. Her face was distinctly unfriendly as she spoke to Tony. "I think you'd better go, Mr. Forrester. Susan's very tired."

He stood up without answering and spoke to me. "If you change your mind, Susan, call me at Oak Hill. I'll give you directions. It's early yet. You'd have plenty of time."

"Tony, you said at Parsons' funeral that you wanted to talk to me about something," I said quickly before he could leave. "What was it?"

He lifted his shoulders in an impatient gesture. "We've already covered it. The trust fund matter."

The disguise was for Amelia's benefit.

He'd wanted to talk to me about his possible divorce. Well, I was past caring about that now. I had much more important things to think about. My life, for instance. And I knew, definitely, that Tony's divorce didn't concern me. I knew that I didn't want to marry him under any circumstances and that my idiotic behavior Sunday night had been based upon a desire to assuage my pride, not upon any love for Tony.

Amelia and Tony left me alone. I was eating the toast and soup when Joe came in. I could feel my chin quiver as I looked at his weary, lined face. He was too young, too nice to look so old and heartsick and tired.

"Oh, Joe, this is such a mess," I mumbled.

He sat down after handing me a little yellow capsule. A sad little smile drew up one corner of his wide mouth, and his eyes flicked over me with a trace of embarrassment. Neither of us said a word for a long three minutes. I swallowed the capsule and gulped a spoonful of soup.

I wanted to burst into frenzied, helpless, hopeless tears. My world had gone to smash, completely. And then I realized that Joe's world, too, was smashed in little pieces.

Well, there seemed to be nothing I could do for myself. But I could help Joe a little, I could restore some of his faith in me, show him that his judgment wasn't as rotten and fallible as he undoubtedly thought it was.

I shoved the tray away and leaned forward to touch Joe's hand. I couldn't make the words come, but if he'd look up from the floor, maybe I'd find them.

He did look up and once more the poor little smile dragged at his mouth. He swallowed, "Yes, Susan?"

"Joe, I—" I gulped painfully. Then I started to cry. I held tight to Joe's hand which he put out to steady me. It was cool and strong and firm and something good to cling to in my nightmare world.

"I'm not in love with Tony," I burst out. "I'm not. I don't want to marry him. I don't!"

My words drowned in a flood of tears, but Joe's face and the genuine smile that lined it was a light in the dark, water in the desert, the ending of pain.

"You mean that?" he said, leaping from the slipper chair to the edge of the bed. I nodded dumbly against the comfort of his tweed shoulder. His shout of laughter was pure joy.

He hugged me to him and banged my back and laughed and pushed me away from him and handed me his big, clean handkerchief. "Mop up that awful face, and I'll kiss you."

He did.

Then he looked at me seriously, a worried frown creasing his forehead. "We'll have to do something, Susan. Get you out of this mess somehow." He smiled again. "I don't think our marriage would be much of a success with you in jail, do you?"

I laughed. "You idiot."

My eyelids weighed about five pounds each. I tried to force them up. I yawned painfully. A tremendous sensation of well-being and relaxation was creeping through my body. From far off I heard another burst of Joe's laughter. The pill and my own happiness were wiping out my abject misery.

I turned restlessly in my bed, trying to hunch myself into a position where I could avoid the early sun pouring through the windows. Finally, I gave up with the realization that there was too much on my mind for me to be able to sleep again. I thought about Joe for a long time, and I felt fine. But I knew I'd have to forget the future for a while and deal with the present. There were murder and suspicion and treachery to be eradicated before happiness could assume its rightful place.

I lay on my back, looking up at the ceiling while I tried to marshal my thoughts and put them into some sort of order. I halfway wished that I had energy to get up and get pencil and paper so that I could make a nice neat list of all the suspects involved in our crimes, with columns for motive, means and opportunity.

Bea, Tony, Will, Mabel, Amelia, and I all had motives—lack of money—and means—the kitchen knife and Joe's morphine—and ample opportunity and not the shred of an alibi for the lot of us.

I wondered if a little investigation might reveal that Opal, too, was minus proper alibis. Bea, of course, could have stolen the morphine for him and let him into the house to commit the crimes. I'd have to do something about investigating the man, but I was not at all sure how to go about it. Even Peggy and young Bill might have committed the crimes if one based the conclusion upon motive, means, and opportunity, but I mentally exonerated them from all complicity. After all, there is such a thing as actions being compatible with character, and those two young people certainly didn't possess either the experience or the "hard-boiledness" for such actions. I was very glad in time to find that I was right about the young people if not about anything else.

When I heard Amelia in the kitchen, I got up. The time had come, I was sure, for us to have the talk I'd been too tired to have the night before.

I put on a comfortable white negligee after I had taken my shower. When I combed my hair and smeared my mouth with cheerful red lipstick, I was surprised to see that my face was only a little pale and hollow-eyed. I'd expected it to be a ravaged mask of lines and wrinkles as a result of the harrowing emotions of the day before. For the umpteenth time in the last few days, I was astonished at the beating the human mind and body can take without disintegrating completely.

Amelia, however, did look tired and ravaged. In answer to my question as to how she'd slept, she shrugged her shoulders eloquently and apologized for waking me by being noisy in the kitchen.

"You didn't," I said. "The sun woke me up. Let's take the tray out on the terrace. We can talk there without disturbing Carlos."

I'd heard Carlos' gentle snore coming from the living room couch as I walked into the kitchen.

Amelia and I settled ourselves comfortably with our coffee and cigarettes. I'd cagily—and rudely—arranged my chair so that I sat with my back to the sun. Amelia, in order to look at me, had to sit so that at least half her face was flooded with unflattering, revealing, morning sun.

I waited for her to begin, but she drained two cups of very hot black coffee without uttering a word. The tension was too much for me.

"You said last night that you thought you could help me—make some intelligent plans was the phrase, I believe." I set down my cup and lit a cigarette.

"Yes," she said very slowly, "I can help you. It is really quite simple." She turned to face me, and I looked hard at her rather raddled countenance, searching for the meaning behind her words. "And when I do," she continued, "I hope you will remember my help and perhaps return it. Not for me, you understand, but for Carlos." She put up her long expressive hand in a gesture for silence, and a mirthless laugh issued from her bluish, heavy lips. "I fully realize that you are not in the least obligated to me, but my son is a young man with his way to make in the world. I came here to help him—through Ella, I'd hoped—and now that she is dead, I must look for help elsewhere."

I could feel my eyes narrowing. "By help, do you mean money?" My voice was sharp, unfriendly.

She nodded emphatically. "Yes, money."

I stood up, angry and desolate and hurt all at once. I was supposed to buy Amelia's help, just as Opal wanted me to buy his silence. Blackmail. I was sick all over.

"But I haven't any money," I said through teeth clenched tight to keep me from bursting into tears. "Only what I *earn*."

Amelia smiled urbanely. "You will have," she said quietly.

"What do you mean?" I snapped.

She stood up, the folds of her beautiful white negligee falling gracefully around her.

"Come inside for a minute," she said, walking ahead of me.

Numb, unthinking, I followed her into the house and down the short hall to my room. She motioned to the little round tufted stool in front of my dressing table.

"Sit down," she said.

I sat. I watched her in the mirror.

Amelia leaned forward and pulled my hair back from my face. She gathered my long bob with both her hands into a knot at the back of my head so that my face lost all the softening effect of my rather thick, waved hair.

"Look," she said. "Where have you seen that face before?"

I looked. My heart turned over three times. I turned quickly, gasping for breath. Every bone and muscle in my body shook with excitement as I looked up at Amelia Ortiz. She smiled blandly with enormous amusement.

"You understand?" she said.

"No, no. I don't. What do you mean?" I fought the strange knowledge that Amelia'd handed me with such aplomb, such evident pleasure.

"Ah, Susan. Don't be a fool. You know who you are now, don't you? You know why you'll have plenty of money, don't you?" She laughed. "You'll share with Bea, half and half."

I struggled up from the dressing table and lunged awkwardly to get a cigarette out of the box. I lit it with shaking hands that had difficulty finding the tip of the cigarette.

"You're not *my* daughter," she said triumphantly. "You're Eleanor Rutledge's daughter. Henry and Ella's grandchild!"

CHAPTER 22

I looked like Eleanor Rutledge. That was certain, and while people had frequently remarked upon my resemblance to Ella Rutledge, I wondered why no one had ever said anything about Eleanor. The set of our eyes, the entire bony structure, our mouths were identical. My long thick hair and Eleanor Rutledge's emaciation had probably obscured the likeness.

Amelia interrupted my concentrated meditation. A lazy smile played over her heavy features.

"You see?" she said.

I nodded dumbly. "But I don't understand. She died at nineteen of tuberculosis." My heart twisted painfully as I forced myself to say the words. "She wasn't ... married?"

Amelia's heavy eyebrows were round above heavy, drooping eyelids. "Yes and no."

My hands were icily comforting as I pressed them to my burning forehead. I shook my head in bewilderment.

"You ... I ... I don't understand any of this. You'll have to tell me."

Amelia turned to walk out of the room. She spoke over her shoulder. "It's a long—and interesting—story. We'll go back to the terrace."

Numb with amazement I followed her. Once more my little world was rocked with violence. I wasn't even Susan Brooks anymore if Amelia were to be believed, and somehow I felt sure that she was telling the truth. I was somebody else entirely different with a different set of parents and grandparents.

Slowly and carefully, I eased myself into a chair. I had some half-thought-out, idiotic notion that this new human being who wasn't Susan Brooks should be handled with care and marked "Fragile." I looked up at Oak Hill, majestic in its beauty. Even my relationship to the old house had changed.

With maddening deliberation Amelia poured out more coffee, sipped it, lit a cigarette. Finally she spoke.

In May of 1914 Ella and Henry Rutledge took their daughter Eleanor to Mentone where they had heard of a man who had success with her type of case. Henry Rutledge returned very reluctantly to the United States early in July. Ella and her daughter were, of course, caught in France at the outbreak of war, and in any case Eleanor was much too ill to be moved. The treatment which the French doctors gave her did, however, greatly help her so that when Ella was notified of Henry's illness in October of 1914, she returned to the United States through the Orient.

Henry took two months to die, and while Ella felt it her duty to stay with her husband as long as he lived, she was, quite naturally, wild with anxiety about her daughter. Immediately after Henry's death, Ella, with a great deal of difficulty, managed to get back to France.

When she returned to Mentone, she went directly to the sanitarium. When she asked to be taken to her daughter, there was much French wringing of hands and rolling of eyes and shrugging of shoulders. It took some minutes for Ella to get the story straight, and all the time the French doctors talked, her heart sank lower and lower.

The lovely, dying Eleanor, just turned nineteen, had left the hospital— with a young man whom she had met when he came to visit another patient. He was a Russian, Prince Serge Obronsky, aged twenty, the Russian prince of Parsons' clipping, of course.

With more hand-wringing, the Frenchmen managed to convey the idea that the two young people had fallen madly in love, and after all, one knew what *l'amour* did to young ladies suffering from tuberculosis.

Ella got the address of the young couple, and half insane with anguish, she was driven through the dusty streets of Mentone to a typical bourgeois villa clinging to the side of a hill, a villa that reached an all-time high in bad taste in its interior. There were gilts in tremendous quantities, ceilings covered with roses and badly drawn cupids, and acres of red plush and pink brocade. The servants who admitted poor Ella were a trio of romantic Frenchwomen passionately thrilled to be serving the young couple.

And in the midst of this unconventional ménage were two beautiful, frantic young people, one of whom was undoubtedly dying, but who were determined to spend their last months together.

They had tried hard to be properly married, but because the young man was under age and because his family flatly and unequivocally forbade the marriage to this outlandish young American who didn't even have her parents with her, they had been unable to be married by the legal French civil ceremony. They had managed, however, to find an obliging unfrocked Italian priest to marry them, and until Serge attained his majority late in 1915, that ceremony would have to serve.

The conventional, dignified, and still devoted Ella did not faint when her daughter explained the situation, but she came very close to it. Her heart was torn in little pieces at the sight of Eleanor and Serge's wild, hopeless love, but it was equally torn at the thought of the daughter of the Rutledges living quite openly in what could only be called "sin."

At first Ella tried to separate the young couple. Eleanor's severe hemorrhage at the end of the interview made her change her mind. The deed was done, and the cruelty involved in the separation seemed somehow to outweigh the conventional demands of her background and upbringing.

Then Ella went to work on Obronsky's parents, who were in Russia, but who were represented in the negotiations by the Imperial Tsarist consul in Nice. The Obronskys flatly refused once more to give their consent to the marriage, large dowry notwithstanding. After all, a distant cousin of the Romanoffs could not marry an American who did not even profess to their Orthodox faith, and even if she did become a Greek Catholic, they had other plans for their Serge.

The discovery of Eleanor's pregnancy, which she kept secret from her mother until it was too late for the doctors to prevent it, was pretty nearly the final blow to Ella's pride and integrity. Eleanor knew, of course, that childbirth would hasten her death, but she and Serge had a romantic notion that they wished to have a child as a symbol of their great love. The embarrassment to the child, as well as to Ella, was left out of their calculations.

Ella had been in correspondence with her niece, Amelia Brooks, and upon receiving the news of Amelia's divorce, she urged her niece to come to Mentone. It was, of course, difficult for Ella to expose her daughter's questionable situation to an outsider, but Ella felt that she could not go through the ensuing months without some help. She had managed to cut herself off entirely from the few casual acquaintances she had made in Mentone before her return to America, the French servants had been sworn to secrecy, a close-mouthed, well-recommended English maid—Parsons, of course—had been employed, and the lips of the French doctors sealed with good American dollars. But the situation was too much for Ella alone.

Late in November Eleanor's child was born. Two weeks later, Serge and Eleanor were married. Within ten days of her marriage, Eleanor was dead. A few days later, Amelia offered to go driving with Serge in an effort to distract him from his almost insupportable grief. There was an accident. Serge was dead when he was pulled out of the wreckage. Amelia was slightly bruised.

Serge's body was claimed by the Russian consul who, up to the last, had done his best with bribery and cajolement to prevent the marriage.

And Ella was left alone with her new grandchild, her niece, the trustworthy maid Parsons, and a broken heart.

Understandably or not, Ella decided overnight that she could not return to America and tell the tragic story of Eleanor's marriage. The young girl, until her illness, had been a conventional, charming, popular girl. With the possible confusion in dates, Ella felt that the attempt to conceal Eleanor's belated marriage was too dangerous. The baby's parents were both dead, and wartime confusion had made it possible to keep mention of the marriage out of the French papers.

Between them, Ella and Amelia cooked up their scheme for crediting the baby to Amelia rather than to her rightful parents. Lawrence Brooks, completely cut off from his family, had died in September. The Obronskys in Russia didn't even know of the child's existence.

Amelia, with a huge sum of money which Ella paid to her, went to South America to marry Ortiz. Ella returned home with the new grandchild and Parsons.

A long and interesting story. That's what Amelia had called it.

A story! That was too easy, too simple. It was a blow, a shock, a source of pain and grief and distress.

I sat thinking, trying to adjust myself for a long time.

"I see," I said. "Then I'm Eleanor Rutledge's illegitimate child."

"Not at all," Amelia said trenchantly. "You're just as legitimate as Bea or Carlos or Bea's children. Your father married your mother at a religious ceremony. What is more, he acknowledged you as his child before he and Eleanor could marry at a civil ceremony." She stood up with an impatient jerk. "Ella made a deep, dark secret of the whole affair, but actually it was all perfectly legal. Ella was a little, well, Victorian. She couldn't bear the idea of having people know about Eleanor's 'impatience.'"

Amelia's voice, as she spoke, had an overtone of annoyance. I could hear the same note creep into my voice.

"But Aunt Ella did keep my origin a secret, and she paid you to keep quiet, too, didn't she?"

Amelia shrugged her shoulders. "Yes, she did."

"How much?" I snapped.

A dark flush crept over Amelia's heavy features. "I think I'd rather not say, and in any case the money's gone now."

I stood up and walked around in front of Amelia Ortiz so that she had to look at me whether she wanted to or not. "And so you came to Ella Rutledge to get more money as the price of continuing to keep the secret she'd kept for twenty-six years, didn't you?"

She lifted her shoulders again in her habitual Latin gesture. I was muddled and unhappy and confused by having to adjust myself to an entirely different origin to the one I'd thought I'd possessed, but I was so *glad* to learn that Amelia and the shady Lawrence Brooks weren't my parents. I had been born in love, not in hate, after all. I could feel courage mounting crazily in my heart.

"And now that you've betrayed Ella's confidence, what do you expect me to do?" My voice shook with anger.

"Don't be a fool, Susan. You can claim your inheritance, and I can help you to do it. I can prove who you are—I have documents, you know, in a bank—and Bea will have to share with you."

"And when I've aired the family linen and forced Bea to hand over half the estate and outraged all my grandmother's decent instincts, I can pay you off for your help," I snapped. "That'll be nice, won't it? Well, I won't do it!"

Amelia sat down. Her face was an even darker red. The color looked dangerous, as though she might burst from the intensity of her emotion.

"Such quixotry is very touching, Susan, but I really can't see that you have much choice. Do you remember the letter Ella wrote the lawyer, the one in which she said the will was unfair to you?"

I nodded reluctantly, but I could feel my jaw jutting angrily. "Can't you see that Ella undoubtedly intended to acknowledge you and that she was killed before she could?"

I sat down with a thump. The pressure of emotion made my head feel like a balloon distended to the point of explosion. "Bea, you mean?"

A smug little smile of gratification had begun to hover around Amelia's mouth. "Or Will or Tony or Mabel. It seems logical, doesn't it? Why else should they be so anxious to pin the murders on you?"

I got up and walked down onto the lawn. The day was already hot in the sun, but I had to think, to make some sense from this chaos.

Parsons and Ella Rutledge had been killed. They both knew who I was. But somebody else had known, too, besides Amelia. Amelia had written to Ella Rutledge, and the letter, with the information I had so recently acquired, certainly indicated very strongly that Amelia's silence was again for sale, at a price. But Ella Rutledge had destroyed her old will and sent for the entire family because she had business to discuss. Before she could discuss it, she and Parsons had both been murdered. Was the proposed discussion to concern me?

I couldn't believe it. My grandmother, as I now knew her to be, had loved me and cared for me all the days of my life, but she had loved her daughter more. After all, she had brought me up as the poor relation in order to protect the memory of her dead daughter. I simply could not believe that she had intended to make any change in my position, not at this late date. The solution of the two killings lay elsewhere, I was sure.

I went back up to the terrace where Amelia sat placidly smoking just as though she hadn't betrayed an old confidence or knocked my life into a cocked hat.

"I don't care who I am," I said quickly. "I don't think this has a thing to do with it, and in any case I don't want Bea's money enough to air the family skeletons. You're out of luck, Amelia."

"You'd rather go to prison?" She smiled. "No, Susan, I think not. If you will let me establish your parentage, we can show the sheriff that you, least of all, had a motive to murder your grandmother. You will not only get your inheritance. You will go free."

I shook my head with irritation. "You'd have to prove first that Ella intended to change her will in my favor, and then you'd have to prove that I knew she was going to do it and that I knew who I was." I sighed. "It's hopeless in any case. I'm not willing to go through with it. I'll have to figure out something else."

Amelia leaned toward me urgently. I think she had begun to feel that her case was hopeless, that I really meant what I said.

"But I *can* prove it, Susan. I can tell that man that I told you Friday night who you were. And Ella's letter to the lawyer and the summoning of the family and the destruction of her old will proves that she was going to acknowledge you—at least to the family."

I shook my head wearily. "It's no use." I stood up and started into the house, but I paused before the French doors. "I know you need money, Amelia, but after all Carlos could get a job. I wish you'd had the decency to keep still about all this."

Her large mouth was taut with anger. "Carlos hadn't even finished his education." She stood up. "I'll get money, Susan, don't worry."

I turned back to look at her, a dull, terrified sensation in my throat. I made her repeat her last statement. I had understood it correctly.

"You mean you're going to try blackmailing Bea?" I asked breathlessly.

Her shoulders rose and fell. "Don't forget that the Starrs didn't want that will changed, Susan. And they didn't know it had been destroyed."

The disgust that I felt for Amelia made the skin crawl on the back of my neck. "Good luck," I said with marked sarcasm. "The Starrs haven't a nickel, and if all this business is true—if my parentage is the motive for the murders—don't forget that you're in very great danger right now. It'll be a lot worse if you try your hand at blackmail."

Her look was bland, imperturbable. "I can take care of myself. You're really a stubborn little fool, aren't you?"

I flounced off into the house and into my room. Amelia's intelligent plans that were going to get me out of the awful mess! They were a hodge-podge of confusion and evil and treachery. I thought, platitudinously, that mother love had strange manifestations, and although half my mind was very happy to reject Amelia as a parent, I wished somehow that I had been spared the knowledge of my romantic birth and parentage. The adjustment, on top of everything else, was just a little too much.

CHAPTER 23

With my mind leaping and whirling under the impact of Amelia's revelations, I slowly got myself dressed. For one second, I'd think of the insane idea that I wasn't Susan Brooks with English parents but that I was actually someone who should be named Susan Obronsky with Russian parents—I had been born during the time American women lost their citizenship upon marriage to foreigners, and Aunt Ella had helped me to be naturalized as the daughter of the British Lawrence and Amelia Brooks.

Then my mind would swing back to Amelia's dangerous plan for blackmailing the murderer.

I needed help, desperately. This turmoil wasn't something I could straighten out unaided, and I searched my mind frantically for the name of someone I could trust. There was no one at Oak Hill—they were all too heavily involved—and even after last night's interview, I couldn't bring myself to dump this load of trouble on Joe. I didn't even think that the famous criminal lawyer that Tony and Will wanted to hire for me would be much help.

Lawyer! I had it. Uncle John Leonard, of course. He could be trusted.

I was even lucky enough to find the kindly old man working in the library at Oak Hill, and I didn't think at all of the fact that Bea might throw me out if she found me in the house.

John Leonard looked up from the papers on the desk as I burst breathlessly into the room. He got to his feet and smiled and asked me what the trouble was.

"Plenty, Uncle John," I said, pulling him down onto the leather couch beside me. "Amelia's told me a fantastic story, and I think it's true, but I don't want her to tell anyone else. Maybe you can help me. She says I'm Eleanor Rutledge's daughter. That I'm not hers—Amelia's—at all, and that my father was a young Russian named Serge Obronsky. He was one of the five million princes in Russia before the Revolution."

Uncle John's lined white skin had turned a pale apricot as I talked. He let out a long, low whistle as I finished.

"Do you believe it?" I asked urgently.

He nodded slowly. "It could be true," he said softly. "Can Amelia prove it?"

"She says she can. She has documents—in a bank."

I told him the whole story in detail as I'd got it from Amelia. From time to time, he interrupted me with a question, and when I had finished, he nodded ruminatively.

"Susan, when you were naturalized, did you have a birth certificate?" he said thoughtfully.

I shook my head. "No," I said, "I didn't. Aunt Ella told the people that I'd been born in wartime France, and we couldn't get one, but that she and Parsons were in the house when I was born. They made affidavits, and I used the same ones when I got my passport."

He was quiet for a few minutes. "You say that Amelia admits that Ella paid her a large sum of money to claim you as her child?"

"That's right, but she says it's all gone now."

He sighed. "I remember Ella's cabling for a large sum to be transferred to her Paris bank. She never would tell me what it was for." He smiled mistily. "She said it was 'philanthropical.'" He leaned toward me. "Susan, why did Amelia tell you this story?"

"She wants me to claim my share—as a granddaughter—of Aunt Ella's estate and then reward her suitably." My voice was bitter.

John Leonard gave me a long, slow look. "You could, you know. You'd share equally with Bea. Are you going to do it?"

"Of course not," I said sharply. "Do you think I want to drag this whole mess out into the open after Aunt Ella spent twenty-six years of her life keeping it quiet?"

The old man smiled and patted my arm. "I think it's quite possible that Ella did intend to make your parentage public, though, Susan. The letter she wrote me would indicate that, you know."

"But we don't *know* what she intended to, Uncle John," I said, standing up nervously. "Besides I can't bear the thought of fighting Bea. We'd have to sell Oak Hill and the furniture and the land and then divide up the money. It's not worth it." I sat down again. "But this is the point. Amelia says she thinks Parsons and Aunt Ella were killed because Aunt Ella did intend to acknowledge me."

John Leonard looked at me sharply and thoughtfully. "There's a serious flaw in her reasoning. I don't agree with her."

"What do you mean?"

He took my hand in his. "Never mind. I may be wrong."

I sighed. "Well, anyway, Amelia says if I won't get hold of the money, she'll get it elsewhere."

Uncle John drew back, a shocked expression making his mouth sag. "You mean she'll blackmail Bea?"

I nodded emphatically.

He rubbed his beautiful thin old hands together nervously. "Good Lord in Heaven, Susan! I never thought I'd live to see the day that Oak Hill was the scene of murder and blackmail and lies and greed."

"Neither did I. All this shabby dirty business. Amelia thinks that the Starrs and Tony and Bea are all mixed up in this thing, but I think she's crazy." Bea's affair with Opal was on the tip of my tongue, but I held it back. There was no need to add to Uncle John's disillusionment. "I was born out of wedlock—even if I was *welcome*—and it looks as though I might die under equally sordid circumstances."

"What do you mean?" He was profoundly shocked.

I told him about my hare-brained trap that had caught me in it instead of the murderer. "I think Atwood's going to arrest me right after the funeral."

"Now, Susan," he said testily, "that man's trying to scare information out of you. He can't arrest you until he places you at the scene of the crime or traces the weapon to you. And don't you talk to him again unless I'm around. You need protection, and you haven't been getting it."

At the scene of the crime. That was a good one. Atwood could place me there soon enough if Opal made his threat good. Right down by the berry vines, and Bea had found me in Aunt Ella's room.

"Well, Tony and Will are going to get me a criminal lawyer—Dwight Murdock, his name is," I said.

"Dwight Murdock!" John Leonard pursed his lips and made a lot more wrinkles around his mouth. "They'll do nothing of the sort. You're not going to be represented by any high-powered lawyer of that type. You're innocent. You don't need the kind of attorney that only guilty people hire."

I wanted to laugh, in spite of the seriousness of my situation. Dear old Uncle John who'd spent his conservative lifetime managing estates and assisting corporations in legal doings would be horrified at the idea of Dwight Murdock.

Uncle John stood up. "Now, Susan, I'm going down to talk some sense into Amelia's greedy head—if possible—and I want you to stay right here. *And—*" He shook a lean old finger in my face. "—if that sheriff shows up again, you tell him you can't say a word until I get back. Dwight Murdock, indeed." He started out of the room, muttering under his breath. I hoped the excitement wouldn't be bad for him.

When Uncle John had gone, my appetite got the best of me. I decided to sneak into the kitchen and get some coffee from Mrs. Griggs. After all, as Ella Rutledge's granddaughter, I had a half interest in Oak Hill and was certainly entitled to some breakfast. Uncle John's pooh-poohing of Atwood's case had made me a little silly—with relief.

A sound of angry voices in the dining room made me turn back from the door to the service wing. Bea and Mabel were glaring at each other.

"You *know* she wanted us to have that money, Bea, and if you had an ounce of decency, you'd pay it to us," Mabel said thickly. "I don't want it for myself—I want it for the children. I *can't* sit by and see them have nothing. I've got to have it!"

"What rot." Bea's voice was entirely nasty.

Mabel's eyes were mean and ugly. "Don't worry. We'll get a lawyer. We'll sue you. You'll have to pay it."

Mabel turned on her heel and pushed past me and went quickly up the stairs. She was so mad she didn't even see me.

Bea's carefully arranged eyebrows shot up.

"And what are you doing here?" she asked.

I didn't answer for a minute. I was thinking, hard. After all, I had a legal half-interest in the Rutledge estate. Opal, Bea, and Amelia were all trying to force me to do things against my will. They were using *threats*. Maybe I could use a few myself. Maybe if I told Bea she could have Oak Hill and welcome, she'd call off Opal with his well-prepared lies.

"I came up here to see Uncle John, and now I'd like to see you," I said snippily.

"Well, you've seen me. Suppose you go."

"Not yet," I said. "I had cocktails last night with your *friend*, Mr. Opal. I want to talk to you about it."

I turned quickly and went back to the library, and Bea followed me as I'd known she would. She closed the door and leaned against it. I was shocked at her appearance. Her face was an unhealthy yellow which she'd tried to disguise with the use of too much rouge.

I deliberately sat down and lit a cigarette.

"You might order some coffee for me," I said. "I haven't had any breakfast."

Bea walked slowly over to the bell-pull and yanked it. "All right," she said urgently, "what have you got to say?"

Jane came in answer to the bell, and Bea ordered the coffee. I waited until she came back with it in order to get Bea good and nervous. Then I took plenty of time pouring the coffee and drinking a little. I'd never even suspected myself of so much latent sadism.

"As you undoubtedly know," I said putting the cup down, "I went over to dear Mr. Opal's for cocktails yesterday. Before I got home, I had been very thoroughly and completely blackmailed. I didn't like it."

"What do you mean?" she snapped. The rouge stood out like twin red flags. Her eyes looked hard and old.

"You know what I mean. You ought to. You cooked the pretty scheme up together."

She slumped onto a chair, her pleated skirt falling limply around her. She shook her head, nervously, quickly. "No, no," she said, her voice barely above a whisper. "I don't know what you mean. I haven't seen him. Really."

I made a snort of disgust. "You don't know, of course, that unless I talk Tony into divorcing you and turn over every nickel I have to you, that you and Opal will tell a few well-timed lies that'll land me in the death house. Oh, no, you don't know a thing about it." I hurled my cigarette at the fireplace in disgust and had to get up and retrieve it from the antique Persian rug.

At a strangled sob from Bea, I turned around quickly. She had her hands over her face.

"My God," she said, looking up at me, "he didn't do that, did he?"

"Did he *not?* He certainly did." Something had gone wrong. I felt like an actor on the stage playing with another actor who was getting his lines wrong. I seemed to be missing all my cues. I'd been prepared for brazen affirmation of Opal's demands. Instead Bea seemed to be going to pieces quickly and thoroughly.

"Are you trying to tell me," I said, puzzled and apprehensive, "that you didn't put him up to this stunt?"

"Of *course* not." She got up from her chair and walked nervously up and down the room.

"You mean you don't want my money? You mean you don't want to divorce Tony and marry Opal?" I could feel myself gaping stupidly.

"No! No!" Her voice was a cry of anguish. She held out her hands and clenched and unclenched them in rhythm with her voice.

"Well, I'll be damned," I gasped. "Then this was all Opal's bright idea. But why did he do it?"

She flung herself down onto the couch and cried and talked at the same time. I had a bad time understanding what she was trying to say.

"Oh, Susan, it's such a ghastly mess. I don't want to give up my children, but Opal *is* in love with me." She stopped to mop up her face. "Susan, Tony's never been in love with me. It was always you. I've always known it, and it's so awful to live with a man who's completely indifferent, and Clare *isn't*. He's so exciting—after all these years when Tony's just barely been able to hide his boredom. But what can I do? Tony says Opal isn't fit to have the children, and I can't give them up, and I can't bear the thought of just years and years and years of Tony being bored and polite."

Bea's wail of distress had poured out in a steady, undammable stream. And I couldn't have stopped her anyway, even if I'd wanted to. I was too dumfounded.

"And Clare does such awful things," she sobbed. "Like threatening you, but I suppose he thought the end justified the means." She even managed a sort of fatuous smile. "I suppose he really thinks you're guilty, and if you'd pay up, I could get a divorce right away and fix a trust fund for the children. You see, Opal does so want to marry me and live here."

I stood up and snorted angrily. "Bea, you are an idiotic, vain fool. The first man who gets you excited and isn't bored with you! Of all the feeble-minded stuff."

She started to cry again, and I let her alone. After all, I hadn't told her about Eleanor Rutledge, and that was something.

"Well, it's your mess," I said trenchantly. "You'll have to work it out to suit yourself, but you might tell dear Clare that substantial members of the best society don't go around blackmailing their cousins-to-be."

"All right," she mumbled into her handkerchief. "All right, but I'm afraid I'll have to marry him, Susan. Do you mind?"

I wanted to hit dear Bea hard. "Do *I* mind? What kind of nonsense is this? What has this got to do with me?"

Her dark eyes, red-rimmed and unattractive, darted anxiously around the room. "Susan, he's going to *make* me marry him. I'm afraid there was something crooked about that oil business."

"Bea, I cannot stand any more of this," I said above the tumult of her anguished wailing, "but I want you to understand just one thing. I have no intention of marrying Tony, and I never did have since the day you married him. Get it?" She nodded tearfully. "So try to keep your wagging tongue quiet around the sheriff, will you?"

I walked out through the French window and stood on the terrace.

Bea was so tangled up with the crooked Mr. Opal that she had to marry him, probably in order to stay out of jail. On the other hand, she was shocked at blackmail, but if she'd been really afraid of Opal, might she not have attempted to buy him off? Might she not have been so involved and desperate and half-insane that shortening a life that was nearly over seemed a small crime?

I had no answers for any of my questions. And I was very glad indeed that my own skin was saved—for the time being.

CHAPTER 24

The funeral was over. All morning long the townspeople had filed past my aunt's bier in the village church, but the funeral had been private, which I thought was a great mistake. After all, the people of Rutledge loved my aunt and were proud of her, and I told Bea that I felt that they should have had an opportunity to pay their last respects. She had cut me off short by saying that there wasn't room for all of them, and they could have a memorial service or something.

As we followed the casket from the church, my heart was leaden with grief. My great good friend, Ella Rutledge, was gone. Maybe she had been my grandmother, maybe my great-aunt, but most of all she had been my friend, and I missed her, and I actively hated the method of her death.

When Uncle John Leonard and I left the cemetery—I had ridden with him, and Amelia and Carlos had gone alone in another car—he told his driver to go over to the Courthouse in Martinez.

"We're going to have a talk with the sheriff, Susan."

I nodded acquiescence. Uncle John was being wise, and I was very glad indeed that he'd fired Mr. Murdock shortly before we left for the funeral. The whole family had risen in righteous wrath at his action, and I noted with amusement their patent disappointment that John Leonard felt I had no need for a fancy criminal lawyer.

Uncle John had also had his chat with Amelia during the morning, and he seemed to feel that he had been fairly successful in persuading her to keep her mouth shut and save her own skin. "I told her, Susan," he reported, "that for the sake of Ella, I might do something for her financially—a couple of hundred dollars a month, perhaps. She seemed reasonably satisfied, but you never could tell with Amelia, even when she was a girl."

The big black limousine wound smoothly through the Reliez Valley, and when I rolled down the window next to me, the hot, dry air did nothing to cool me or to lighten the almost unbearable depression that the funeral had caused. My black dress looked and felt hotter than anything I'd ever had on my back. Uncle John, frail and slim inside his black broadcloth, looked as though he might become really ill at any minute.

Aunt Ella was out of all the mess that her death had left behind. I hoped desperately that our talk with Atwood would do something to bring decency and order back to our lives once more.

Atwood was waiting for us in his office. He pulled up the usual golden oak chairs with which public buildings are furnished and took Uncle John's hat and stick and shoved an ash tray over where I could reach it. He was, in fact, downright courteous, which is a characteristic that Uncle John seems to bring out in most people.

"I'm glad you came, Mr. Leonard," he said. "Maybe we can get somewhere."

"I hope so, Sheriff," Uncle John said quietly. "I've just seen my oldest and best friend buried." He closed his mouth tightly in an effort to dam up the emotion that threatened to engulf him. "Well, we won't talk about that. First of all, I want to tell you that there will be no more browbeating of Miss Brooks. This girl's had about all she can stand. If you want to question her again, you'll have to do it in my presence."

Atwood looked quickly at me and then back to Uncle John. He folded his thick hands in front of him on his desk. "You want Mrs. Rutledge's murderer caught, don't you, Mr. Leonard?"

"Naturally." His tone was incisive.

"Even if Miss Brooks is the murderer?"

John Leonard nodded emphatically. "*Especially* if Miss Brooks is the murderer—which she isn't—because if she is, she is one of the most perverted, evil criminals of history. A young girl whose disposition and character are so outwardly good would have to be a monster of wickedness to commit the crime of which you've accused her." He spoke slowly as though choosing his words carefully for his little speech. His profile seemed to become sharper and older as he spoke.

Atwood sighed deeply. I took off my big black hat and laid it on the floor. It was heavy and hot, and it looked as though we might be with the sheriff for a good long time. I leaned forward in my chair.

"Sheriff Atwood," I said, "I know you think I searched my own house. Actually I was asleep—doped—when the searching was done. But why would I beat my own dog almost to death? Can you answer that?" I waited anxiously for his answer.

He coughed and muttered and turned to Uncle John.

"Mr. Leonard, I want to tell you what I've been up against the last few days." He sighed again, and Uncle John nodded solemnly. "I was called over to Oak Hill, the most important house in the community, to investigate the death of a servant. I hadn't been there an hour before I found good, irrefutable evidence to the effect that the servant had been killed by someone in the house."

He told in detail the story of the wheelbarrow, the gloves, the keys to the tool house.

"Frankly, Mr. Leonard, I would have given my right eye and a year's salary if that maid had been murdered by some tramp or a professional criminal. That kind of crime is simple, so's the method of solving it, but what happens?"

"Well, what?"

"Everybody in the place clams up. Won't talk, won't cooperate, and if they do talk, they tell mostly lies. They all act—even the servants—as if I was some kind of a heel coming over there just to make trouble and disturb them. "Why," he pounded the desk in emphasis, "even when Mrs. Rutledge is murdered, that fine old lady who never did anything but good in her life, they still can't think of anything but their own skins. Innocent and guilty alike. Once in a while, one of them gets mad at somebody else, and then they spill something." He turned to me. "You got mad at Mrs. Ortiz and told me about the letter, didn't you, Miss Brooks?"

"Yes," I said, "that's right."

"And Mrs. Forrester got mad at you and told me about you and Mr. Forrester, and I saw something with my own eyes to confirm what she said."

I could feel myself blushing like an adolescent.

"What do you mean, Atwood?" Uncle John was visibly excited.

Atwood, reluctantly enough, told him the well-known Tony Forrester-Susan Brooks true love story. Uncle John just "hummed" when he'd finished.

"Then, Mr. Leonard," he continued, "I hear down in Rutledge that it's common gossip that Mrs. Forrester has been carrying on with this Clare Opal for over a year, and I ask her about it, and she says, very insulted, that they're just good friends and I have an evil mind, and he says the same thing. I even went to Forrester with the story trying to see if it had anything to do with the case—I didn't want to either—and he pooh-poohed the whole thing."

John Leonard was certainly getting an earful. I was very sorry that I hadn't enlightened him before I let Atwood do it. It would have been kinder.

"Next I get a report from Long Beach that Will Starr's been mixed up with a blonde waitress who's threatening to make trouble between him and his wife if he doesn't ante up. He calls me a liar and says he just befriended the woman when she was broke, and his wife knows all about it." Atwood shrugged his heavy shoulders. "Mrs. Starr backs him up, and that's that. Forrester and his wife are in debt up over their ears—margin accounts with brokers and stores and God knows what—and they say it's none of my business and for me to get out. Mrs. Ortiz says she didn't steal any letter and that Miss Brooks just made it up to be nasty and to save her own skin, and if she did make an arrangement with Mrs. Rutledge when Miss Brooks was born, it has nothing to do with the case." He got out a lively purple and white handkerchief and mopped his forehead.

"All right, Atwood, go on." Uncle John's voice sounded a hundred years old. I offered to get him a drink of water, but he said he didn't need it.

"Why, Mr. Leonard, Mrs. Forrester even had a fit when I tried to find the hypodermic needle after Mrs. Rutledge was killed. She said I was deliberately messing up the house." He snorted with indignation. "Well, I couldn't find it. But why the murderer bothered to hide it, I don't know. He stole it from the nurse—hers was missing from her bag—when he knocked her out with the ash tray." He turned to me. "Incidentally, Miss Brooks, I did search your house the day after Mrs. Rutledge was killed, but you never would have known it if I hadn't told you, and I didn't make that mess you found."

I looked him right in the eye. "Neither did I." I offered the man a cigarette, and he took it.

"Then we come to alibis, Mr. Leonard. Friday night during the time the maid was killed, Miss Brooks admits she's out of her house, and her mother says she thinks she was gone for an hour—plenty of time, you see. Mr. Forrester, who was drunk he tells me, goes to sleep out by the pool. The young Starrs are in bed, and Mr. and Mrs. Starr likewise, in separate rooms. And Mrs. Forrester is alone in her bed, she says, although I have a good hunch she's lying."

"Why?" I asked urgently.

"Because Clare Opal's servants tell me they heard him take his car and go out at ten o'clock, and he didn't get back until after two. I think he was with Mrs. Forrester."

So! Atwood was certainly anything but dumb.

"Then on Sunday the whole family is down at the pool, and all of them have a good chance to steal the doctor's morphine." A purplish flush crept over his face. "Of course, I'll never forgive myself for not putting guards all over that house. I oughta be impeached."

Uncle John sighed. "Frankly, I wondered about that, Atwood."

"Mr. Leonard, to tell you the truth, I thought the doctor'd made a mistake. That he'd lost it some place else. And I knew, too, that there's a trick to giving morphine. You have to know how much, you can't put it in a drink because it's too bitter. I had an idea that if the murderer did steal it, he took it so he could commit suicide in case he wanted to." He sighed from the soles of his shoes. "I was wrong. Then after the murderer used it to kill Mrs. Rutledge, I find out that Mrs. Starr was a nurse once and that Clare Opal was an orderly in a hospital when he was going to Fresno State College and that he went out Sunday night and didn't get back until four in the morning!"

I tottered over to the water cooler and filled a paper cup and drank the contents. I needed it.

Limp and sticky, I slumped down in my chair. Uncle John used a fine white lawn hanky to dab delicately at his pale forehead.

"You've certainly been thorough, Atwood," he said evenly.

"But where does it get me, Mr. Leonard? Nowhere. That's where." He gestured toward me. "You blame me for browbeating Miss Brooks, but can't you see that it keeps coming back to her? She finds both bodies, her room and her house get searched, somebody writes her a note telling her to come down to the Farm House. Her mother turns up unexpectedly after twenty-six years, and last night I find her messing up her own shop in the dark. What am I going to do? Let everybody off scot-free just so they won't be annoyed, Mr. Leonard?"

The purple handkerchief came out again to do its customary mopping. I didn't blame him. I could actually feel myself getting sorry for the man.

"Listen, Mr. Leonard," he said, leaning across the desk, "there's something else going on up there at Oak Hill that I haven't yet found out. I *know* that. I've dug up a lot of information. I've uncovered a lot of past history that's better left covered—and Lord knows I've held out on the newspapers—but there's something else, and if I can just get those people to talk, I'll get somewhere. Somebody must know something that'd help me get proof on one of those people. They've got too many motives. That's the trouble. But there must be somebody who knows some fact that would shed a little light."

My heart was banging around in my chest like a wild bird in a cage. I looked at Uncle John and then back at the white hanky that I had rolled and fidgeted until it had become a grimy little rag.

Uncle John said nothing. Apparently, he'd decided that my strange birth had nothing to do with the case. Otherwise, I felt sure he would have told Atwood, because Uncle John had a good, healthy respect for the law and for justice.

Uncle John straightened himself in his chair.

"All right, Atwood," he said, "I'll see what I can do. I'll talk to each member of the family separately and see if I can get them to 'open up,' as you put it. You've been more than fair to them, withholding a lot of scandalous information from the newspapers. They should be made to appreciate that."

I coughed to get Atwood's attention. "Did Peggy Starr tell you about hearing the elevator and the wheelbarrow the night Parsons was killed?" I asked.

"What!" Atwood's voice was a scandalized shout.

I nodded. Then I told him the story as I'd got it from Peggy. When I finished, Atwood turned to Uncle John.

"You see? That's just one more example of what I'm up against. The Starr child knows the exact time the murder was committed, and her father won't let her tell me." He muttered a few swear words. Then he hunched his shoulders in a shrug. "Not that it'll make any difference when they all insist they were in bed."

We all did a lot of thoughtful sighing. Then Uncle John stood up and shook hands with the sheriff.

"I'll do my best for you, Atwood," he said, "but you mustn't question Miss Brooks again without me." He put his hand on my shoulder protectively. "You see, there was an unusually close relationship between her and Mrs. Rutledge. I know that. Anyway, Susan is constitutionally incapable of cold-blooded, premeditated murder." A tiny smile crinkled at the corners of his mouth, and Atwood's face deepened in color slightly.

"Well," he said sceptically, "if you say so."

Down in the car, Uncle John made a fine suggestion.

"Susan, how would you like to dine with me? We'll drive over to San Francisco and cool off, and we'll have a good dinner together," he said. "We'll get away from our troubles for a while. We won't even mention what's happened—at all."

I smiled and nodded vigorously. "Wonderful, Uncle John. I'd love it."

Looking back now, I still think of that evening as something rare and choice and perfect in my life. It stood out from the days before and immediately after like a piece of fragile bone china on a shelf full of dime-store pottery.

As we drove across the Bay Bridge, we watched the red streaks of the sunset fade in the sky and the first stars come out. We felt the air that had been ugly in its heat cool to sea-spray freshness.

We drank perfect dry Gibsons in the serenity of Uncle John's book-laden living room that overlooked the Bay. We ate a simple, beautifully cooked dinner and drank an old, but not too old, St. Julien.

After dinner we listened to a fine French recording of the *Iberian Suite*, because, we decided, Debussy seemed to match our meal, and we had good talk and a deep feeling of serenity and peace. There was, of course, a strong undercurrent of distress and sorrow, but we overlaid it carefully with our enjoyment because we had to. We'd both had too much in the last few days.

We drove back to the country together as Uncle John had more work to do at Oak Hill. Although he was old and tired and very sad, he helped me out of the car and went up to the door with me, and I kissed his dry, thin skin and thanked him with all my heart for the fine evening.

Carlos opened the door before I could put my key in it.

His huge dark eyes were filled with tears and distress, his young face limp and pasty.

"Susan, where is Mama? I look and I look, and I cannot find Mama."

The old, hot lump backed up into my throat.

"When did she go?" I said, grabbing at the door frame.

"Four hours." He looked at his rather elaborate strap watch. "Yes, four hours. I go to Oak Hill where she says she is going, and they say she has not come. She has not been there at all, and I cannot find her."

His voice trailed off into tears.

CHAPTER 25

We found Amelia, but finding her took a long time and the help of Atwood and his men.

Uncle John and Carlos, who was decidedly out on his feet with apprehension, and I stood on the front steps watching the play of flashlights as Atwood's men combed the grounds, and when one of them called out, "Here she is, Sheriff," we ran in the direction of the voice.

Twenty feet off the driveway just inside the main gates from the road, we heard the men's voices.

"She's dead, all right!"

Carlos grabbed at me for support.

"You'd better stay here, Carlos," I said.

"No, no. I must see."

He pulled away from me and plunged into the high, thick shrubbery. I went after him, sick and trembling, with a desire not to see, but to hang onto the poor boy.

One glance was enough to tell me that Amelia, deservedly or not, had met death in the same manner as Parsons. The indecently ugly gash in her throat thrust up at my eyes.

I pulled Carlos away and hugged him to me to keep him from looking. He screamed softly and whimpered like some pathetic child, and when Atwood asked us to get away and stop tracking up the ground, I half-pulled and half-carried Carlos into the driveway and up to the house.

Somebody sent for Joe. We needed him, because Carlos became totally unmanageable and almost incoherent. He screamed and flung himself on the floor and tried to attack us singly and as a group. Once he got away from us and ran into the dining room and got a knife from one of the Adam knife cases standing on pedestals which flank the sideboard.

Tony, shaken and shocked like the rest of us, managed to get it away from him, but he got a bad cut on the hand before the struggle had ended.

"Hit him, Tony. Hit him and knock him out," Will shrieked, from a good safe distance.

"Get out, all of you," I muttered. "I'll take care of him."

I grabbed a brandy decanter from the sideboard and managed to persuade Carlos to drink some. He choked and sputtered and screamed again. I held him tightly by the shoulder.

"Carlos, listen to me," I said firmly. "You must trust me. I was in San Francisco with Mr. Leonard all evening. I didn't kill your mother. I'll help you."

His sobs gradually subsided, and he gasped for breath and took the brandy and the cigarette I gave him. His enormous brown eyes, swimming in tears, darted around the room as though seeking escape from the bloody and horrible reality of his mother's death. He was no longer a rather ridiculous, pampered young man dressed in absurd, foppish clothes. He was a pathetic grief-stricken young animal, unable to understand why he was so hurt, in such unbearable pain.

Joe's dear good face poked around the edge of the dining room door, but I motioned him to go way. Carlos' hysteria was disappearing, and I wanted him to be able to talk, to tell me what had happened. If Joe gave him a sedative, he might go to sleep.

I sat down in a chair next to him and took his hand. He had, unfortunately, been entirely incoherent when Atwood had questioned him at the start of the search for Amelia.

"Carlos," I said, in a voice as level and controlled as I could make it, "you must tell me what happened so that we can catch the person who did this awful thing. When did your mama go out?"

He looked at me with an entirely blank expression and shook his head. I realized that English was too much for him. I tried French and that was no better.

Uncle John came quietly into the room and beckoned to me. I got up and went over to him. "Atwood has to talk to the boy," he said softly. "Can he talk?"

I shook my head. "Not English."

"I can interpret then," he said and went out.

When Atwood and Uncle John came back, they pulled chairs up to the table and sat opposite us. Atwood asked Uncle John to convey his sympathy to Carlos, and when he heard the good familiar Spanish, the boy looked almost comforted. He and Uncle John talked for several minutes, and when they had finished, the dear old man turned to Atwood with a painful little smile twisting his lips.

"The boy is, of course, frantic with grief, Atwood, and he's threatening all kinds of bloodthirsty vengeance. He thought his mother the finest woman in the world, and anybody who'd kill her could only be a monster."

Atwood's face was drawn and grim. "I don't know how good she was, but you can tell the boy that we're going to get the killer if I have to lock up everybody in this house. Ask him when he saw his mother last."

Uncle John and Atwood and Carlos talked back and forth for a long time. Occasionally Carlos' emotion would be too much for him, and I'd give him water or another cigarette and hold his hand until he managed to become coherent again. He told Uncle John that his mother had gone out at about seven—it was dark then—saying that she was going up to Oak Hill to see somebody, but she didn't say whom. We all ground our teeth in frustration at that statement. She did say, however, that she would be gone only a few minutes and that she would see about dinner for the two of them when she got back.

When she hadn't returned by eight o'clock, Carlos, who had the appetite of a growing boy, went up to Oak Hill to look for her as the telephone was too much for him. When he arrived at the big house, the family, except for Bea, were at dinner. They invited him to join them, but he'd said, no, he would go look for mama. Apparently all of them had been totally indifferent to Amelia's disappearance, which was an interesting touch.

Carlos had gone all around the garden, the tennis courts, and the pool and had finally given up and gone home. He'd even asked the servants if they had seen her, and they denied having laid eyes on Amelia all day except at the funeral.

He went back to my house and waited until ten, at which time he'd had the bright idea to go over to Anne and Joe's but nobody was home. Of course, by the time Uncle John and I returned from San Francisco, Carlos was frantic with nervousness.

"Ask him if he has any idea who'd want to do his mother harm," Atwood said.

Uncle John and Carlos talked, and I watched the expression on Carlos' face.

"He says nobody. His mother was a very good woman. There was no reason for anyone to kill her. He apparently knows little of his mother's affairs," Uncle John said. "He knows that they are in financial difficulties and that they came here to see if Mrs. Rutledge would help them. He says his mother may have learned something about the other murders."

I looked down at my hands quickly. I waited for Uncle John to start on Amelia's blackmailing activity, and a heavy feeling of embarrassment at my own position in the matter was welling up in me.

"Has he any notion of what it could have been?"

Atwood's voice cut into my preoccupation.

Uncle John shook his head and he looked directly at me as he did so. "He says he hasn't any idea."

The shaking head was a signal. I knew that, but I was painfully uncomfortable. How could Uncle John hope to keep silent now when Amelia was dead?

Atwood looked at me for a long painful minute. "How about it, Miss Brooks? Have you any ideas about why your mother should have been murdered? Did she tell you anything?"

I shut my eyes and shook my head. I could trust neither my voice nor my eyes.

"Miss Brooks!"

Atwood's voice snapped out, and I jumped nervously.

"Miss Brooks, I know good and well that you didn't kill your mother. You've got a cast-iron alibi, but are you going to clam up again, or are you going to cooperate?"

I sighed wearily. "I'm cooperating," I said. "This thing—it's sickening. Three murders. Please."

"I guess that's all, Atwood," Uncle John said, standing up. "You know Susan is innocent, and she doesn't know anything. Let's go in the library, and I'll help you question the others. Susan, you might look after your brother."

His voice accented the last word very strongly. I had a hard time keeping still. Keeping Aunt Ella's secret was important, to be sure, but how on earth did that nice old man reconcile concealing the motive for Amelia's murder with justice? What if Amelia had tried blackmail? There was no longer the slightest doubt in my mind that I, Susan Brooks, or Obronsky or whatever, was actually the underlying cause for the deaths of all three of the women.

Somebody in our own family group, and I included Opal, because I had heard Atwood order him picked up, had learned of my true relationship to Ella Rutledge and had killed her and Parsons and Amelia to keep that secret.

Preoccupied and listless and worried, I patted poor Carlos' shoulder from time to time.

Then I got it! Like the well-known bolt from the blue. There was a great big gap in my reasoning.

If my position as Eleanor Rutledge's daughter was the underlying motive for three murders, I should have been the logical victim!

It would have been simpler to kill off one twenty-six-year-old female rather than two old ones and one middle-aged one. I almost shouted aloud with relief. I wasn't guilty, even indirectly. And Amelia must have known, or have learned during the day, something else about the first two murders which made hers necessary.

At last I understood why Uncle John had kept silent. He had spoken in the morning of the flaw in Amelia's reasoning. There was even a possibility that Amelia, for some obscure reason of her own, had been lying about the whole business.

"Susan," a quiet little voice said at my side, "I am so 'ongry." I jerked myself back into the present.

"Of course you are," I said, "and the brandy made it worse, didn't it?"

Glore brought Carlos a tray, and the boy wolfed his food. Hunger, I am told, is not a sign of heartlessness but a fairly common reaction after intense emotion.

"Glore," I said when I had thanked him for his sentiments of sympathy, "did Mrs. Ortiz telephone here this afternoon or evening?"

He shook his jowly head slowly and thoughtfully. "No, Miss Susan, I'm sure she didn't. I answered the telephone all afternoon when we came back from the funeral. This evening, too." He sighed and seemed to have something else to say. Finally he continued. "It's a terrible thing for poor Mr. Carlos, isn't it? All alone and unable to speak English."

I said yes it was awful, and Glore quietly left the room.

Well, Amelia hadn't telephoned to make an appointment with her proposed blackmailee, that was certain. She'd probably managed to speak to her victim at the funeral, I decided.

"Susan, what shall I do now?" The poor little voice interrupted my thinking again.

"What do you mean, Carlos?" I said gently.

"I have no 'ome," he said, very seriously.

I groaned inwardly. "Well," I said, "you stay with me for a while. I'll look after you. Maybe you'd like to go to the University of California after a while."

He smiled pitifully. "You are a good sister."

His mother's death had allayed Atwood's suspicions about me very thoroughly, so the least I could do was to look after her baby.

"I am very sorry about the knife. I was perhaps crazy." Carlos' shock was disappearing, and his fine South American manners returning.

I smiled a little and looked over at the knife case that was still open. It was a very handsome mahogany one, urn-shaped and richly carved, and it stood on a pedestal cupboard. I went over to close it as I had no faith in the ancient brass hinge at the back, and I could see the fine carved top with its graceful finial smashing into little bits if it fell off. There were two empty slots in the red velvet holder inside the case, and I put Carlos' knife that he'd waved so menacingly in one of them. Then I took it out as I decided it really ought to be washed.

For no sane reason on earth, I walked over and opened the other knife case on the pedestal cupboard at the other end of the sideboard. The knife slots were all empty with the exception of one.

My face got dry and my mouth hot very quickly. The only knife in the case was an ordinary kitchen one.

I ran to the dining room door and pulled it open and tried to go into the library but was stopped by one of Atwood's men standing guard before the door. A quick glance showed other men standing in front of the other doors opening into the hall.

"I think I've found the knife that was used to kill Parsons," I said. "Please tell the sheriff, will you?"

Then I ran back to the dining room and stood guard over my find, first stamping on the buzzer to summon Glore. "Glore," I said pointing at the knife in the second case, "did you put that kitchen knife in there?"

"Why, no, Miss Susan. We don't use that case. We haven't used it since I came here. It's split down the back, and while the wood was mended, Mrs. Rutledge told me distinctly not to use it." He looked outraged at this upset in his traditional domestic arrangements.

Atwood and Uncle John came in, and I told them about the knife and how I'd happened to find it. Atwood looked properly impressed and carefully removed the knife with a handkerchief and gave it to one of his men with instructions to dust it for prints. "Of course, there won't be any," he said irritatedly, "but send it in to the laboratory. We may find blood on it." He looked quickly at Uncle John. "And how much good that will do us I couldn't tell you."

"There's a knife missing from the other case," I said, "unless Glore has it in the pantry."

Glore didn't have it in the pantry and he was very upset to find it gone. "I can't imagine, Miss Susan. I didn't need any of these knives for dinner tonight, and I haven't looked in the case all day."

Atwood chewed the inside of his cheek in thought. "It was probably used on Mrs. Ortiz. You see anybody hanging around the sideboard this afternoon?"

Glore thought long and carefully. Finally he shook his head. "No, sir," he said.

"Hell," Atwood said tersely and stomped back to the library with Uncle John following him.

Well, we'd found one of the weapons. If we could only find the hypodermic, that would be nice and neat, of course, but why on earth the murderer had taken the trouble to hide knives and needles that couldn't possibly be traced was beyond me.

When Atwood's man told me an hour later that I was wanted in the library, I took Carlos with me, leading him by the hand as though he were two instead of twenty.

The faces of Atwood and Uncle John were in shadow but the desk lamp shone brightly onto a stained, dirt-encrusted silver steak knife lying on a piece of newspaper on the desk.

"That's what did it?" I said.

"Yes," Atwood said quietly as he folded the newspaper over it and handed it to one of his men. "It was wiped off and stuck in the ground near a rose bush. The butler says it came out of the knife case all right."

I made Carlos lie down on the couch, and I covered him up with a little handwoven blanket. Then I sat down in a chair near the desk, my shoulders stiff and painful from fatigue.

"Are you getting anywhere?" I said.

Atwood and Uncle John shook their heads in unison. "No proof, Miss Brooks," Atwood said. "Nothing to link the killer to the scene of the crime or the weapon. We're just as bad off as we ever were." His face sagged with weariness and discouragement. He ran a thick, pudgy hand across his eyes as though they hurt. Then he opened his notebook and gouged at the pages with a stub of yellow pencil. "This time," he continued, "I managed to separate the members of the household and keep them quiet and separated until I talked to them. Even so there was plenty of time for the necessary covering up from the time the murder was committed until we found your mother's body. She must have been killed soon after seven o'clock, because she left your house then, and she was never seen up here. We figure that the murderer hid in those bushes off the drive, hit her with the usual ash tray, and dragged her into the bushes to cut her throat."

My stomach jerked and swayed unpleasantly. Uncle John's poor old face was livid, and his long hands trembled uncertainly in mid-air.

"Alibis?" I asked.

Atwood snorted. "The usual, except for yourself. Mrs. Forrester had gone to bed, Opal was out, and he still refuses to say where, Starr was strolling around the grounds in the direction of the Farm House he says—a quarter of a mile away from the drive entrance—Mrs. Starr was sitting down by the pool, Mr. Forrester was in here in the library punishing a bottle of Scotch, and the two young people were at the north end of the house playing tennis under floodlights."

Everybody was around the place, but then, too, they were all separated, and there was no one, Atwood said, to substantiate their whereabouts with the exception of the two young Starrs whose tennis game was watched by Magruder.

"Then there's nothing you can do, is there?" I said hopelessly.

Uncle John roused himself from his silent preoccupation. "We have a plan, Susan, but we need your help to carry it out," he said quietly. "You see, my dear, we simply must end this thing. We can't let this murderer go on and on and on, decimating the population of Oak Hill until his acts reach the proportions of a massacre. This murderer has been so fiendishly clever. He's chosen his times when no one had an alibi. He's used weapons from the house that were accessible to anyone, and he's had the good fortune to delay discovery of his crimes. But it just can't go on. Why," he gasped, throwing up his hands, "the lives of the survivors, even if they're safe, will be utterly ruined. You'll all be ostracized from the decent companionship of your friends for the rest of your lives. No one's going to associate with suspected murderers! No one!"

He was right, entirely right. I'd seen enough of the attitude of the townspeople to know that I'd not only be good and lonely but that my business would simply disappear, and I certainly wouldn't be able to marry Joe with the crimes unsolved. I'd ruin him professionally if I did.

Bea and Tony, even if they patched up their tangled matrimonial affairs, would have to bring up two little children under a black cloud of ugly crime. The Starrs and their children, too, would be looked at with loathing and suspicion by the good burghers of Long Beach. Of course, something had to be done and quickly, but *what?*

I was about to speak when the door to the hall opened, and Glore ushered in a weeping, inarticulate Katherine, Bea's maid.

"Now, Katherine," Glore said sternly, "you stop crying and tell the sheriff. It's your duty." He led her over to the desk. "You see, sir, Katherine was out walking late this afternoon—six-thirty, it was, and she saw something down along the creek road."

It took a lot of coaxing to get Katherine to mop her tears and open her mouth. "Well," she finally sobbed, "I'm going to quit anyway. I told Mrs. Forrester I'm not going to work anymore in a house full of murderers, and I don't want a reference from her anyway." Her ordinarily attractive young face was red and blotchy, her eyelids puffy. "I saw *her*," she said, leaning over the desk toward Atwood. "And I'd helped her to bed not a half an hour before, and she said she wouldn't need me anymore. And I saw *him*, too."

She stood back, her legs and back straight and triumphant. "He was in his station wagon parked on the road leading to Doctor Hilliard's, and she got in with him."

It took quite a bit of questioning and checking and repetition to get Katherine to state coherently that she had seen Bea Forrester get into Clare Opal's station wagon and sit there talking to him for some minutes between six-thirty and seven o'clock.

Katherine had watched them for a few minutes, and when nothing exciting happened, she had turned back to the house in the gathering twilight. She had spent some time in the servants' sitting room until Bea, back in her bed, had rung at eight o'clock to say that she'd have some dinner after all. Katherine, of course, had said nothing of her mistress's clandestine roadside rendezvous until after Amelia Ortiz' death was discovered.

Katherine's eyes darted rather wildly around the room as though a tongue-lashing from Bea might leap out of a bookcase any second. "You see, sir, she's been going out at night a lot to meet him. I *know*."

"How do you know, Katherine?" Atwood snapped.

"Well, sir, there'd be dust on her shoes in the morning when I'd put them away clean, and you only get that along the creek road. The real road into the village is paved and so's the driveway, and the paths have got bricks." She glanced hastily at me and then away. "Sometimes I've looked in her room late at night, and she wasn't there, and Selma and Robert have seen the station wagon down there off the road under that oak, and they've seen Mrs. Forrester walking back." She blushed painfully, and I felt for her. Selma and Robert would be good and mad when they learned that Katherine had divulged their own nocturnal wanderings. "But *please* don't tell her I told you this. My life wouldn't be worth living, sir, and I've got to stay till the end of the month."

Atwood dismissed Glore and Katherine, and I sighed from my boots. "Now, what?" I asked.

Uncle John curled his long upper lip in distaste. Bea's cheap behavior being reported by the servants was revolting to him. Atwood shrugged his heavy shoulders. "That only confirms what I suspected all along. I can get Opal in here and try to sweat him, but what good will that do? He can refuse to talk, and then I'm right back where I started. Same with Mrs. Forrester." Atwood got up from his chair and walked heavily around the room. "Why in hell didn't somebody see somebody up at the gates instead of a quarter or half a mile away. *Why?*"

Carlos stirred uneasily on the couch and then dropped back into the heavy, youthful sleep he'd been enjoying all through the excitement.

"Then what's your plan?" I asked.

Atwood went back to the desk and sat down. He looked from Uncle John to me and back again. "The only thing I can do, Miss Brooks, is to set a trap and make the murderer walk into it." He looked intently at me, and John Leonard reached over and took my suddenly cold hand in his hot, dry one. "I want to use you for bait, Miss Brooks."

My heart labored heavily, and a chilly little trickle of water ran down my spine.

"I don't like it, Atwood," Uncle John said softly. "I don't like it at all."

"But, Mr. Leonard," the sheriff interrupted, "I've told you I'll protect her. Actually, she won't be in any danger at all. I'll have men posted all over the place." He turned to me. "You see, Miss Brooks, I know now, of course, that you aren't the murderer—unless there are two around here, and I don't think there are—so you're the only one in the house I can use for my trap." The desk light shone into his face as he leaned forward, accenting the satanic peaks of his hair and ears. "I can't use the boy, because he wouldn't keep his head or understand what was being said to him. You can see that I've got to use you, can't you?"

I nodded reluctantly. It was all very logical and undoubtedly necessary, and I was terrified. I also thought it was crazy. It sounded more like something out of a book than something that was happening in my life. But then everything that had happened at Oak Hill in the last five days was fantastic, dramatic, unreal.

I was still frightened. Suppose something went wrong. Suppose Atwood's men weren't close enough. I had no desire to die just so that Atwood could catch a murderer and save his own political career.

But Atwood was a good, eloquent talker. So good that Uncle John finally joined him in his arguments. Somehow I hadn't the courage to refuse.

We talked for a long time. Then we sent for Glore and told him to have sandwiches and coffee in the dining room. Atwood dismissed his men from their posts around the house as separators of the family and guardians of doors. In a strangely detached fashion, considering the deadly danger that would soon surround me, I listened to him give orders to the men concerning their new posts and their actions in case I was attacked. They were to be stationed all along the road leading to my house, as well as inside my house.

"What'll we do with Carlos?" I said when the last sheriff's deputy had left the library and ostentatiously slammed the front door.

We looked over at the sleeping boy on the leather sofa. "Might as well leave him here," Atwood said. "It's only a couple of hours till morning, and I want them to think you'll be alone in your house anyway."

I gulped and steadied myself on the back of a chair and then walked out into the hall to start my act. Uncle John and Atwood made quite a thing of their departure, and I went over to the dining room door.

Someone sitting in that room had murdered three times and would soon try again. And why not? A murderer is only executed once, so why not take another chance when blood is heavy on your hands?

CHAPTER 26

Glore had put two big silver candelabra on the long polished mahogany table. Their saffron flames stirred uneasily in the draft from the doors to the hall as Glore closed them, and I sat down. I took a sandwich from the plate in front of me, and I gulped a little coffee. Then I looked at the faces around me. My mind asked a thousand silent questions. There were no answers.

Did you, Mabel, pudgy and dowdy and no longer attractive, kill three times to save your faithless husband from financial disaster or to help your nice young people?

And you, Bea, spoiled and childish and unhappy in your marriage that was made principally to spite me, did you kill and kill and kill so that you could live luxuriously with that sleek, unscrupulous man who now sits at Oak Hill's gracious table?

Or did you do it, Tony, so that you could pay your debts and go on living as you have since your marriage and keep your two babies?

And how about you, Will? Are you, middle-aged and mousy and a failure, one of those stupid men who try to recapture youth with a cheap blonde? Did you have to murder viciously and cruelly because you had to pay for your middle-aged idiocy?

Or you, Clare Opal? Did you persuade poor, silly Bea to help you murder three women because you were afraid of being poor again or even of going to jail on account of your crooked dealings in oil?

A voice broke into my unspoken cross-examination.

"You're not hungry, are you, Susan?" Tony's face sagged with weariness. He'd temporarily, at least, lost his good looks.

I shook myself back into the present. "Yes," I said. "I am. I was thinking." I made myself bite into a sandwich and swallow it.

"You were in there with Atwood for a long time, weren't you, Susan?" Mabel's expression was blatantly smug. "What's he going to do with you?"

Apparently Mabel was far behind the times. I had a nice time bringing her up to date. I even managed a faint gust of a laugh.

"He's not going to do anything with me, Mabel. I have a nice alibi." I told her in detail where I'd spent the time from the funeral until the discovery of Amelia's body. Her beady little eyes blinked with fear as I spoke. I looked quickly around the table. There was blank dismay on Will's face, and varying degrees of surprise on the others.

"Oh," Mabel said flatly. "So you were with Mr. Leonard. Well."

We lapsed into silence again, and Glore walked around slowly filling the coffee cups and passing the sandwiches which everyone refused. Bea started violently at the sound of the coffee splashing into her cup, and Opal looked bluntly at Tony on the opposite side of the table and then at Bea.

My own hand rattled the coffee cup against the saucer, and I looked down at the stain in my lap where coffee had splashed. Tony was stirring in the chair beside me, and before he got up, I'd have to force myself to say the words. The words that would build the trap for the murderer who sat at this table.

The hall door was closed, and I knew that Atwood's men were taking up stations in the grounds and along the road and in my house.

The room was heavy with silence and tension. A drop of candle grease sizzling in the flame sounded like an explosion in my nerve-taut ears. The ring of a spoon against the blue Wedgewood cup was a sharp crack.

The five white masks that the family wore for faces were white blurs reflected in the dark red wood of the table.

"You don't seem much moved by my mother's murder." I heard the hysteria in my voice. It belonged there, but not for the reasons my listeners thought it did.

A rush of protests flooded over me. "It's dreadful," Mabel's flat, toneless voice said. "We're sorry, of course," Will said pedantically, pompously. "Frightful," Clare Opal contributed. Tony squeezed my hand with his big brown one, and I looked down at it, fascinated by the fine gold hairs that gleamed so brightly under the candle light. Bea only shook her head slowly.

"I think that Atwood's entirely incompetent," Will said with a thick quaver. "My God, we'll all be murdered off one at a time while he sits idly by, doing nothing to protect us." He turned to Mabel. "Come on, we're going to bed, and we're going to lock our doors, too."

He stood up, his oxford gray bathrobe hanging limply around his paunchy body.

"Atwood isn't going to be idle long," I said. "I'm going to call him in the morning."

The words came out sure and strong.

"What for, Susan? Do you think you can tell him why your mother had to be put out of the way?"

I whipped around in my chair at the sound of Clare Opal's voice, smooth and clear. I hadn't expected that much help from anyone. Then my heart twisted painfully. Had he accented the words, "your mother," with strange sarcasm, or was that another product of my ragged nerves and timorous imaginings?

I stood up and turned on my heel and walked out of the room. I flung back a brief torrent of words over my shoulder.

"I've remembered something," I said, "and tomorrow I think I can get proof."

I leaned back on the couch in Oak Hill's library, panting and shaking. The leather felt cold and sticky through my black dress, and I lit a cigarette jerkily. Carlos, my brother-who-probably-wasn't-my-brother, slept quietly on beside the tumult of my heart.

I smoked a cigarette slowly and thoroughly, and once I thought I heard a footstep on the terrace outside the French window. Pretty soon now I'd have to get up and walk out of the house and down the dark lonely road and give somebody a chance to murder me. But half my mind told me I'd be safe. Our plan was too crude, too obvious. Certainly this crafty murderer who'd eluded capture so effectively couldn't fall for anything so childish as the few words I'd flung down as a challenge.

The other half of my mind was bleak and empty of everything but fear. *I was afraid to know the identity of the murderer.*

Shuddering and weak, I put out my cigarette. Then I stood up and walked into the hall where the light from the heavy crystal chandelier glowed reassuringly. The black and white marble floor stretched off ahead of me to the door, and on my left the staircase swept gracefully up to the second floor, its rich red carpet making a brilliant contrast to the white panelled walls and the accented pattern of the floor.

I leaned against the wall, waiting for courage to walk out of the silent house.

Black and white. Black is wrong. White is right.

My glance trailed across the floor aimlessly. Black and white.

But one white square wasn't white. It was white and gray. A gray shadow across the white.

I looked up at the chandelier, its crystal prisms winking in the reflection from the electric lights wired inside the frames from which the crystals hung.

Then I looked down at the floor again. The funny little gray shadow was still there, and there were no other little gray shadows under the chandelier in the pool of light that it cast on the marble floor.

I stood under the fixture looking up past the wire frame to the chain that went high up to the second floor ceiling. I was dizzy when I looked down at the floor again. And then I turned quickly to look up through the carved mahogany balustrade. Someone had moved in the upstairs hall. I knew that someone had been watching me as I looked at the chandelier.

The hall was deadly quiet again. I shivered and then shook myself in an effort to throw off the eerie sensation of being watched. I was crazy, I decided, full of jitters and fear, and I was still in the house. I still had to face the long walk down the dark road.

Again the little shadow caught my eye, and again I looked up at the chandelier. And then I saw the thing that made the shadow. A little grayish white thing with metal that winked in the light from the globes.

I tried to swallow without success. I knew what it was. I wanted to call out, to bring Atwood or one of his men running, to tell of my discovery. But I had to be sure before I spoiled Atwood's careful trap.

I swung myself around the newel post with my left hand and ran silently up the heavily carpeted stairs.

Halfway up I stopped to look into the chandelier. I couldn't see anything. The prisms were in the way.

I ran to the top and leaned over the balustrade and looked down in the complicated frame of metal and glass and wires.

Down in the chandelier, caught on the wire, was the hypodermic needle that had killed Ella Rutledge.

I leaned dangerously far out, hoping to push the chain that held the fixture to the ceiling. I wanted to dislodge that little instrument of death and send it crashing down to the marble floor below.

I pulled back, my hands slipping clammily on the wooden rail. My heart hammered so hard that my whole body felt like one great pulse. The needle! The needle!

Stunned and sick and fearful, I watched the lights in the chandelier go out. The hall was plunged in black darkness.

A scream of horror froze in my throat.

Then things happened very quickly.

A big hand was clapped over my mouth. I was dragged, rigid with fear, toward the stair rail. The heavy wood dug into the small of my back.

Then the lights flashed on, and two men leapt from behind the dark red curtains on either side of the hall window.

There was a harsh crack-crack from a gun, and sulphur blotted out the strong male smell of tweeds and Scotch and lavender shaving soap.

Tony Forrester's handsome face wasn't handsome any more.

CHAPTER 27

Three months have passed since that violent, bloody September dawn. The fall rains have made the hills and the ground in the orchards softly green. The sun shines gently and cleanly upon the valley, and the nights are sharp and the good smell of oak fires floats down the road to hasten my steps toward the gracious old house on the knoll.

Chrysanthemums in all their brave colors flame outside in the garden and inside in well-polished brass bowls. The fire crackles gaily on the library hearth, and the pungent smell of a teaspoon of rum in a cup of tea mingles happily with the damp woolly smell of the dog and the buttery warmth of toasted English muffins.

There is a sick, dull ache in my heart because the four-poster bed in Ella Rutledge's room is empty, but there are even things that help to assuage that grief. Joe Hilliard says that my grandmother couldn't have lived long in any case, and at least Tony gave her a painless, easy, death.

So once again our lives are back in the old channels from which they were so rudely wrenched.

It took a long time for the ugly snarl of Tony's crimes to be untangled, and there are some things, perhaps, which I shall never know, and many more which Atwood will never know. Between us, Uncle John and I have kept the secret of my birth.

Tony, of course, knew it. In his safe deposit box in the bank we found an old letter which Aunt Ella had written him at the time of our engagement explaining my rather dubious background and enjoining his silence. I suppose that he told her it made no difference, but when he jilted me and married Bea, she knew that Tony was interested in money. He knew, undoubtedly, that Aunt Ella, in an effort to keep her daughter's secret, would never acknowledge me and make me a joint heir with Bea, so he chose the heiress and let love shift for itself.

Then, of course, when Amelia's threatening letter came, Aunt Ella changed her mind and sent for her family to tell them who I was, and Tony must have known what she intended doing. Uncle John says that Tony's feigned ignorance of Aunt Ella's affairs was not correct and that he had ample opportunity in the office to know exactly what money she had left. With Bea wanting to marry Opal, Tony decided that there was only one way to ensure his future and quite incidentally that of his children—to keep Bea in control of the Rutledge estate. The murder of three old women was the result.

I was, of course, the logical victim, but we have decided that Tony let me live for two reasons. One of them was because he hoped to pin the crimes on me. The note was written with that idea in mind, and it did work, to a certain extent. I found the body, destroyed the note, and Atwood was suspicious. The other reason for not killing me was that if Aunt Ella did leave a letter or document acknowledging me as heir and the crimes went unsolved, he thought he could marry me. Parsons came first because she probably caught him in his initial attempt on Aunt Ella, and then too, she knew the secret of my birth.

Some spark of kindness or decency in his twisted brain made him choose the morphine for Aunt Ella, and of course, as a doctor's son, he undoubtedly knew how to administer it. We think that he may possibly have given his mother hypodermics during the last months of her illness from cancer, but when Amelia threatened him, he went back to his old method with the ash tray and the knife.

I feel quite sure that he would never have tried to kill me if I hadn't found the needle. I think he might have tried to marry me—and I still blush hideously and painfully when I think of his rapacity which I confused with love. But the trap which Atwood and I planned was too simple, too easy. Atwood did, of course, find Tony's fingerprints on the needle, and Tony tried wildly and insanely to kill because he knew that the prints were there. I shall never know why he threw the needle into the chandelier when he could so easily have wiped it off and left it anywhere in the house, as it couldn't be traced to him. Uncle John thinks that Tony might have planned on planting it on me and that he had to get rid of it quickly when I came into the hall and headed for Aunt Ella's room.

I remembered, a long time afterwards, a little swish of sound in the hall behind me when I was on my way to discover her body. I think that noise was made by Tony throwing the needle into the chandelier. Only panic could have made him do it of course. At least it's a theory.

Atwood has been very despondent over the fact that the deputy aimed for Tony's head instead of his feet when Tony was attempting to push me over the balustrade, because he (Atwood) would undoubtedly have enjoyed a sensational trial, but the rest of us are glad that Tony went as he did, and some day, I suppose, we may even be able to rationalize his insane behavior into something that makes sense.

Atwood says that he suspected Tony all along, and I think that perhaps I did, too. I was so very reluctant to find out who the murderer was that I can only account for my reluctance by subconscious suspicions, but Atwood says that Parsons' murder involved a lot of bloodshed, and yet he never could find any bloody clothes. A pair of swimming trunks, of course, was the answer to Tony's freedom from bloodstains.

Uncle John and I think that Tony searched my house and my room at Oak Hill because he was afraid that Aunt Ella had given me some documentary proof of my birth, but Atwood, in his happy ignorance, holds to the theory that Tony was madly in love with me and regretted having written the note which caused me to discover Parsons' body and did the searching as a bit of chivalrous red-herring casting. And we are quite willing to let him keep his theory as long as we can keep our secret.

Tony beat the dog to silence her barking the night he searched my house. She, out of all his female victims, is hale and hearty and fat.

The only reason we can think of for Tony's putting the kitchen knife used on Parsons in the Adam knife case is that he wanted to keep it handy in case he needed it to plant on me, and he knew, naturally, that the case was not in use. He left the steak knife that he used on Amelia in the garden because he didn't have time to replace it. He knew that Glore and Jane would be in the dining room between seven and eight setting the table. Then too, he was in a hurry to get back to the library before anyone discovered his absence.

The deed to my house and office which I kept unopened in my safe deposit box was the height of irony, and I still tremble inwardly when I think of it.

About two weeks after Tony's quick and painless execution, I went into town and got out the deed and took it over to the County Courthouse to record it. Bea and the servants had long since left Oak Hill and the house was shut up tight and seemed likely to stay that way indefinitely as Bea had stated firmly that she would never live in the house again. She would wait the decent interval and marry Opal, but never again would she set foot in Oak Hill.

I looked desultorily at the deed and handed it over to the clerk. I had never bothered to read it, as descriptions of rural real estate are complicated and childish gibberish to the layman. I mean that stuff about "the northwest corner of the southeast section running in a line 100 feet south along the creek known as Putah, Willows, or Cottonwood," and so on and on and on. The clerk glanced up rather avidly when he saw the names on the deed. Then he started to read the description of the real estate.

He was a rather slight and colorless young man, and as he became more colorless, I watched him closely as he read.

Suddenly he jerked up his head. "Gosh, Miss Brooks, I've been reading about you folks in the papers, but I understood your cousin, Mrs. Forrester? Is that it?" I nodded. "I understood she owned Oak Hill, but according to this you do."

I leaned on the counter to steady myself and the big room with its racks and racks of huge canvas-bound books spun around me. "Say that again," I gasped.

He said it again. Four or five times, and he got the recorder and several other clerks and the county clerk, and they all said the same thing.

Ella Rutledge, two and a half years before her death, had deeded the whole valley, the land in the village on which my shop stood, and all improvements thereon to Susan Rivington Brooks. For two and a half years I had been a big landholder, and I hadn't even known it.

And now I, Ella Rutledge's granddaughter, am mistress of Oak Hill. Bea and I are going to share the proceeds of the sale of the eastern end of the valley, which is only fair, even if she doesn't know it, and Mabel and Walter are going to get their bequest, too. And when the decent interval has elapsed Bea will join Opal in Santiago and her children will take his name and discard the name of a murderer, because while Opal is unscrupulous, he stops short of a major crime. Somehow, I think he may even make a woman of my cousin.

Bea says that she doesn't see how I can bear to live in the old house where all these awful things have happened, but I've told her that I think houses are like people. Sometimes they have to have tragedies in their lives to give them character.

And, after the proper interval following my marriage to Joe next spring, I hope very much that Oak Hill's rooms will be filled with cries and laughter of new young lives that will surely drive out the ghosts of old, unhappy ones.

THE END

Printed in Great Britain
by Amazon